A Brush with Death

Evie Jacobs

A Brush
with Death

Chapter 1

Special Agent Marcus Anderson ducked under the crime scene barrier tape and entered the Society Hill residence of Mickey D'Amico, better known in the criminal underworld as Mickey the Fish. A man who'd cultivated an impressive network of criminal associations through his work as a fence, and whose body lay face down on the kitchen tile, surrounded by a puddle of blood, a bullet wound in the back of his head.

The lead investigator, Eric Erickson, stood in the center of the room, staring at a message written across the wall in something dark and red. *Mickey the Rat.*

Marcus joined the other agent and peered at the epitaph. "Blood?"

"Looks like it, but forensics will know for sure." Erickson inhaled a breath that somehow added inches to his already imposing stature. At six-foot-one, many considered Marcus to be a tall man, but even he'd describe the other agent as towering.

Erickson shook his head, his expression tight. "I've spent months cultivating this relationship. It's a shame to see it end like this."

Marcus rubbed the back of his neck. "Where does this put your investigation?"

Erickson shrugged. "The guy had dealings with almost every illicit organization on the East Coast. Could've delivered a lot of information."

"Guess that's exactly what someone was worried about." Marcus stared at the red scrawl for a beat, then let his gaze wander the room. He tilted his chin at the body. "You sure it's him?"

The corpse in the kitchen wore athletic shorts and a T-shirt.

"We haven't flipped him over yet. Might be hard to make a positive ID given the hole in his face. But yeah. I'm sure. Barracuda tattoo on his forearm. Webbed toes. Can't be many men fitting that description."

Right. Webbed feet. The reason for the moniker Mickey the Fish.

"Saw the medical examiner van outside. When are they getting in to do their thing?"

"Soon. I wanted to look around the place first. Seems Mickey has done well for himself."

Indeed, the townhouse was lavish. From an expensive kitchen remodel to the ritzy light fixtures and furniture. And then there was the artwork. Paintings and sculptures everywhere.

Marcus's gaze snagged on one piece in particular. Filling the space between two windows, the large image stretched from floor to ceiling and featured a series of evenly spaced, perfectly aligned dots. He stared, fascinated by the way patterns emerged and shifted in the colors, almost like one of those hidden-picture posters.

"You think all these are real?" Marcus had a hard time believing a guy like Mickey D'Amico had a penchant for art, but he had an equally difficult time thinking the man would bother to display something that wasn't genuine.

"Probably. And if so, where did they come from?"

It wouldn't be difficult for a fence like Mickey to get his hands on stolen merchandise, but for him to have amassed a collection like this, something else had to be going on.

"You get to figure that out without me." At least until he got back from vacation.

The other agent's brows drew together. "When does your leave start?"

"Technically? Already did, but I got the call from headquarters and thought I'd see if I could help."

"Appreciate it, but I think we've got it covered. I need to let forensics and the medical examiner in. After that, I'll assemble a team to search the premises."

"And the artwork?"

"That'll be cataloged and inventoried." Erickson let out a loud sigh. "Philadelphia PD can handle the rest."

"Sounds like everything is under control. Guess I'll see you in three weeks."

"Three weeks? You sure you'll be able to forget about work for that long?"

"You're one to talk." Erickson was well known for his near-obsessive fixation on the Alario crime syndicate. "I'm driving to Florida tomorrow. My mom moved into a retirement community, and I want to check on her, make sure she's okay. She's been all alone since my dad died."

"What about friends?"

Marcus shrugged. "She goes to activities at the senior center, and I've got an aunt who lives in the same complex, but she's in Seattle for the summer. I'll feel better if I can see how Mom's doing with my own eyes."

"Good luck. Hope it goes well."

Marcus grasped the other agent's outstretched hand. "I'm expecting a lot of sitting around Mom's place watching Wheel of Fortune."

Erickson laughed, then turned his attention back to the crime scene. A twang of regret vibrated in Marcus's chest. He hated to leave at the start of an investigation, but his mom was alone, and he needed to make sure she was okay.

*   *   *

After a day and a half of driving, Marcus pulled up to the gate outside the fifty-five and older community in Fort Lauderdale, Florida, and rolled down his window. A guard with a clipboard stepped out of the little hut in the middle of the road.

"Who are you visiting?" The guy looked at least a decade older than Mom. His name tag said Mort.

"Violet Anderson."

The guard looked at his list. "Is she expecting you?"

"Nope. I'm her son."

Mort turned back toward the gate. "Let me call and tell her you're here."

"Is that necessary? I was hoping to surprise her."

"I'm sorry, sir. Can't let you in without the resident's permission."

Marcus flashed a smile he hoped conveyed respect, reached into the center console, and pulled out his wallet. "Maybe you could bend the rules this one time?" Feeling like a total douche, he let his wallet fall open to reveal his FBI identification.

Mort took a step closer. "You with the Bureau?"

"Left Philly yesterday morning. Mom doesn't know I'm coming."

"Well..." Mort took a deep breath. "I suppose it wouldn't hurt, seeing as you're law enforcement." He leaned into the guard shack and pressed a button to open the gate. "Welcome to Riviera Villages."

Marcus waved. "Thanks. Appreciate it."

The GPS on Marcus's phone navigated him along a winding road lined with tall, shady trees. Everything in this neighborhood looked identical. Small one-story homes, barrel-tile roofs, white stucco facades. He found his mom's bungalow without issue, and since there was no curb, he parked his truck on the strip of grass between the sidewalk and the narrow street.

Mom had a tiny front yard decorated with flowering bushes and several small, spiky plants he guessed were pineapples. He smiled. She'd been so excited when she discovered she could use the top of a pineapple to grow more pineapples. After a glance in the visor mirror and a half-hearted attempt to tame his messy hair, he reached for his hat, then discarded the idea. Mom wouldn't care what his hair looked like. She'd just be happy to see him. He'd waited too long to make this trip to check on her.

He got out of the truck and made his way to the front door, glancing at the numbers screwed to the stucco. He pressed the buzzer. Nothing. He pressed it again.

"Yeah, yeah. I'm old. Give me a minute to get there."

The voice was male. Marcus glanced at the house numbers again, then at the street sign on the corner. Six-two-one Redfish Way.

The door flew open, and an older, but fit-looking man in striped boxer shorts, a sleeveless undershirt, and black socks stood in the entryway. "Yeah? What do you want?"

What the—? Too stunned to respond, Marcus stared.

"Well? You could hardly wait for me to get here, and now you've got nothing to say? Spit it out."

Marcus was pretty sure his mouth was moving, but no sound emerged. Jesus, he was an FBI agent. Time to pull his shit together. Finally, he rasped two words. "Violet Anderson."

The man adjusted his glasses and stepped closer. His gaze slid from Marcus's head to his feet, then back up again. "You're a big fella, aren't you? Hard to get a feel for size from a photo on the back of the piano."

A hard lump rose in Marcus's throat, and even as he swallowed it, his brain refused to process what was happening. The man turned around and yelled into the depths of the house. "Hey Vi, your son is here."

"Stop it, Freddy. That's not funny. My son is hundreds of miles away."

Just two days ago, Marcus had been at the scene of an execution with blood and brain matter splattered across the kitchen floor. That was nothing compared to the horror that filled his gut as his mother shuffled toward the door from the back of the house, wearing nothing but a bathrobe in the middle of the afternoon. He squeezed his eyes shut, trying to block the image now seared onto the insides of his eyelids.

With a deliberate, conscious effort, he unclenched his fists and opened his eyes.

When his mom saw him, delight lit up her face, and despite his heart pounding in his ears, he could still hear her when she exclaimed, "My baby!"

"Hi, Mom." He gave her a tight hug.

She stepped back to look at him. "What are you doing here? Why didn't you tell me you were coming?"

"I wanted it to be a surprise." And it was. Just not in the way he'd hoped.

"I guess you've already met Freddy." His mom motioned to the underwear-wearing man now standing behind her.

"Hiya." Freddy waved.

"Hello." What grown man went by a name like Freddy?

His mom tugged on his arm. "Come in." She shooed Freddy toward the back of the house. "Go put some clothes on so I can introduce you properly."

Tempted to tell his mom to do the same, Marcus pressed his mouth shut and suppressed a shudder as he stepped inside. The room was small and cluttered with furniture, photographs, knickknacks, and mementos, most of which he recognized. What he didn't recognize was the woman standing before him telling a strange man to get dressed.

Marcus couldn't hold it in for another second. "Mom, what's going on here?"

"What do you mean?"

So that was the way she wanted to play this? He waved his hand to the hallway Freddy had disappeared down a few moments ago, then motioned to her bathrobe. "Who is that man?"

"I told you. That's Freddy."

Marcus resisted the urge to pinch the bridge of his nose. "As I've gathered. Who is he to you?"

"Oh." She straightened. "My boyfriend."

Marcus struggled to contain his frustration. "For how long?"

"About four months."

"*Four months*? You've only lived here for *four* months."

"Your Aunt Barbara introduced us when I visited in January. He was one of the reasons I made the move."

"Why have you never mentioned him?"

"For one thing, it's none of your business. For another, I knew you'd overreact."

"And you've been intimate with him?"

"Grow up, Marcus. It's not like I'm going to get pregnant."

He sputtered. What he wouldn't give for a memory wipe right about now. If there was ever something he wanted to forget, it was hearing his mom say those words. "What about Dad?"

"Your father has been gone for almost two years. I'm only sixty-eight. I have plenty of good years ahead of me, and I plan to enjoy them." She gripped his hand, glanced over her shoulder, and whispered loudly. "Besides, we're only having a bit of fun."

The spot above Marcus's right eyebrow throbbed. Time to put an end to this. "Get rid of him. You and I need to talk."

She put her hands on her hips and glared at him like she'd done when he'd been a mischievous little boy. "I'll do no such thing. You came to spend time with me. And that means spending time with Freddy."

He shook his head, trying to make sense of the situation. Had his mother just given him an ultimatum? She kept talking, but the words came at him like feedback on a telephone.

"Where are you staying?" she asked.

Good question. The original plan was to stay at her place, but that hardly seemed viable now. "Hotel."

"Oh, that's perfect. Freddy and I were about to get ready for our bridge game. You go check in. We'll meet for dinner."

Marcus nodded numbly.

Freddy emerged dressed in black pants and a light blue dress shirt. "Vi, you better get ready. We don't want to be late."

She reached up to pinch Marcus's cheek. "I'm so happy you're here." She steered him to the front door and nudged him over the threshold. "I'll text you when we're done."

Perhaps dinner would be an opportunity to talk without Freddy hovering in the background. Then an unpleasant realization dawned. *No.* Surely, she wouldn't bring her new boyfriend to dinner with the son she hadn't seen in almost six months. He turned, intending to ask, but the door closed before he had a chance.

Stunned, he stood frozen on his mother's front porch, staring at nothing in particular and realizing that this trip was going to be nothing like he'd planned.

Chapter 2

If Ava Montoya had learned anything about working as a beat reporter for a small suburb, it was that there was nothing more tedious than a city commission meeting. Or so she'd thought. That was before she attended her first community hall.

Seaside city commissioner Martin Singh and a developer named Jared Meeks were presenting their plans for a new beachfront project they hoped to build along State Road A1A. They'd come with artist's renderings, a fancy plastic model, and promised everything from increased property values to job creation and economic development.

The locals weren't buying it. Several had gotten wind of the plans and turned up to voice their concerns. Loudly.

"What about the extra traffic this shopping center is going to cause?" asked one woman who lived in a condo across the street from the beach. "A1A is only a two-lane road."

Other residents nodded and grumbled their agreement.

"How long is construction going to last?"

"What about the noise?"

"This development is going to bring crime to our community!"

One red-faced man stood up and shook his finger at the men at the front of the room. "We don't need another big empty mall like the one at the end of Las Olas in Fort Lauderdale!"

The crowd clapped, and Commissioner Singh patted the air with his hands in a calm-down motion. It had the effect one might expect. Nothing.

"You're a hypocrite, Singh!" shouted a woman sitting in the second row.

The sentiment didn't surprise Ava, but rather that it took this long for someone to say it. Singh's embrace of the proposed development was surprising, especially considering he'd been a fierce advocate for preserving Seaside's small-town charm. His recent campaign slogan, *Keep Seaside Scenic*, seemed rather disingenuous now.

A chant of "Singh's a sellout" drowned out any attempts to continue with the meeting.

Ava packed up her computer with a sigh. She needed to get a quote from the commissioner justifying his support for the development, but she had enough to write a basic article, and this had gone on much longer than she'd expected. While she'd hoped to get names of people willing to talk on the record, she had another job to get to. One that paid better than working as a journalist at a dying local newspaper.

Happy to leave the meeting behind, she hurried into the turn-of-the-century Chevy Camaro she inherited when her nana died last year and headed west to the interstate. She arrived at On a Roll with two minutes to spare. Despite the low hourly wage, the generous tips made the job worthwhile. Some weeks she pulled in as much cash slinging drinks as she did writing articles.

"You're cutting it pretty close." Her coworker fixed a hand on her hip and a scowl on her face.

"I realize that, but I'm here. On time."

"Yeah? Well, I'm outta here." The lunch shift bartender left before Ava could respond.

She logged into her digital timecard, grabbed an apron, and scooted behind the bar. She had one customer, a disgruntled-looking man with golden brown hair, tired eyes, and a light scruff of beard. He stared at the television on the wall, but it was obvious he wasn't watching. Trying not to stare, she couldn't help but notice he was handsome in a world-weary sort of way. Or the enticing flex of his biceps when he lifted the pint glass to swallow the last gulp of beer. His gaze met hers.

"You want another?"

He nodded.

"What are you drinking?"

"Stella."

She got a clean glass, filled it from the tap, then wiped the bar before setting it down in front of him.

"You're not a regular. New in the area?"

He bobbed his head indifferently. "Yep."

"Bad day?"

"Uh huh."

"Geez, stop monopolizing the conversation. Let someone else have a chance."

He didn't take the bait. Or smile. Clearly, this guy wasn't interested in small talk. Fine with her. She had things to do, and while the bar wasn't busy now, it would be in another hour when the happy hour crowd arrived. She should enjoy the peace and quiet while she still could. God help her if those middle school teachers showed up.

She went to the refrigerator, took out a jar of cherries and one of olives, and busied herself with refilling the condiment tray on the end of the bar.

An order came in. Eight specialty drinks. She lined the various glassware onto the bar top, filled the cocktail shaker with ice and started pouring. When she finished, she moved the drinks onto a round tray set atop the serving stand.

The hairs on the back of her neck bristled like she was being watched. She glanced at her lone customer. Sure enough, his hazel eyes bore into her with the intensity of a dying sun.

"Did you need anything else? You want to see a menu?"

He blinked, then looked into his glass as though he wanted to crawl inside and disappear. "Uh, no. I'm meeting someone for dinner."

Her interest piqued. "A blind date?"

He snorted. "My mom."

Strained parental relationships were something she understood. Of course, her mom would never be caught dead in a chain restaurant like this. She nodded at his nearly empty glass. "Another?"

"That would be great." She stared for a moment, transfixed by the way his throat moved up and down as he swallowed the last of his beer.

Now she was the one staring.

Right, beer.

She grabbed a clean pint glass, filled it, and slid it in front of the somewhat-less-cranky man. "What time is dinner?"

He spun his glass through a condensation ring on the bar. "Whenever Mom finishes her bridge game."

"Killing time, then?"

"More or less. I live out of state. Drove down to spend time with her, only to discover she's got a boyfriend."

"Hey, good for her."

The guy grunted. The scowl returned.

"Not good for her?"

He shrugged. "She seems to think so. I'll get over it. What choice do I have?"

"Is she bringing the boyfriend to dinner?"

"Most likely."

"So watch their interactions. See how he treats her, how they get along. Whether he's a good guy. Maybe then you can put your mind at ease."

Just then, a pretty, older woman with chin-length gray hair, wearing a purple dress with a matching chiffon cardigan, breezed into the room. A trim man with a full head of white, wavy hair and a neatly clipped beard trailed behind.

Was this his mom and her boyfriend? If so, props to the cranky guy's mom. Gramps was hot. "So, it *is* good for her."

The guy at the bar shot her a look. "What was that?"

"Nothing." She smiled.

The woman looked around the bar, her gaze falling on the lone customer. She grasped his face and kissed him on the cheek. "Marcus, go tell the hostess we need a table."

His eyes swept the empty room, and Ava saw the sarcastic comment forming on his tongue. For some reason she didn't understand, she couldn't let him start his dinner off being obnoxious.

"Open seating," she interrupted. "Sit wherever you like. Unless you prefer the restaurant. Then you'll need to see the hostess."

His mother gave her a sincere smile, then turned to her son. "We can eat in here. Is that what you want?"

"Sure." He stood and pushed a credit card across the bar.

Ava totaled his tab, swiped the card, and then handed it back. "Enjoy your dinner."

He answered with one of his caveman-like grunts she found so attractive and trudged toward the booth where his mother waited with her boyfriend.

The guy—Marcus—slid onto the bench seat across from his mom and the older man. A family having dinner. Something she saw all the time. And yet, Ava couldn't break her gaze from Marcus's revealing face that projected his every thought and emotion.

"Hello? Earth to Ava."

Trance broken, Ava pivoted to greet her friend sliding onto a barstool. "How's it going?"

"Great."

She had to smile. Patrick was a perpetual optimist. The opposite of cranky Marcus over there. Her gaze again trailed toward the table where a server now stood, taking their order. She dragged her focus back to her friend.

"How'd that beach development meeting go?" he asked.

Ava feigned a snore, and Patrick laughed. He also worked at the newspaper. The difference was, he had an actual future in journalism. Unlike Ava, who'd probably still be going to Seaside City Commission meetings when it was time to retire.

"Amanda says she's set aside two tickets for the shindig at the art museum. It'll be great for networking."

This again? The dishwasher beeped, giving Ava an excuse to turn away and roll her eyes. They'd only been over this about a zillion times already.

"Why are you being so difficult? It'll be fun. An opportunity to dress up."

"I have nothing to wear."

"That's a lie. I've seen your closet. It looks like a high-end department store."

That much was true. Ava loved to get dressed up, especially since the way she looked was the only thing anyone seemed to care about. She amended her statement. "Fine. I have nothing I *want* to wear."

"So, buy something. Go check out one of those consignment stores you're always trying to drag me into."

She lifted a glass from the dishwasher and rubbed it with a towel. "Why is it so important to you that I go?"

"You need to cultivate your professional relationships. I don't understand why you don't even try."

Another conversation they'd had before. There were only so many times Ava could explain to an overachiever like Patrick that when not-good-enough was always the outcome, it was only natural to stop trying.

She narrowed her eyes. "What's the real reason you want me to go?"

"Amanda's working. I want to support her, but she'll be occupied for most of the night. I need someone to hang out with."

Ah, that made sense. Patrick had been dating Amanda, a public relations rep for the museum, for a couple of months now. Ava had never seen him so smitten. "So, you want to go with Amanda, but she's going to be busy, and I'm the backup?"

"It sounds bad when you put it like that," Patrick teased. "But seriously, I think it's an opportunity for you to make some connections."

"Fine. I'll go, but I don't want you harassing me to talk to people the entire time."

"I'll agree but only if you agree to introduce yourself to Ian Vanderbrook."

"Who?"

Patrick let his mouth fall open. "You aren't serious?"

She smiled. Provoking him was so much fun. "Celebrity artist. Big deal. Yadda yadda yadda." She flicked the dishtowel against the bar. "And why should I introduce myself to this man?"

"He hasn't given an interview in over a decade, but they say he's a sucker for a pretty face." Patrick motioned toward Ava's face. "And you have one of those."

She suppressed a groan. He had no idea how insulting it was for him to assume she would get an interview because of the way she looked. "I'll think about it."

Despite Patrick's assumption that she didn't care, she had thought about the show and the charity auction. Specifically, that a big-name artist like Ian Vanderbrook would agree to an off-the-map exhibit opening. It didn't make a lot of sense.

But what did she know?

Marcus reached for his wallet at the same time Freddy went for his.

"My treat," the other man said, extracting a wad of bills.

No way was Marcus going to let this lothario buy him dinner. He yanked a card from its slot and slammed it on the check. "I insist."

When the server returned, Freddy shoved the cash at her. She left Marcus's card on the table and sauntered over to the bar where she made change and chatted with the pretty bartender.

Throughout dinner, between his mother regaling him with stories of Freddy-the-big-spender and his by-the-bootstraps success story, he'd found his gaze dragged back to the woman behind the bar. She laughed and smiled at the server, and there was something captivating about it. She had perfectly tousled dark brown hair, light brown eyes, and lips painted in the most ridiculous shade of red.

He'd considered staying for another drink after his mother and Freddy left—what else did he have to do? But then, some other guy showed up, parked his ass on a barstool, and had been nursing a beer ever since.

"...And Freddy has tickets." His mother's voice rose an octave in her excitement.

"I'm sorry, what?"

"To the gala at the art museum. Freddy is on the board of directors. Ian Vanderbrook is going to be there."

Marcus didn't know who that was, but he wasn't about to admit it and give Freddy another excuse to gloat. Smiling and pretending to care while the man recounted his high-school-dropout-to-dry-clean-franchise-owner story had already taxed his patience.

Then the words *museum* and *gala* registered. Marcus stifled a groan. He'd come here to spend time with his mother, and if she wanted to go to an art show, then that's what he'd do. "When is it?"

"Tomorrow night." She gave him an appraising look. "I don't suppose you packed a suit?"

He shook his head. Work rarely required a suit. Why would vacation?

"There's a big outlet mall out west. We can go there tomorrow. It'll be my treat."

"Are you sure a suit is necessary?"

"Yes, Marcus. This is a big deal."

The server returned with Freddy's change on a tray, plus three peppermint candies. Marcus unwrapped one and popped it into his mouth.

Finally, this exercise in awkwardness could be over. As they stood, Marcus's gaze returned to the bartender. She threw her head back and laughed at something the guy at the bar said. Barstool guy rubbed a hand along his jaw and smiled at her. And why wouldn't he? If Marcus made her laugh, he'd be clambering for every crumb of adoration she doled out too.

In the parking lot, he gave his mom a hug and a kiss on the cheek.

"Tomorrow, we shop for a suit." She beamed, and he realized he could never stay mad at her, boyfriend or not. "No putting it off, hoping you won't have to go."

"Wouldn't dream of it. I'll pick you up at nine."

Freddy held open the door of his luxury sedan, and Marcus's mother climbed into the passenger seat. As much as it stung to see her with a man who wasn't his father, he believed Freddy's feelings were genuine. And he made her happy. That counted for something.

Marcus waved, then glanced at the restaurant. Temptation to go back inside gnawed at him, but she already had a guy to keep her company. What could she possibly want with him?

Chapter 3

Ava had maxed out her credit card on a beautiful gown she'd found in a couture shop in Fort Lauderdale. A black strapless dress with a built-in bodysuit and an embroidered see-through skirt. She'd paired the ensemble with a pair of stiletto-heeled thigh-high boots.

She poured herself a Pinot Noir, hoping to calm her nerves. Patrick texted to say he was on his way, and while history said otherwise, she hoped they'd put the Ian Vanderbrook nonsense behind them.

Why couldn't he understand she liked things the way they were? She was content with the small house in Wilton Manors left to her by her grandmother. Her two jobs earned enough to pay her bills with the occasional splurge, and it wasn't like she was alone. She had Nana's big fat tuxedo cat for company. As long as she continued to supply him with food, water, and a clean litter box, Mr. Belvedere seemed happy enough to let her stay.

The truth was, she wasn't a very good reporter. Her fondness for writing drew her to journalism, but she found much of the job to be intrusive and uncomfortable. Asking personal questions, probing this scandal or that. It just wasn't for her.

Besides, she wasn't good at thinking on her feet, coming up with follow-up questions.

She let out a deep sigh. Maybe she'd be happier if she quit the newspaper and found another job to supplement her income. Of course, then she'd really be a failure. What would her parents tell their country club friends? *Our pride and joy is a pediatric surgeon*, they'd say of her older sister Isabella. *But we just don't know what to do about poor Ava. Will she ever find her way?*

Ava gulped the last of her wine and poured another half glass. The doorbell rang, and Mr. Belvedere bolted from the room.

She opened the door, and Patrick's mouth gaped. "Wow. In that getup, you'll attract Vanderbrook's attention whether you want it or not."

Shit. Had she overdone it? She stepped aside so he could enter.

He looked her up and down. "You know we're going to an art gallery, not the Academy Awards?"

The comment poked at her insecurities. "Yes, I'm aware."

"So why the dress?"

What was she going to say? That her appearance was her armor? Or that his never-ending nattering about Ian Vander-brook triggered those familiar feelings of never measuring up? "I like it."

"Well, you look amazing."

"Thank you." She might not be the smartest or the most interesting, but she could at least be the prettiest. "You don't look so bad yourself."

This might be the first time she'd ever have described her friend as handsome. A few inches shy of six feet and with a somewhat doughy physique, the word that typically came to mind when she thought of Patrick was *nondescript*. Tonight, however, he was striking. His blond hair had been cut and styled, and the dark blue suit he wore fit him perfectly.

"This is all Amanda's doing. I guess she didn't want me to look like a slob for her big night."

Amanda had done a great job. The only thing that didn't fit with his new suave image was the red polka-dot tie. She looked again. Wait, those weren't polka dots. She stepped forward to inspect the garment. "Puppies? You are going to a ritzy social event and wearing a necktie with puppies?"

He tugged the tie from her grasp. "It reminds me of Beagle Bailey." Patrick and his spoiled little dog were inseparable. "I figured they were small enough no one would notice."

"Should I assume the tie wasn't Amanda-approved?"

"I've been dressing myself for over three decades. I think I can pick out a tie," he said, side-stepping her question.

She finished her wine and grabbed her tiny handbag, cinching it around her wrist. The thing only had space for her phone, cash, a couple of credit cards, and a press pass.

Once inside Patrick's SUV, he launched into another lecture. "You're talented. I don't understand why you don't care."

"You're wrong. I do care." Her throat tightened at the admission. Sometimes she wondered if she cared too much. She glanced over. Seeing his stricken expression, her indignation evaporated. He was trying to help. She needed to remember that. "I appreciate your concern. I do, but sometimes it's a bit much. Just because you were born to be a journalist doesn't mean I was."

He shook his head. "But you were."

"No, Patrick, I wasn't. But if you believe I can land this interview, I'll try, but just to be clear, I think it's tacky to bring up work at an event like this."

He scoffed. "It's expected. Trust me." Then his face softened. "And thank you. Just knowing you'll put in the effort means a lot."

"Can I ask you a question?"

"Shoot."

"If an interview with Ian Vanderbrook is such a big deal, why aren't you doing it?"

A moment passed before Patrick answered. "For one thing, it's not the type of story that interests me. For another, career-wise, it'll have a bigger impact for you."

Sometimes Ava forgot how selfless Patrick could be. "It means a lot to know you have my back."

"I'll always have your back. Besides, you're much prettier than me."

Ava ignored his deflection. "What about you? Why are you so eager to attend this thing? You see Amanda all the time."

"As far as Amanda knows, I'm there to support her, but between you and me, I may have a lead on a story. I'm hoping to meet with a source tonight."

"At the museum?"

"Or nearby. He's supposed to reach out."

Patrick was notoriously tight-lipped about his investigations. Asking questions would get her nowhere. "Well, good luck."

"If I'm right, it could be big." Patrick looked like a kid unwrapping a bicycle-shaped present on Christmas morning, and if his instincts told him he was onto something big, he probably was.

She envied his ability to sniff out stories and find people willing to tell him their secrets. This was the requisite skill she lacked. That special something that made people trust him. It was a rare and valuable quality for a reporter, and she doubted he'd be working at the local newspaper for long. He'd already had articles picked up by the wire, and one of these days he'd stumble onto something big.

Patrick found street-side parking a couple of blocks from the museum. Ava climbed out of his vehicle and waited for him to come around the front of the SUV. A light breeze tickled her bare shoulders. She inhaled a hint of salt in the air, and for a moment, didn't mind the outing or the reason for it.

They approached the museum entrance. Ava reached for Patrick's arm. "Can you do me a favor and give me some space for a bit? I need some alone time before I have to turn on the charm."

"Sure, but for the record, you have nothing to worry about."

Had she not been so nervous, she might have stopped to admire the elaborate decoration of the lobby. Instead, she snatched a glass of champagne from the first server she saw and took off into the exhibit.

Damn. For a luxury car, this thing was small. Marcus unfolded himself from the backseat of Freddy's Mercedes and glanced at the museum with its decorative twinkle lights. He opened the front passenger door and helped his mom out of the car.

They stood to the side, waiting for Freddy to get his ticket from the valet. Mom turned and straightened the lapels of Marcus's suit jacket. "You look very handsome tonight." She stretched her arm to pat his cheek. "So much like your father."

The comment—and the mention of Dad—gave him pause. Maybe her forty-five-year marriage wasn't just a blip in the rearview mirror after all.

"Ready to go inside?" Freddy appeared beside his mom and offered his arm. Marcus couldn't help but notice Freddy had selected a silver tie that matched his mom's dress. Had Dad ever bothered to coordinate with his mom's outfits?

Marcus followed them up the steps and into the museum, where Freddy handed over three tickets. Despite loathing the reason he was here, Marcus appreciated the décor. Tiny white lights hung from the ceiling in gentle waves. Red and orange spotlights shot colorful beams up the walls. The entire setup was impressive. Absently, he accepted a program from an usher and a glass of champagne from a server.

"Exhibit's this way." Freddy motioned for Marcus to follow.

He trailed behind, trying to ignore how his mother and Freddy drifted toward one another. Or the way Freddy whispered in his mother's ear, making her giggle.

Marcus wanted his mother to be happy. But watching her flirt with a man who wasn't his father was asking a lot. Then Freddy's hand moved down until it found his mom's ass and squeezed.

Nope.

Marcus shuddered as he veered down an exhibit alleyway. Finding a corner to hide in, he opened the glossy program he'd picked up at the entrance. *Ian Vanderbrook.* He snorted. Surely that wasn't his real name.

Vanderbrook's first painting exhibited in a traveling museum show when he was twelve-years-old. As a teenager and into his early twenties, he lived in South Florida and derived inspiration from the Everglades. In recent years, he's all but disappeared from the art world, choosing instead to travel the globe. An extended visit to Africa rekindled his passion for his art, and the latest exhibit reflects the beauty he found on the continent.

Marcus glanced at the savannah scene in front of him. The predominant colors were red, orange, and yellow, though there were splashes of blue and purple as well. Bright and vibrant.

He wandered. The paintings were eye-catching, but masterpiece seemed like a stretch. Then again, who was he to criticize any of this? He paused every so often to study the work and read the description. Occasionally, other visitors engaged him in conversation. Mostly, he nodded and shrugged.

Turning the corner, he spotted a lone figure leaning against a wall, staring at her phone and sipping on a flute of champagne. His breath caught, and he stopped to stare. The bartender from last night. God, she was beautiful. But what drew his attention was how the light filtered through her skirt, revealing her thighs above sexy black boots.

Her gaze shifted, and she looked straight at him. Her lips—still painted dark red—parted when she saw him.

His feet were moving toward her before he realized it. "Hiding from someone?"

"Possibly."

"Your date?"

Her eyes held steady for a moment. "No, my friend Patrick. He's pushing me into talking to people I don't want to talk to."

"People?"

"The artist. Ian Vanderbrook." She waved at the exhibit. "Want to walk with me?"

"Sure." He set his empty glass on a nearby table and shoved his hands into his pants pockets. "Why does your friend care if you talk to Ian Vanderbrook?"

"He says it'll be good for my career."

He tilted his head in question.

"I'm a reporter. Bartending is a second job." She held out her hand. "I'm Ava, by the way."

"Marcus." She was pretty enough to be on television. "Do you work in TV?"

"Newspaper." She narrowed her eyes. "And yes, they still have those."

He chuckled. "Is there a reason you don't want to talk to this artist guy?"

"Not a good one." She chewed on her bottom lip as though trying to decide how much to share. "I don't enjoy cornering people. Patrick says to someone like Vanderbrook, it's expected, but I think everyone—famous or not—deserves a little privacy."

Marcus considered it for a moment. "Patrick is probably right. Vanderbrook is probably used to being approached by journalists and fans, especially at events like this. But that doesn't mean he likes it."

"Right?" She scrunched her nose. "But I promised I'd try."

"Was Patrick the guy at the bar the other night?"

Surprise registered on her face. "You noticed?"

Well shit. Why not come out and admit to staring at her throughout dinner? "Yeah."

"That's him. He's around here somewhere. His girlfriend does PR for the museum."

So, Patrick wasn't a boyfriend. Marcus wanted to exhale a sigh of relief. But why did it matter? He'd only be here for a few weeks. Not enough time to start a relationship, even a casual one.

They stopped in front of a painting of elephants. Ava pushed her hair behind her ear, and Marcus stared at the slope of her neck rather than the artwork.

"What do you think?" she asked.

"I like it." He also liked the way her dark hair fell over her shoulders. The dark rims around the edges of her light brown eyes. That pert little nose and the pout of her lips.

"Really? Why?" She looked up expectantly.

Crap. She was asking about the painting. "Um...." He tore his gaze from her face. "There's intelligence in their eyes. This one in the foreground—" he pointed to the most prominent feature. "He looks kind of sad, like he's lived a hard life."

"Huh." She was apparently unconvinced by his bumbling reply. "But what does it add to the body of work on Africa? For something to be important, it seems like it ought to have something to say, and in my mind," —she waved her hand at the painting— "this isn't making much of a statement."

She was right. Obviously. He searched for a response and pointed toward the canvas. "These shiny bits are nice." God, what a tool.

Tilting her head and considering his comment as though it hadn't been inane, she studied the piece. "It has an interesting shimmer. I wonder how he did that."

They started walking again.

"I've admitted to hiding out to avoid interviewing famous artists. What brings you out this evening?"

"My mom's new guy is on the board of directors. I'm here with them and also in hiding."

"That bad?"

He shrugged. "Mostly just weird. But your suggestion that I pay attention to how he treated her? It helped. He appears to care for her, and they seem to get along well."

"I'm glad." Ava leaned over and squeezed his arm. "But why the cloak and dagger?"

"I'm relieved she's happy, but I shouldn't have to watch him feel her up."

"Ew."

"You don't have to tell me."

They rounded the corner, with Ava leading the way, but she halted. Marcus nearly collided with her but steadied himself by grasping her shoulders. A sweet floral scent with just a hint of spice enveloped him, the effect as intoxicating as a narcotic. "What's wrong?"

She didn't answer, but looked around, then tugged on the sleeve of his jacket. "This way."

He allowed himself to be dragged to a door behind one of the portable exhibit walls. "Where are you going?"

Shaking her head, she yanked it open and hauled him inside a brightly lit hallway. The door slammed shut. She leaned against it, her breaths heavy, like a criminal evading capture.

A laugh bubbled forth. He couldn't help it. "What's going on?"

"I saw Patrick talking to Ian Vanderbrook. He's trying to help, but it's too much. The interview is a big deal, and I don't need the attention or the pressure."

"Wow, you're really determined to avoid this guy." Seemed like a dramatic reaction, but what did he know? He was just glad to have her to himself. "How did you know there was a door here?"

"Saw it on my first loop of the exhibit while scoping out possible exit strategies."

He shook his head, equal parts impressed and amused. "Do you often sneak through unlocked doors marked *Staff Only*?"

"Don't you?"

"Not if I can help it." Though he had to admit, this was the most fun he'd had in a long time. "Do you worry about getting caught?"

She dug into the little bag secured around her wrist and yanked out a plastic identification card on a lanyard. "That's what the press pass is for. Everyone knows nosy reporters go where they don't belong."

He smiled, realizing he'd done something similar to gain access to his mom's neighborhood. Perhaps they were compatible in other ways as well. If only he had more time to find out because even though they'd just met, she was surprisingly easy to talk to.

Again, he stared at the curve of her neck and the way her hair skimmed her bare shoulders. Those big eyes and full lips. He had a sudden urge to run his thumb along her jawline.

She craned her head. "Do you hear that?"

"Hear what?"

"Voices." Taking off at a quick clip, she headed down the hall toward a door with a narrow window. She held a finger against her lips.

Curious, Marcus peered through the glass. A paint-streaked wooden table, tubes of acrylic, and canvas stretchers. Clearly a studio, possibly a classroom. A shadow fell on the work stand, but the arguers were not visible. Which was just as well.

"Be reasonable. Two days isn't enough time." Desperation coated an accented voice.

Another, deeper voice responded. "You've forgotten who works for who."

"I did as you asked. You promised me a show." The accent became more pronounced. A heavy quiver threaded the words. "We had a deal."

Ava turned to Marcus, eyebrows raised.

"And we still do, but right now, you are in no position to bargain." There was a pause. "I own you."

The first voice let out a bitter laugh. "That's where you're wrong."

Marcus had been around enough criminals to know they were not kind to eavesdroppers. Whatever this was, getting caught listening would not end well.

Movement on the other side of the door spurred him into action. Before he could think better of it, he pushed Ava against the wall. Then, like the hero in an old, campy detective movie, he leaned in and pressed his mouth to hers.

Chapter 4

Marcus hadn't meant to kiss her and certainly not like this. But he was glad he did, because after a moment of brief resistance, her lips softened. Her mouth was warm and plush. Confident and inviting.

Closing his eyes, he gave in to the kiss. One of his hands found the small of her back and the other wound into her hair. Ava let out a breathy moan, and when her lips parted, he took it as an invitation, slipping his tongue inside. She tasted of champagne and cherry lip gloss. Lost in sensation, he dragged her against him.

There was an intimacy in the kiss that went beyond attraction. Something about this woman drew him to her. He wanted to savor her. Protect her. Worship her.

Now it was his turn to moan. How easy it would be to lose himself. Here. Now.

A sudden shove propelled him forward, thrusting him into Ava and pinning her against the wall. The offender grunted an apology, and though Marcus's body approved of the closeness, his investigative instincts were hard to ignore. He tore his gaze from her just in time to see the back of a short, stocky man in a gray t-shirt, jeans, and a long dark ponytail hurrying away.

Marcus turned and found himself staring into Ava's eyes, her look of shock and confusion mirroring the emotions tearing up his insides. The moment was heavy, but then he realized he was still pressed against her. He stepped away.

She blinked, and the dazed look gave way to excitement. "What do you think that was about?"

Truthfully, a couple of things came to mind. Blackmail. Coercion. Things he didn't want to get involved in. "Don't know, but it's none of our business."

"Aren't you curious?" Ava darted toward the studio door where the owner of voice number two was presumably still inside.

Marcus stopped her. This situation—these people—could be dangerous. The last thing they needed was to be seen.

"Come on. We should get back to the party." He reached for her hand and tugged her down the corridor.

Someone spotted them as soon as they stepped into the exhibit hall.

The guy from the bar waved his hands. "Ava!" He was standing with a thin woman in a green gown. Her tense stare pinballed around the room.

Ava pulled on Marcus's sleeve. "Come on. Might as well introduce you to Patrick and Amanda."

Patrick had just shoved a small sandwich in his mouth when they approached. He wiped his palms on his pants and extended his hand to Marcus. His gaze slid between Marcus and Ava, and though he said nothing, there was something obnoxious in his cocked eyebrow.

"Patrick, this is Marcus. He was at the bar the other night. We just ran into each other."

Taking the other man's hand, Marcus squeezed harder than was necessary and didn't release his grip until the corner of Patrick's mouth twitched into a grimace.

"Marcus, this is Patrick O'Donnell. Patrick is a colleague at the paper, though it's only a matter of time before he moves on to bigger and better things."

"You could too with a little effort."

The comment struck Marcus as condescending. "I think she's pretty amazing as she is."

Patrick turned to the haggard and distracted woman beside him. "My girlfriend, Amanda Soto. She had a hand in putting all this together."

Marcus shook Amanda's hand. "The event is wonderful. I hope you'll get to enjoy some of it."

"You and me both, but at the moment, that seems unlikely. Security has been a nightmare. Not only do we have to deal with the protection of the exhibit, but we've got the paintings for the auction to think about as well."

Though tempted to ask for more information, Marcus kept his mouth shut. He was here to enjoy himself.

Patrick had no such qualms. "What's going on?"

"Everyone's worked up about the paintings Vanderbrook donated. They were removed for display about thirty minutes ago."

"When did the museum receive the paintings?" Patrick asked.

"The ones for the auction came last week. Well, except for the *African Sun* donation—we've had that for months, since the rest of the series arrived…"

Marcus followed Amanda's gaze to a tall, well-dressed man headed their way, his eyes focused on Ava. Marcus recognized him from the brochure.

Ian Vanderbrook.

The artist, though at least a decade and a half older, was handsome, but Ava was more interested in Marcus—the man who'd kissed her so thoroughly her knees had gone weak. The man now standing awkwardly at her side.

Patrick hurried to seize the moment. "Mr. Vanderbrook, have you met my colleague, Ava Montoya?"

Of course they hadn't met. Patrick knew that. When would he get it through his thick head that none of this mattered?

"Nice to meet you, Mr. Vanderbrook."

He was tall with a square jaw. His short dark hair had a disheveled, just-got-out-of-bed look that created a sexy, absent-minded professor vibe.

"Ian, please." His voice was smooth and deep.

Patrick gave her a double thumbs-up from behind the man, and she considered how to ease herself into asking for an interview. A newspaper article was undoubtedly the last thing on the artist's mind. It was certainly the last thing she cared about right now, with her brain still stuck on kissing Marcus and the pleasurable tingles he'd coaxed.

Not wanting to be impolite and worried he'd bolt, she turned to introduce him. "This is my friend, Marcus."

Vanderbrook stuck out his hand, but she didn't miss the question in his raised eyebrow. "Nice to meet you."

"Likewise." Marcus returned the handshake, though his voice seemed to have dropped an octave.

"So..." Ian drew out the word as he pivoted back to Ava. "Are you enjoying the exhibit?"

"It's wonderful, though I know very little about art."

"I could show you around? Answer any questions." He offered his elbow.

Ava caught Patrick's impatient glare. This was her chance, and if she passed up the opportunity to ask this man questions, Patrick would never let her hear the end of it. She looked at Marcus. He offered a small but encouraging nod.

"It would be an honor."

Patrick grinned like a cartoon villain.

Ava wove her hand through Vanderbrook's offered elbow and allowed him to lead her toward the exhibit. She couldn't help but glance back at Marcus, still standing with Patrick and Amanda, but staring at her.

"Is there anything specific you'd like to see? Anything you're curious about?"

Had she been more like Patrick, she would have seen that as an invitation to ask about a formal interview. But she wasn't Patrick, and she wouldn't misinterpret the offer. "I must confess, I know very little about any of this. How about you give me a newbie's orientation?"

The corners of his eyes crinkled when he grinned down at her. "It would be my pleasure."

"Is this your first time in this museum?"

He chuckled. "Oh my, no. I've only been in this building a few times, but I was at the original location often when I lived here."

"So, what is your advice for someone new to the art scene?"

Looking pensive, he ran the back of his fingers beneath his chin. "When I'm in a new gallery, I like to pretend I can pick one piece of art to take home with me. As I go through the museum, I ask myself questions about which I'd most like to own and why."

This was not something Ava would have thought of, but she could see how it might make the experience more enjoyable. "That sounds fun. And a good way to stop and think about the pieces."

"The exercise helps me clear my head, but it might be useful for someone just wanting to spend an afternoon appreciating art."

A server carrying champagne stepped in front of them. Vanderbrook gave Ava a questioning look. She nodded, and he plucked two flutes off the tray. She accepted one and took a sip.

"Fort Lauderdale has a nice variety of pieces from notable artists, though much of the work is on loan from private collections."

She considered this for a moment. "People spend a lot of money on their art. Why turn around and loan it to a museum?"

"Lots of reasons. Loaning art is a way to see it hanging in a museum without having to give it away. There's vanity. Collectors want people to see it and know it belongs to them. For others, it's about sharing their collection with the public."

They ended up in front of the three paintings that had been set up for the auction. Ava noted that two of the paintings appeared to feature South Florida. One was of the Everglades. The other a beach scene. The third was obviously part of the Africa series. "Why did you select these paintings?"

"Did you know I lived in South Florida as a teenager?"

Ava shook her head. Perhaps that explained his connection to the museum.

"This is where I became interested in the preservation of plant and animal life." He pointed at the two Florida paintings. "I painted these while I lived here. They seemed a fitting donation given that the proceeds will go to the Everglades Restoration Fund."

She stared at the painting titled *River of Grass*. Through some sort of optical illusion, the blades of grass almost seemed to move. And to think a high school student had painted it. Her own adolescence had been filled with failure and uncertainty. To be so skilled at such a young age was something she could scarcely imagine. "That's very generous of you."

"Hardly. The renewal of habitat is so much more important than keeping these paintings for myself." The words sounded scripted, and she caught a flicker of regret in his eyes.

"And what about this one?" She pointed at the extraordinary savanna scene and leaned forward to see the title. *Masai Mara Reserve in the Morning*. The background was painted in shades of orange and red, and in the foreground were an acacia tree and a line of buffalo. Again, she noted the same shimmering quality that appeared in the other paintings. A mirage in acrylic.

"Pure enticement." He didn't elaborate, and they stared at the paintings in companionable silence for a beat before Ian's attention returned to her. "Do you feel you've gotten the full tour?"

"I do, thank you." She blushed. "Though I'm pretty sure I'm still a newb."

"Do you want my advice?"

"Of course."

"Anytime you look at art, slow down and take it in. How you view a piece of artwork is intensely personal. Every person sees something different, and their experience is unlike anyone else's. Look for what you like and what you don't like. Think about whether it speaks to you, and if so, what it's saying."

"It's almost as if you know what you're talking about," she quipped.

He smiled, and his eyes did that crinkly thing again. "Now, how about we get you back to your date?"

Was she that obvious? She'd only just met Marcus, but could still feel his kiss lingering on her lips. She opened her mouth to speak, but no sound came out. Ian walked her toward the cafe table where she'd last seen Marcus. Patrick, who was leaning against the wall typing furiously into his phone, was the only one left.

"Thank you. I appreciate the tutorial."

Ian dug into his suit pocket. "Here's my card in case you'd like to talk again professionally."

How did he—? "I never mentioned I was a journalist."

"No, but your friend did." He tilted his chin in Patrick's direction. "He thinks a lot of you."

Ava wasn't sure how to respond. Despite Patrick's pushiness about her career, he was a good friend. She took the card and tucked it into her bag. "Thank you."

"I hope we meet again."

"So do I." And she meant it. The man had been more forthcoming and easier to talk to than she'd anticipated, though why he was so agreeable to an interview was a mystery. "I'll be in touch."

He tipped his head, then turned to leave.

When Patrick looked up from his phone, she shoved him in the shoulder. "You told him I was a reporter."

"I knew you wouldn't do it." He grinned. "How'd it go?"

"Great. I think I'll follow up on an interview."

"That's my girl."

She ignored his condescension. "How is your night going?"

"Not bad. I'm about to step out to meet with my source, but I'll be back before the auction."

Ava nodded. With the dreaded Ian Vanderbrook introduction behind her, she could relax and have a good time.

Now to find Marcus.

And maybe get some more of those kisses.

Chapter 5

M arcus had wandered away from Patrick not long after Ava left with the artist. Besides the fact that the guy didn't lift his eyes from his phone the entire time, they had nothing in common, and Marcus saw no reason to stick around waiting for Ava to return. Watching a celebrity flirt with the woman he had just pinned against a wall was like a kick in the balls.

She could have any man she wanted, and compared to someone like Ian Vanderbrook, Marcus was about as appealing as a pair of used underwear.

Other than an impromptu kiss in a hallway, what else did he have to offer? Anyone could see that Ian Vanderbrook was more successful, more attractive, and more desirable. Despite the obvious age difference, the man had a refined air about him. The hundred-dollar haircut. The bespoke tailored suit. There was zero chance the artist bought his clothing from an outlet mall overrun with sunburned cruise ship passengers.

Ava would be a fool to turn down any sort of interest from a man like that.

He had no shot with her. Hell, he didn't even live in Florida, and he had no interest in a long-distance relationship—or any relationship, for that matter. As far as he was concerned, his professional life was more important than anything personal.

Marcus made a beeline for the lobby and the cash bar he'd spotted on his way into the exhibit. He ordered a beer and then looked for some tucked-away corner where he could hide. He'd just found the perfect spot when his mother's voice carried over the portico.

"Woo hoo! Darling." With the way Mom's silver dress glittered and her excited waving, she was impossible to miss.

And he loved her for it. Because despite all the things that had changed—Dad's death, the move to Florida, her new boyfriend—she was still Mom. The wacky woman who believed in telepathic communication and who'd followed him like a paparazzo on his first day of college. And despite being a man in his mid-thirties, there was something comforting about knowing some things in life would never change.

He made his way across the lobby to where his mother stood beside Freddy, who was deep in conversation with a tall, older man.

"Where have you been?" His mother's voice was a tad loud.

"Do you remember the bartender from the burger joint the other night?"

"The cute girl with the big lips you kept staring at?"

Leave it to Mom to cut to the chase. "Yes, her. She's here. We walked around looking at paintings for a bit, but then she had something to do for work."

"Is she a server?" His mom twisted as she looked about the room.

"She's a reporter. That artist came along, and she went off with him."

His mother took another big sip of wine. "He's a good-looking man."

"So I'm told."

She flattened his tie against his chest. "Not half as attractive as you."

"You might be partial, but it's nice to hear." He crossed his arms and gave her a pointed look. "You called me over like you had something to tell me."

"Freddy has someone to introduce you to." She tugged on Freddy's sleeve. "Marcus is here."

Freddy adjusted his glasses and peered at Marcus. "Ah yes. This is George Gerou, the director of the museum. George, this is Vi's boy. He's an FBI agent."

The other man leaned forward and offered his hand. "Is that so? Are you local?"

"Based in the Northeast. I'm just here to check in on Mom."

His mother swatted his arm. "I can take care of myself."

Perhaps she could, but he worried. At least she seemed happy and wasn't staying home to watch game shows and the evening news.

"George has done a lot for the museum, not to mention the local art scene." Freddy took a sip of his beer. "He's the one who brought in the Ian Vanderbrook exhibit."

Marcus tried to look impressed, though in truth, he didn't care. "I don't know much about art, but I know the name Ian Vanderbrook." Or at least he did now. "Quite exciting. You must be proud."

Gerou rolled back on his heels. "Yes, it's a real coup to get a big name like Vanderbrook in here. It's been a lot of work, but it's worth it."

"By work he means wining and dining," Freddy said. "George could charm a donation from the Vatican."

Gerou laughed and clapped Freddy on the back. "You're overselling my skills."

Marcus looked around the space. "This building looks new."

"Just celebrated our five-year anniversary," Gerou said. "Freddy had no small hand in making that dream a reality."

Marcus turned his attention to Freddy, who had apparently done a bit of everything. "I ran a contracting business in New York City for twenty years. Helped George secure the funding and permits, found him an architect, things like that."

"Oh, Freddy is being modest. We'd still be in that tiny building off Federal Highway if it hadn't been for his connections."

Marcus sipped his beer and did his best to feign interest. Clearly, his mother was impressed with Freddy. He should pretend to be as well.

Beer almost drained, he looked at the bar, and his chest tightened when he spotted Ava chatting with the bartender and accepting a glass of red wine. She threw her hair over her shoulder and laughed. The guy beamed, looking pleased with himself, and Marcus knew how he felt. He had no claim on her—he knew that, and yet little prickles of jealousy plucked at his chest.

He shook it off but couldn't stop staring. Her dress did something to him. The sheer skirt revealed her perfectly round ass covered by some sort of leotard, and those thigh-high boots stimulated his imagination in a way completely inappropriate for a public space.

Something smacked him in the chest. He startled and looked down at his mother. "That is some dress. Do you think I could get away with wearing something like that?"

He stared at his petite mother with a mixture of horror, revulsion, and relief. The thought of her wearing something risqué like the dress Ava had chosen for this evening was not an image he needed, but it also killed any hint of arousal. For that, he was grateful.

"Go talk to her." She gave a not-so-subtle chin jerk toward the bar where Ava was still smiling and laughing with the bartender. "Or do you need me to do it for you?"

Mom would be the perfect excuse to approach her again. Ava had seen his mom at the restaurant, so it wouldn't be that unusual. He was about to suggest it, then saw the eager look on her face.

"Would you like to meet her?"

Mom gave him an enthusiastic nod. "I haven't seen you this taken with a girl since your junior year in high school."

Marcus groaned at the memory. He'd had a hopeless crush on Brandi McVeigh, the captain of the cheerleading squad. When Marcus showed up for the blind date his mom had orchestrated, he found Brandi making out with a much older guy. She shoved twenty dollars at him, told him to keep his mouth shut, then got into the passenger seat of the guy's car and drove away.

After going to the movies alone and lying to his friends about the outcome, he vowed never to involve Mom in his love life again.

"This is an introduction only." He stressed the word *only*. "Don't embarrass me or try to manipulate the situation."

"Is that how you see me? Some meddling shrew who doesn't know when to shut up?"

He raised an eyebrow and received another smack in the chest with his mother's handbag.

"I'll be good, I promise."

"I'm not sure I believe you." Sure, he could go for another beer and try to pick up the conversation where they left off. Or he could take his mom over there, knowing Ava would give them her full attention. "Let's go."

Ava's smile widened as they approached. Marcus felt a grin stretch across his face, and something loosened inside him.

"Ava, this is my mother, Violet Anderson."

Mom rushed forward to grip Ava's hand. "It's so nice to meet you. I noticed you at the bar the other night, and Marcus said you'd been chatting."

She returned his mom's greeting with a smile. "Yes, I noticed you and your handsome date as well."

"You'll have to fight me for him."

Ava let out a delighted and surprised laugh and glanced up at Marcus with a twinkle in her eye. "I think he's a bit out of my league, but I can appreciate an attractive man with white hair."

"Nonsense. You're stunning." His mom took one of Ava's hands in each of her own and spread her arms wide. "And look at that dress."

"Thank you. I bought it this morning on Las Olas."

"We should go shopping sometime. I'm always on the look-out for a flattering new outfit. I need something that says va-va-voom."

Marcus groaned, and both women turned to look at him. While Ava's gaze conveyed amusement, his mother shot daggers with her annoyed glare. Dismissing him, she turned back to Ava. "My son likes to pretend I'm a half-dead, sexless lump of wrinkles and cellulite."

He clenched his jaw, but didn't respond. What would be the point?

Mom's attention was back on Ava. "Marcus tells me you're a reporter. That sounds exciting."

"It can be," Ava hedged. "I don't think I'm going to be doing it for the rest of my life. I'm not very good at it."

"No one is good at something when they first start. You should have heard Marcus complain when he went through FBI training. Where did you do that again, honey?"

"Quantico."

A look of respect filled Ava's gaze. People often responded with awe and admiration when they found out what he did, but something about seeing that look on Ava's face sent his body temperature up a degree.

"Right. I knew it was on a military base." Mom continued her chattering, unaware of the heaviness of the moment. She squeezed Ava's arm. "You're still young. Surely, you've not been a reporter for very long?"

Ava patted his mother's hand, still resting on her arm. "I'm twenty-nine. I graduated with a degree in journalism when I was twenty-two, but I've only been working at the newspaper for about a year. Before that, I bummed around, going from job to job. Most recently, I was writing copy for a medical supply company."

"See! You're still new," his mother said, convinced of her own wisdom. "You just need to give it time."

"Thank you for the encouragement. It means more than you know."

Something sad flickered in Ava's eyes, and Marcus decided it was time for a conversation change. He opened his mouth and said the first dumb thing that came to mind. "How was your conversation with Ian Vanderbrook?" Dammit. That guy was the last thing he wanted to talk about.

"Turns out Patrick had already spoken to him about me. He gave me his card so we can schedule an interview."

Bing bong. The unmistakable alert of a message over the PA system. "Guests, please make your way to Exhibit Hall A. The charity auction will begin in ten minutes."

His mother squeezed his hand and gave him a wink. "I'd better find Freddy. I'll see you two inside."

Another perfect setup orchestrated by Mom. He had to hand it to her. The woman was savvier than he gave her credit for.

He peered down at his companion. "Shall we?"

Ava wove her hand into the crook of his elbow. "Let's do this."

Chapter 6

There was a buzz of energy in the room as the auctioneer picked up his gavel. Ava glanced at Marcus and his towering form beside her. He had strong features. A mouth that was quirked into a perpetual grin, hazel eyes constantly lit with amusement, and facial hair that was somewhere between scruff and beard.

And funny? Without a doubt. He had the ability to make her laugh, while projecting a protectiveness that made her feel safe. Of course, now that she'd learned what he did for a living, that made a lot more sense. And damn if she didn't want to soak up every bit of his power and confidence. Wrap it around her like a blanket. Let it smother her, if that's what it took to get more of him.

And then there was the kiss. That unexpected, wonderful, bone-melting kiss. How could someone she'd just met make her feel so many things with the touch of his lips? She nearly groaned, remembering the emotions he'd drawn from her, the way she'd felt desired, cherished, safe.

They stood near the back wall. Marcus's mother and her companion sat in wooden folding chairs in the front row to the left of the podium. Seaside City Commissioner Martin Singh was also in attendance, sitting in the back. He glanced at Ava several times.

Marcus leaned over to whisper in her ear, his breath tickling the hairs on the back of her neck. "My mom seems to be enjoying herself."

She nodded. Indeed, Mrs. Anderson had done her part, flinging her paddle and driving up the price of the first two paintings. Ava had to give the woman credit. By all appearances, she was having a grand time, and Freddy seemed happy to sit beside her, watching her have fun. "Your mom is amazing."

He gave her an odd look, but the truth was, she meant it. When talking about her son, Violet Anderson exuded pride, and her encouragement regarding Ava's career had been patient and genuine. A sentiment she'd never experienced from her own parents, who preferred to ignore her shortcomings rather than accept them.

Ian Vanderbrook stepped to the front of the room. "Thank you all for coming." His voice boomed, thick and deep. "Plants and animals have been important themes in my work since I lived in South Florida as a young man, and it is an honor to have this opportunity to contribute to the Everglades Restoration Fund."

Polite clapping filled the room.

"As you may have heard, I spent some time in Africa and was struck by the generous spirit of the people. It was this, combined with the beauty of the continent, that inspired the *African Sun* series." He put his hands together and bowed slightly. "I appreciate your continued support of my work, this museum, and especially the preservation of plant and animal life."

There was a drumroll, and the lights dimmed. A spotlight drew attention to the center of the room, where *Masai Mara Reserve in the Morning* was illuminated. The crowd gasped. Even Marcus appeared awed by the beauty of the piece.

The piece glittered and looked somehow even more impressive than it had earlier. "I take back everything I said about his work not having value. This is amazing," Ava mumbled.

The auctioneer began the bidding. In a flurry of activity, the price climbed higher and higher, until the man behind the podium began his chant. "Going once. Going twice. Sold to bidder number seventy-five."

The room erupted in applause.

"Jesus, that's a lot of money," Marcus muttered.

The crowd dispersed. Martin Singh made a beeline straight for Ava.

"Miss Montoya, so good to see you again." The commissioner's voice swelled with a good-natured familiarity. "I'm sorry we didn't get to speak at the rec center the other day. I imagine you have questions about how our development will enhance the community."

"I haven't written my article yet and have some questions about the residents' concerns." But now wasn't the time to discuss it. "Can I follow up with you early next week?"

"Splendid. If I don't hear from you by Tuesday morning, I'll have my secretary set something up."

"Who was that?" Marcus asked once Singh was gone.

"Commissioner for the city I cover. He's involved in a controversial development project. He thinks I'm going to provide good publicity."

"That happens a lot, doesn't it?"

Ava tilted her head and considered his question. "What does?"

"People underestimate you."

Little did he know how often the phrase, *just a pretty face*, was used to describe her. Still, she liked thinking he hadn't figured that out yet. "You're sweet."

"I try." He turned to face her, something that might have been regret filling his eyes. "So, I guess that's it."

"Guess so." She didn't want the night to end either, but scanned the crowd, looking for her ride. "I'm not sure where Patrick got off to." Guilt washed over her. Patrick arranged for her to talk to Ian Vanderbrook, even brokered an interview, and she'd not even noticed his absence from the auction. "Have you seen him?"

Marcus shook his head. "Not since you walked off with Vanderbrook to look at the exhibit."

Something niggled at Ava's subconscious. "He said he was going to meet with a source, but promised to be back for the auction."

"Maybe it took longer than he expected."

"Maybe..." But if that was the case, why hadn't he called? Or sent a text. She typed out a quick message.

—*Where are you?*—

"There's Amanda. She'll know." Ava grabbed Marcus's hand and tugged him across the room to where Patrick's girlfriend stood with her boss. "The event was spectacular. Thank you so much for inviting me."

There was a glow in Amanda's eyes that told Ava the night had been a success. "You're welcome. I can't tell you how relieved I am there were no major disasters."

Amanda gestured to the man standing beside her. "Ava, have you met Mr. Gerou? Patrick said you might be working on an article about the exhibit. Mr. Gerou knows more about the operation than anyone else."

The museum director reached over to shake Ava's hand. "Did you enjoy yourself?"

"It was magnificent."

"Glad to hear it." Gerou shifted his attention toward Marcus. "And what did you think?"

"Fantastic."

Gerou nodded, but then his gaze wandered. "Forgive me, but I see someone I need to speak with." He tipped his chin and walked off toward a man who looked a lot like Jared Meeks, the developer behind the Beachside project. The men shook hands and then left the room together.

"Speaking of Patrick—" Ava turned to Amanda. "Have you seen him?"

Amanda's lips pressed into a thin line. "I haven't. I was hoping you might know where he was."

"He told me he was going to meet someone about a story, but said he'd be back for the auction."

"Probably got held up. He's your ride, isn't he?"

Ava nodded. "I sent a text, but he hasn't responded."

"If you don't mind waiting for me to take care of the cleanup, I'll give you a ride home."

Truth be told, Ava didn't want to wait around any longer than necessary. "Thanks for the offer, but I think I might just call a rideshare."

"Let me know if you change your mind." And with that, Amanda was gone.

Marcus cleared his throat. "If you don't mind riding in the back of Freddy's car, we can give you a ride to my hotel, then I can get my truck and take you home."

"Sounds like a plan." More time with Marcus was exactly what she wanted.

~ell~

They pulled up to Marcus's hotel, and he climbed from the backseat of Freddy's car, intending to hurry around the back to offer a hand to Ava—because God knew how she could walk with the heels on those boots.

"Marcus, come here. I want to say something to you," his mother called from the front passenger seat.

Hopefully, she wanted to make plans for tomorrow and wouldn't comment on his love life. Or, God forbid, offer advice. "Yes?"

"Have fun with Ava. I like her. She's a nice girl."

"I'm only giving her a ride home."

His mother ignored his protest. "Unlike Freddy and me, you're still young. Sex has consequences. If you don't have protection, there are other things you can do."

He sputtered, unable to form a response. His gaze strayed from his mother over the roof of the car to where Ava stood watching. Had she heard? Mom's stage whispers were never very quiet. "Nothing is going to happen."

"I worry about you. You forget to have fun. She likes you, and tonight, enjoy yourself."

"Mom—" She couldn't have missed the warning in his voice.

"Call me tomorrow and let me know how it goes." With that proclamation, she rolled up her window, and Freddy sped away.

He was left standing in the middle of the circular drive, confused and troubled by his mom's foreplay comment. He shook it off, and with three long strides was standing in front of Ava. "I need to go up and get my keys. Do you want to wait in the lobby or..." Leaving the thought unfinished, he rubbed a hand against the back of his neck.

"I'll go with you if that's okay."

Ava. In his room. *Don't read too much into it.* Unfortunately, his body had other ideas.

"After you." He gestured toward the hotel's automatic doors and followed her inside. Her round little ass, combined with the sway of her hips, did nothing to stop his cock from stiffening against the zipper of his pants.

Falling in step beside her, he put his hand on the small of her back, guiding her through the lobby. "Elevator's this way."

The ride to the second floor was short, and before he knew it, the doors dinged open and he was directing her to his room.

What was happening here? Was she just coming up so he could get his keys, or was she hoping for something else? He wasn't against a vacation fling, but he liked Ava and didn't want to assume something that would ruin their developing friendship. Besides, he'd outgrown the meaningless-sex phase of his life.

He pressed his keycard against the pad and nudged the door open. She stepped past him and took a seat at the end of the king-size bed. He snatched his keys off the top of the TV cabinet, still unsure what she was thinking.

"Your mom is great."

He looked at Ava perched on the edge of the bed. "Most of the time." When she wasn't doling out hook-up advice.

"I mean it. She's very easy to talk to. I wonder how things would have been different if my parents had been more encouraging."

He set the keys down and sat beside her. "Your parents weren't supportive?"

"Not at all." The matter-of-fact tone of her voice tugged at something in his chest. She continued with a sigh, but the words sounded mechanical, rehearsed. "School was hard for me. My parents assumed the problem was that I didn't try. When I did poorly, they'd yank me out of one school and enroll me in another. I attended ten different schools between first and twelfth grade."

"I can't imagine." Marcus grew up with the same group of kids, elementary to high school. "My experience was the opposite. The kids in kindergarten were the same ones at graduation."

"Sounds like a dream."

"Not really. Everyone remembers every stupid or embarrassing thing you ever did. There were times I would have killed for a little anonymity."

She nodded, but the sad look on her face ignited a need to wrap her up and pull her close. Instead, he clasped his hands together and leaned forward to rest his elbows on his knees.

Ava continued. "Thank God for Nana. She was the one person I could always count on."

"She passed away?"

"Last summer. She left me her house. That's when I moved down here and started working at the newspaper."

"I'm sorry for your loss."

"Me too."

Ava frowned, and this time he didn't resist the need to touch her. He wrapped an arm around her shoulder and tugged her close.

"You want something to drink? I picked up a couple of six packs the other night."

"Sounds great."

Marcus pushed himself off the bed and retrieved two bottles from the mini-fridge. He twisted off the tops and tossed them into the garbage.

Zzzzziiiipppp. He turned just in time to see Ava with her skirt shoved up her thighs, tugging off one of her boots. Part of him wanted to tell her to put it back on, but maybe if he couldn't see the sexy boots, he wouldn't fantasize about them.

Ava removed the other boot, massaged the arch of her foot, and groaned. "Man, that feels good."

The thrum of her moan wrapped itself around him and squeezed until he forgot to breathe. He stood, a beer bottle in each hand, staring. He knew beautiful women. Hell, he'd slept with a few of them. But none had ever had the ability to turn him on with something as simple as a sound.

"Here." He thrust a bottle in her direction.

She reached for it, scooted back on the bed to prop herself against the pillows and took a long pull. He kicked off his shoes and settled beside her, sipping his beer.

"So, FBI?"

He turned to find her staring, with an appreciative gleam in her eye.

"I bet women love that."

He smiled, but didn't respond. Were there law enforcement groupies? Sure. Women who got off on a gun and a badge? Absolutely. Had he indulged a few fantasies? Without a doubt. "And what about you? What's your opinion?"

She shrugged. "If you're asking whether I've ever watched old episodes of *The X-Files* and fantasized about being locked in a bunker with Mulder, the answer is yes."

He laughed. "You're a little young to have a thing for Mulder, aren't you?"

"I don't know. A strong, attractive man willing to entertain all possibilities. I think that type of sexiness is timeless."

Once again, he found himself staring at her mouth. She must have noticed because her tongue darted out, wetting her bottom lip. And then, without conscious thought, he was leaning toward her.

"Was that kiss at the museum just pretend?" Her murmured words beckoned him closer.

He took her beer and placed both on the nightstand. "You tell me."

The first brush of their mouths was light, tentative, but the feel of her lips was also a revelation. Satin and silk. Sweet and delicious. He nipped at her lip, delighting in her groaned response. Hoarse, raspy, and filled with desire. Quite possibly the sexiest sound he'd ever heard.

She returned the bite, sucking, then dragging her teeth against his lip. His answering growl was feral and left no doubt of his desire. He urged her back onto the pillow, fitting himself against her, his erection pressing into her leg.

"Well, that is *not* pretend." She let out a delighted gasp when he ground against her.

For a moment, he wished he had a snappy response, but his lustful brain had no resources to spare, so he replied with a trail of kisses that went up her neck from collarbone to ear. She dragged her lips across his face until her mouth was on his again. This time, their kisses were hot, desperate, unrestrained.

Good God, what was it about this woman? He'd only just met her, but sensed she had the power to destroy him. And he'd let her. Gladly.

Her fingers danced up his neck, settling on the short hairs at his nape. Nails raked into his scalp, and her tongue stroked against his. Something possessive took root, and he wanted to lay claim, to make her his. *Slow down.* She'd given no sign she wanted more than a kiss.

He pulled away, panting and rolled onto his back. "Well? Real or make-believe?"

"Hmmm." She put a finger against those red, swollen lips, pretending to consider his question. "I could almost believe it was real, but I might need some more convincing."

He drew her against his side and kissed her long and slow. He wanted nothing more than to continue what they were doing—and then some.

They broke apart, and her mouth cracked into a yawn.

"Maybe I should take you home? I've obviously exhausted you." He waggled his eyebrows. "And we can save the persuasion for another time." He held his breath, worried she'd say yes to going home, but no to seeing him again.

"I'll take a rain check on the kissing, but I don't have to leave right now." She gazed up, uncertainty glittering in her eyes. "If that's all right with you."

"More than all right." He draped an arm over her shoulder, snuggled her against him and kissed the top of her head. She nestled into the crook of his arm, and he gripped the remote, clicking through until he found that old comedy about two guys headed to Aspen to return a briefcase full of cash. He settled in to watch, happier than he'd been in a long time.

Then, something—or someone—was jostling his shoulder.

"We fell asleep."

"Sorry?" He blinked sleepy eyes, his gaze finding Ava.

"Can you take me home? I need to feed my cat."

He sat up, rubbed his palm against the scruff on his jaw, then reached for his shoes. He glanced at the time. Two o'clock in the morning. "Sure. Give me a sec."

She slid her feet into her boots and zipped them up. "Ready when you are."

He grabbed his keys and wallet from the dresser, then turned to look at her. Her hair was flattened against the back of her head, and the makeup around her eyes was smeared. And still, she was stunning.

He held the door open. They exited his room and then the hotel.

The flicker of streetlights lit up the cab of his truck, and he sneaked glances at the woman in the passenger seat. Even hours later, he could still taste her on his lips and feel her warm body beneath his. Should he ask her on a date? Tell her he wanted to see her again?

Ava navigated him into an older neighborhood filled with small, one-story houses. "Turn here. Then take the first left."

He drove slowly, following her directions, not wanting the night to end.

"I'm the first house at the end on the right. The one with the two big palm trees."

They traveled past five houses before arriving at a small single-story with a Chevy Camaro parked in the driveway. There was a second vehicle parked on a patch of gravel beside the road.

"Weird. That's Patrick's SUV. He didn't say anything about stopping by."

Prickles of unease worked their way up Marcus's spine until they bristled the hairs at the back of his neck. A nearby streetlight cast shadows into the vehicle, revealing—if he wasn't mistaken—a figure slumped against the window.

He'd barely shifted into *park* before Ava had her door open and was getting out. "I'll see what he wants."

Events from the evening came careening back. Patrick leaving to see a source. A no-show at the auction he promised to attend.

Leaving Ava without a ride home. No calls. No text of explanation.

Marcus was out of his truck before he realized he'd moved. "Ava, stop!"

Already rounding the back corner of the vehicle, she threw him a smile. "Let me check first."

He lunged for her, uselessly attempting to grab her hand, but she was already at the driver's side door.

Chapter 7

P atrick was dead.

Ava gasped for air and pinched her eyes shut. Nothing would ever erase the image of Patrick slumped against the driver's side window, his nose pressed against the glass, and that vacant look in his eyes.

The realization knocked at her chest, stealing her wind like a belly flop off the high dive at her parents' country club. She folded her arms against her stomach, bent at the waist, and took a slow, ragged breath.

She exhaled, then straightened.

Blue lips hanging open. Gray skin. The splatter of blood on both the window and the tan upholstery of Patrick's headrest.

And that goddamn tie. For some reason, she couldn't stop staring at the dark stain now coating his stupid puppy-printed necktie.

She lurched for the door handle, an anguished cry tearing from her throat.

"Don't touch it." Marcus's voice was sharp, and before she knew it, he'd dragged her from the car, his perusal trailing the length of her body.

She turned back toward the car, needing to get to Patrick. Marcus's big hand clasped hers and wouldn't let go. She tried to pull away, but he tugged her back. Gently, but firmly, he cupped her face in his hands, locking her in place with his steady gaze.

"Sweetheart, I'm sorry, but there's nothing we can do for him now."

"But...he's...I..." she stammered. There had to be something.

He guided her away from the SUV and onto her front porch, where he pushed her into Nana's old rocking chair. "Stay here while I call the police."

He stepped from the porch into the yard and punched a button on his cell phone.

"I'd like to report a death." He was quiet for a few moments, then gave Ava's address. "Gunshot." Another pause. "No, I haven't checked for a pulse... Yes, I'm certain he's dead."

He returned to the porch without disconnecting the call. "Someone should be here soon."

Marcus sat on the ground beside her. One of these days, she should buy another rocking chair, she thought dazedly before returning her attention to Patrick's SUV. She could feel Marcus's worried gaze, and she was glad he was here, but she couldn't talk about it. Not now.

They sat like that for an indeterminable amount of time. A few minutes? An hour? She didn't know.

Sirens sounded in the distance. They grew louder. A sheriff's cruiser stopped in front of her house.

"Wait here." Marcus made his way to the end of the driveway, where he spoke to a young patrolman. She couldn't hear the conversation, but saw him motion toward the car.

The officer gestured for Marcus to stay put, then walked around the back of Patrick's vehicle. When he arrived at the driver's side window, he staggered backwards and covered his mouth. Maybe this was his first dead body. She could sympathize. It wasn't something she'd ever wanted to see. Not something she'd forget either.

After a moment, the policeman tilted his chin toward the radio pinned to his shoulder. He shooed Marcus back to the porch, but followed close behind.

The officer flipped open a notebook. "Can I see some identification, please?"

Marcus reached into his back pocket and removed his wallet, letting it fall open to reveal his badge.

The younger man's eyes got huge. "FBI?"

"I work out of the Philadelphia field office. I'm here on vacation."

Ava fished her driver's license out of the bag cinched to her wrist and handed it to the officer.

He recorded the information and handed her license back. "I'm going to secure the scene. The investigative team is on its way. They'll want to talk to you, so please stay put."

She stared after him.

Patrick was dead. Her house was a crime scene. And the whole thing felt like it was happening to someone else.

Marcus squatted beside the rocking chair, concern etched across his features. "How are you doing?"

"Oh, you know. The usual." The words contained a fury so contradictory to the numbness she felt inside, it surprised her.

He took her hand and squeezed. "You're allowed to be angry."

Her bottom lip quivered. Nope, not now. She could break down later. But now she needed answers. She needed to be strong for Patrick. And she needed to know why this happened.

More police cruisers showed up, blocking the road, their blue and red flashing lights illuminating the neighborhood. At least she lived at the end of a dead-end street. Only a few houses would be affected by the crime scene.

The sky lightened, bringing more vehicles and more people with it. Perhaps she was wrong about the effect on the neighborhood. The police operation now encompassed the length of the road, with the entire community standing around watching.

And the whole time, Marcus stayed on the concrete beside her chair, holding her hand. Thank God he'd been here. What would she have done if she'd arrived home alone?

Alarm filled her chest. She moved to sit beside him. "If I had come straight home last night, do you think I could have prevented this? Helped him?"

He wrapped a strong arm around her shoulders and hauled her against him. "You can't think like that."

"But I wasn't the least bit bothered when he didn't return to the museum." Her chest tightened. Oh God, she'd been glad he wasn't there because it gave her an excuse to spend time with Marcus. "I wasn't here when he needed me."

His voice grew hoarse. "And what if you had been here? They might have shot you too."

An involuntary sob shook her entire body. Marcus tightened his grip, and she buried her face in his chest. "Could it have been random? Wrong place, wrong time?"

She felt him shrug. "Random crimes like this are rare, but you can't rule anything out. For now, we just have to wait and see what the police find."

"This is connected to his meeting last night. I just know it." She straightened while still leaning into Marcus. "He knew the shooter."

"It's possible, but we can't know for sure. Not yet."

Her brain raced through the details she'd been too shocked to think about before. Window rolled up. Patrick's body collapsed onto the driver's side door. No bullet holes in the glass. "Someone was in the passenger seat."

Marcus gave her a sad smile, but one also tinged with surprise and admiration.

"You already figured that out, didn't you?"

"It crossed my mind, but I have more experience with this sort of thing."

Speaking of... wasn't he an investigator? "Why didn't you look for clues? Shouldn't you be down there demanding to know what's going on?"

"It's a crime scene. I wasn't going to walk around destroying evidence. And despite what you see on television, I can't just waltz in and press for information without cause. If you want, I can flash my badge and see if they'll tell me anything as a professional courtesy. But there's always a chance it has the opposite effect."

As much as she wanted answers, she didn't want to be alone. "No, I'm glad you're here."

Ava spotted an older man in black slacks and a sheriff's department pullover. He appeared to be the one in charge, and then, as though he could feel her watching, turned to stare back at her. Then, with his hands on his hips, he strode toward them.

Marcus stood, then tugged her to her feet.

"Travis Kelly, detective in charge of the investigation." The man held out his hand to Ava and then to Marcus. "I understand you discovered the body upon returning home?"

Finally, things were happening. "Yes, Marcus gave me a ride. Patrick's car was here when we arrived."

The detective flipped over the cover of a tiny spiral notebook similar to the ones provided by the newspaper and jotted a note. "Are you acquainted with the deceased?"

"He works with me at the *South Florida Gazette*. He's a reporter." *Was*. He *was* a reporter. He wasn't anything now.

She shook away the unpleasant thought and waited for the detective's next question.

"Are you aware of any threats he might have received? Can you think of anyone who would want him dead?"

"Everyone liked Patrick." Or at least that was what she'd always believed. "We were at a party at the art museum when he said he needed to meet a source for a story. He said he'd be back to take me home, but he never showed."

The detective gave her a probing look that dragged up and down her body, no doubt taking in her attire. She glanced at Marcus, still wearing his black suit pants and a white button-down dress shirt. He'd discarded the tie and jacket at the hotel.

"What time did the party end?"

"Around ten."

He flipped back to the previous page in his notebook. "Yet the call wasn't made until nearly three o'clock in the morning. What were you doing for five hours?"

Indignation surged. "We were at Marcus's hotel."

"Can anyone vouch for you?"

Marcus gave a clipped response. "There are cameras outside the front door of the hotel, as well as in the lobby. You can see for yourself."

The detective turned his scrutiny on Marcus. "You in the habit of marking security cameras?"

"As a matter of fact, I am." He didn't elaborate, returning the detective's glare with one of his own.

Annoyance flickered across Detective Kelly's face. "I suppose you're the FBI agent."

"That's correct."

"Can I see your badge?"

The detective took Marcus's ID and copied his badge number into his notebook. He handed it back. "Agent Anderson, Miss Montoya, we're going to be investigating for a while. I'd like you to stay here in case we have additional questions."

"Okay, if we wait inside?" Marcus asked.

"The house is fine. We'll let you know if we need something." He trudged back to the crime scene.

Ava unlocked her door, and they stepped into her small sitting room. Mr. Belvedere lifted his head and gave a slow, bored blink from his perch on the back of the couch.

"Make yourself at home." She dropped her keys and her bag on the counter and nodded to Marcus. Would word of Patrick's death have made the morning news? "You can turn on the TV. I'm going to get Mr. Belvedere his breakfast."

Once the cat was munching on chicken with gravy, Ava went to the bedroom and changed into sweatpants and a T-shirt. When she emerged, Marcus was looking out the window.

"Anything new?"

He startled and jerked the curtains closed. "It looks like they've finished collecting evidence from the car—at least what they can do here."

"Does that mean they'll leave soon?"

"The medical examiner just arrived. It'll be a while, but once they remove the body, they'll tow the car and everyone will clear out."

She flinched at his words. *Remove the body.* She hadn't eaten since dinner last night, and still her stomach rolled at the thought of her friend being shut in a body bag and taken to the morgue.

Marcus steered her to the couch. "I'm sorry. I'm used to it being part of the job, but I know he was your friend."

"It's okay." Though in truth she doubted anything would ever be okay again.

There was a knock on the door, and Detective Kelly entered. "We're about to pack things up, but I have a few questions."

Ava took a deep breath. She could do this.

"Was Patrick a drug user?"

She narrowed her eyes. "What are you implying?"

"Do you know of him purchasing narcotics?"

She didn't know when it happened, but she was standing. "No. Never. Absolutely not." Could she be any more declarative?

The detective pursed his lips, but didn't respond.

"This is about the story he was working on, something to do with the museum. It's the only explanation."

"Do you know who he planned to meet? The topic of his story?"

"No." She had no idea what Patrick was working on. He never shared that information. "But if you have his phone, that's how he communicated with his source."

The detective didn't respond. He sifted through his shirt pocket and dug out a couple of business cards. "Please let me know if you remember anything that might be helpful."

Ava took the card and stared at it for a long moment before looking up and catching the detective's gaze. "Please find out who did this."

He tipped his head. "I'll do my best."

The door shut. She turned to Marcus. "Why are they asking about drugs?"

"They must've found something when they searched the car."

"Patrick barely even drank."

Marcus didn't respond, but his look spoke volumes.

"He was an investigative journalist. He was meeting someone about a story." She lifted her chin. "If they won't look for the truth, I will."

Chapter 8

Marcus watched Ava's anxious pacing and mumbling and contemplated whether he should intervene. Discovering a body was traumatizing under any circumstance, but Patrick, who had presumably been waiting to see her when he was shot, had been a friend, someone who supported Ava professionally.

So far, her reaction had been a mixture of numbness and anger, both of which were understandable. She worried her lip and continued the endless circle from the back of her couch to her dining room table.

"Do you want to talk? About Patrick? Or what we saw?"

Her marching came to a sudden halt. "Beagle Bailey!"

"What?"

"Patrick's dog. Someone needs to take care of Beagle Bailey." Her eyes had gone wild, but at least now she had a purpose.

"Do you have a key to his place?"

She nodded.

"Let me check with the detective and see if he'll let us go get the dog." Truth be told, he was glad to have something useful to do.

"Patrick wouldn't want him to end up in a shelter." The corners of her mouth turned down, and her chin quivered.

God, he wished he could go back in time, tell Patrick not to leave the museum and keep Ava at his hotel with him. Anything to shield her from all this. He stepped forward and drew her into a hug.

Her body trembled with a shaky inhale, but then she thrust him away. "Find out about Beagle Bailey? Please?"

Marcus trotted down Ava's driveway and caught the detective as he was about to get into a dark sedan. "Patrick had a dog. Ava wants to know if we can go get it."

The man regarded Marcus with caution and appeared to weigh his words. "My team can handle the dog. I have people heading over there now."

"She doesn't want it to go to a shelter."

The detective pursed his lips. "Give me half an hour to find a deputy who can go with her."

"Your people are busy. I'm happy to drive her over and coordinate getting the animal."

"We haven't secured the property yet. We don't know if it's safe."

"I'm not looking to interfere with your investigation or violate protocol. I just want to retrieve the dog."

The man put his hands on his hips and squared off to face Marcus head-on. "I suppose you think because you're FBI, you can handle this on your own?"

Marcus saw no reason to be coy. "Of course I can."

There was a long, exasperated exhale. "Respect my deputies. Do as they say. Touch nothing, and remove nothing from the apartment other than things you need for the dog." Detective Kelly wagged his finger in Marcus's direction. "Don't think I won't hesitate to charge you with tampering with a crime scene. I don't give a damn who you work for."

Beneath the man's gruff exterior, Marcus saw compassion. "Thank you."

The detective turned away, apparently done with the conversation.

Marcus made a visual sweep of the crime scene, but as an outsider, he couldn't know what investigators had learned. He bounded up the driveway and through the front door. Ava stood at the window, anxiety clear in the crease of her brow. "Well?"

"We're good to go. Whenever you're ready."

She extracted a keyring with a rectangular fob from a drawer in the kitchen and grabbed her bag from the front-hallway table. "Patrick's in-case-of-emergency keys."

Marcus guided her toward his truck. Her steps slowed as they neared the bottom of her driveway. A medical examiner's van with its back doors open was parked catty-corner to Patrick's SUV. Two men wheeled a bag on a stretcher toward the van and rolled it inside.

Ava watched, her features drawn, her lips pressed into a thin line. Marcus wanted to ease her distress, but nothing he said would make the situation any better.

"You ready?" He put a hand on her shoulder and steered her to his pickup.

He kept his eyes on the road as Ava directed him to Patrick's condo, but he couldn't help the occasional glance. She'd said nothing when they wheeled Patrick's body into the transport vehicle, and even now, she didn't acknowledge it. In fact, other than to give him street names, she'd barely spoken.

They drove for a few miles along the beach, past stores, bars, and hotels before she spoke again. "Take a left at the next stoplight."

Following her directions, he drove one block, turned left, then right into a condo's parking area. He eased his truck into one of the guest spots and killed the engine. No police cars.

"The detective said there'd be deputies here, but I don't see any sign of them."

"Can we still go up?"

"We're probably supposed to wait, but I say we do it anyway."

She offered him a slight nod. Tension rippled through him at her wary demeanor.

"You okay?" He wanted to touch her, to offer comfort as more than a friend, but that was impossible. Especially now.

Her entire body seemed to collapse. She yanked on the handle, and the door popped open.

This time he did touch her, grabbing her arm to halt her from getting out of the car. "You're not doing this alone." His hand slid down to grasp hers, and she entwined her fingers with his.

"That means a lot."

After a beat, he released her hand and climbed out of the truck.

The building appeared to have about eight stories and, like everything in South Florida, a stucco façade. Stone balconies with a lattice pattern made him think the structure dated back to the 1970s.

She walked to the entrance and held the key fob against the electronic entry pad. The door clicked, and she pulled it open to reveal a dated lobby that included an abandoned doorman's desk, a relic from when the condo must have paid a person to watch the door.

"Patrick's place is on the third floor. There's an elevator, but I always take the stairs."

He held open the door to the stairwell and waited for her to enter, noting her slumped posture and the way she trudged, each step seemingly more difficult than the one before. Once they reached Patrick's floor, she led him down a long hallway.

A door opened, and a stooped-over older man with wispy white hair stepped from his unit with a plastic bag. His face brightened at the sight of Ava.

"Hello, Mr. Johnson. How are you?"

"Feeling pretty good." He held up the bag. "Good enough that I thought I'd give Patrick a break from carrying my garbage to the dumpster."

Ava stumbled at the man's words. She stopped walking and chewed on her bottom lip, probably wondering if it was her job to tell this man Patrick was dead.

Marcus saved her from having to decide. "We're here to pick up Patrick's dog, but if you'd like, I'd be happy to grab your garbage on our way out."

The man chuckled. "Appreciate it, but it'll do me some good to get out of the apartment. I don't get much exercise these days."

"You'll work up a sweat. It's hot out there." Marcus placed a gentle hand on Ava's back, urging her forward.

Mr. Johnson waved them on their way.

They continued down the hall. Marcus glanced at Ava, trying to gauge what she was thinking.

"Most of the residents on this floor are elderly. Patrick helped out whenever he could. Household repairs, computer issues. Sometimes he even stopped by for a game of bridge." She shot Marcus an uncertain look. "They're going to be devastated."

"Sounds like he left an impression. That means something."

They neared the end of the hall.

"Patrick loved living here. It's a quick walk to restaurants and bars. Not to mention, the beach is only a block away."

She lifted the key to fit it in the keyhole but stopped and pushed on the door. It swung open. "What the—"

Marcus held her back before she could step inside. "Let me go first."

Someone had tossed the place. Couch cushions on the floor, drawers from the TV console pulled out and dumped. He noted the deep cut through the cushions where someone had removed the stuffing and cut a long slit across the back of the couch.

She burst past him. "Where's Beagle Bailey?"

Faint whimpers came from across the room. She followed it to the galley kitchen.

"Be careful where you walk," Marcus warned her, then entered the room, stepping as best he could over dumped-out pasta and flour. She opened the pantry door, and a brown and white face appeared.

"Bailey!" She scooped the little beagle into her arms and let him coat her face with doggy kisses.

Marcus considered the disordered apartment. "Someone was looking for something."

Still clutching Beagle Bailey, she shoved past him into the main room to a desk in the corner. "Patrick's computer is gone."

"Is it possible he had it with him? Maybe it was in his car? Or at his girlfriend's place?"

"His work computer, maybe, but his personal laptop stayed here." She shifted the dog to one arm and pointed at the empty desktop and shot Marcus a meaningful look. "This has something to do with his story. I just know it."

He rubbed a hand against his rough jaw. She was likely right—it seemed too much of a coincidence for it to be anything else, but that meant whoever did this would kill to protect their secret. And they knew where Ava lived. "We need to call the detective."

"What we need to do is find out who killed Patrick."

He shook his head, realizing where this conversation was going. "You need to let the police do their job."

"The police aren't going to figure out what he was investigating. I'm a reporter, and Patrick was my mentor. I know how he thought."

What she was suggesting was dangerous, and Marcus couldn't let a civilian get involved in a murder investigation.

"It's not a good idea."

"You can either help me or get out of my way." She turned to gather things for the dog.

He didn't speak. What was there to say? But he sure as hell wasn't going to let her do this on her own. Not when there was a cold-blooded killer on the loose. "We still need to call the police."

He pulled out Detective Kelly's card and dialed. By the time he finished explaining what they discovered, Ava had located a canvas grocery bag and filled it with dog food, a water bowl, toys, and a doggy bed—all while still cradling the dog.

"I think I have everything." She set Bailey on the floor by the front door and clipped a leash onto his collar. Then she turned and leveled a hard stare at Marcus. "I appreciate your concern for my safety, but this is something I need to do."

She gave a nod of finality, and Marcus didn't bother arguing. He recognized the gleam in her eyes. He'd seen it before on agents who'd lost a partner. It was the look of determination, the quest for justice.

And—most concerning—revenge.

Chapter 9

Monday was always the worst day of the week. But no Monday compared to this one.

Ava sat in her car outside the newspaper office for twenty minutes before working up the nerve to go inside. Her breath caught when she stepped into the small lobby. Everywhere she looked, she saw reminders of Patrick. The large beige tiles and the shiny white handrails on the stairs that he said looked like they'd been lifted from an '80s office sitcom. The pile of newly printed papers in which he almost certainly had an article. The building security guard, who always referred to Ava and Patrick as the dynamic duo.

"Hey, Sam. How're you doing?" She waved to the uniformed man sitting behind the linoleum counter watching the camera feeds.

A sad, haunted look lingered in his eyes. "Still can't believe he's gone."

"I know. Me either."

The stairs, just fifteen feet away, felt like miles. If crossing this drab room was a challenge, how daunting would it be to step into the newsroom?

She held in a groan. This wasn't about her. This was about Patrick and finding his killer. "I need to finish some work. We'll talk later?"

"Sure, whenever you're ready."

Halfway across the lobby, her eyes snagged on the stack of newspapers beside Sam's desk. Had they reported Patrick's death already? And if so, what did they say about the current drug theory? *Keep going.* She got herself to the stairs and gripped the slick handrail. She'd made this journey countless times before. Today would be no different.

Finally, her feet were in motion, and she climbed until she arrived at the second-floor offices of the *South Florida Gazette*. Stopping to look around, she noted a strange energy. The newsroom looked normal, but something was missing. The obvious answer was Patrick, who by now would have downed two cups of coffee while swapping story ideas with other reporters.

But that wasn't it. Something else was bothering her.

And then it hit her. The familiar, excited buzz of the newsroom. Instead of the clacking of keyboards, ringing of phones and animated chatter, the room was quiet. No one was working. Instead, they were paired off and whispering.

Ignoring her colleagues' curious glances, she kept going and had almost made it to her desk when Joe Sanchez stepped in her way, arms wide.

"Ava." His voice had a gentle rumble. He drew her in for a hug. "How 'ya holding up?"

She'd never been close to the managing editor, but she liked him. His jet-black hair with a slight curl, chubby tan cheeks, and a deep dimple accentuated his affable demeanor. He drew back, his gaze studying her face.

This would likely be the first of many conversations just like this. She winced, but saw no reason to give any answer that wasn't the truth. "I've been better. Still trying to believe it's real."

"Is it true? That you—" Joe averted his eyes.

Under different circumstances, Ava might have taken pleasure in seeing the gregarious man at a loss for words. Patrick certainly would have gotten a kick out of it.

"That I found him?" She gulped down the hard lump rising in her throat and blinked back tears. "Yes, it's true."

He put his hand on her shoulder. "You know, you don't need to be here today. No one will think twice if you take some time off."

"I appreciate that, but there's nothing for me to do at home other than think. I'm pretty sure I'd rather be at work where I can be productive."

"Whatever you feel is best, but take care of yourself."

She nodded, unable to open her mouth for fear that rather than words, a big sob would emerge.

"We all liked Patrick." He shook his head. "His death is a great loss for the paper."

She tried not to flinch at the callous words. Truly, Joe didn't mean to imply that Patrick's only value lay in his work. Plus, she didn't need something else to feel bad about. She'd already spent much of the previous night tossing and turning, agonizing and admonishing herself for taking Patrick for granted.

"You and Patrick were tight. Do you know anything about services?" he asked.

Oh God, a funeral. Ava hadn't even thought about that. Patrick wasn't religious, nor was he close to his family. A small ceremony for friends was likely the best she could do. Maybe a service at the beach? He would've liked that. She'd ask Amanda what she thought. Though Amanda and Patrick had only dated for a couple of months, Amanda deserved an opportunity to participate in the planning.

"I don't have any details yet, but I'll let everyone know when I do."

"Guess a lot of it depends on when the police department releases the body."

Pain stabbed Ava in the chest. *The body.* There was that phrase again. A vision of Patrick slumped against the window. His mouth open. His expression lifeless. An unwelcome tightness spread across Ava's face and stung her eyes.

She gave a stiff nod and stepped past Joe, making her way toward her desk and plopping into her office chair. She propped her elbows on the desk and let her face fall into her hands. Figuring out what Patrick had been working on and who he met last night was her sole focus now.

She needed to find Patrick's notes and pretend he was here to help. Time to try out those investigative skills he'd tried so hard to teach her.

She grabbed her notebook and started making a list of everything she knew. First, Patrick had a meeting with a source connected to the museum. Unfortunately, she had no way of knowing whether the meeting happened. Second, someone broke into and trashed his apartment. The perpetrators were looking for something, but whether they found it was anyone's guess. Third, his personal computer was missing.

Her gaze drifted toward his workstation. The monitor, keyboard, and mouse were there, but no computer. The police probably had it. The computer was unnecessary if she could access his folder on the office network, although she knew for a fact that he rarely kept research on the company server.

Returning her attention to her list, she could see only one logical conclusion. Whoever killed Patrick worried he had evidence, and they were desperate to cover their tracks.

She tapped her pen against the spiral binding of her notebook. Where should she look next? Marcus worked in law enforcement. He might have some ideas. But no, she couldn't talk to him about this. As much as she wanted to see him again, yesterday morning at Patrick's apartment, he made it clear he believed she should leave the investigating to the police. His caution came from a good place, but she didn't trust the police to follow the clues. At least, not the right clues.

She let out a loud sigh. Loud enough, a colleague spun in his chair and shot her a concerned glance. Offering a weak smile, she turned back to the notepad, but found her mind wandering to Marcus.

He'd stayed with her yesterday morning, sitting on a bench outside Patrick's building until the police arrived.

Too stunned by the empty spot in her yard where Patrick's SUV had been, she'd not invited him in when he dropped her and the dog at her house. She regretted it as soon as he drove away.

Once inside her house, she'd spent a good deal of the night trying to get Beagle Bailey settled while soothing an agitated Mr. Belvedere. After that, she tossed and turned, torn between thoughts of her last night with Patrick and wishing Marcus were there to hold her and make her feel safe. But, as wonderful and attractive as Marcus was, Ava didn't have time for a fling. All of her energy needed to focus on finding Patrick's killer.

Shaking away the memories, she typed in her login credentials and opened the newspaper's email client. The first thing she saw was a message from the corporate office with the subject line: Death of Gazette Family Member. An immediate wave of sadness crashed over her. She closed the program and turned off the monitor.

Coming to work today had been a mistake. She picked up her phone and punched in the four-digit PIN to listen to her messages.

"Ava, this is Martin Singh." His obsequious tone made her cringe. "Just checking to see when you'll be available to talk about Beachside at Seaside. I'm eager to share the exciting details."

She deleted the message. That stupid article was the last thing she cared about right now.

Desperate to speak with someone else who would be missing Patrick, she called Amanda.

"Hello?" Amanda picked up on the first ring. Her voice sounded raspy.

A lump of regret rose in Ava's throat. She swallowed it down and did her best to keep her voice even. "How are you holding up?" What a stupid question.

"Not good." A weary sigh traveled through the phone. "Just trying to make it through the day."

Ava could sympathize.

"I'm sorry you had to find him...like that." Amanda's voice was thick.

When they spoke last night, it had been to express disbelief and promise to take care of one another. They'd not gotten into the details. "I wish I knew why he was at my house."

Amanda sniffled, then blew her nose. "I feel so guilty. I was angry with him for missing the auction. I thought he'd abandoned me."

"I assumed he'd gotten caught up in his story. I never imagined..." Ava forced the regret back before it spilled out. "How'd you hear?"

"A detective interrupted my lunch yesterday with the news. I'd been trying to call Patrick all morning, but his phone went straight to voicemail, so I thought maybe his battery was dead."

"Makes sense." But did it? Patrick kept his entire life on that phone. Having no way to contact him should have raised concern.

"I waited for him to check in after I got home, but then I fell asleep and when I woke up and still hadn't heard from him, I figured maybe he'd overslept."

Ava didn't respond. Not only did Patrick rely on his phone, but he was up at the crack of dawn. Always.

"Did Patrick say anything about who he was meeting last night?"

"The police asked me the same question, but no."

If Patrick was going to confide in anyone about a story connected to the gallery, it would have been the girlfriend who worked there. "Did he tell you what he was researching? He said his story was related to the museum."

"He asked me last week if I could find him a brochure from an old exhibition." There was weariness in Amanda's tone.

"What was the exhibit? Did you give him the brochure?"

"I don't recall the name, but I wrote it down. He was interested in a particular painting, and no, I never got around to looking for it. The gala preparations kept me busy."

"Of course, I didn't mean to upset you. I just want to know what happened and why."

"I'm taking a few days off, but when I get back to the office, I'll look for the brochure he wanted."

"Thank you. I appreciate it."

There was a long pause. "Patrick was your friend. You should give yourself a chance to mourn."

"I know. I will."

After she found his killer.

Chapter 10

"Hi, honey." Marcus's mom met him on the path to her front door. Reaching up, she patted him on the cheek. "How are you feeling today?"

Lonely. "I'm good."

A look of doubt shadowed her features, but for once, she didn't respond and allowed him to help her into the passenger seat of his truck. He jogged around the front and got inside. "So, what are you in the mood for?"

"A sandwich, I think."

Though close to dinnertime, they were headed out for a late lunch. Because, unlike Marcus, Mom had been busy. First Pilates at the senior center, then jewelry making at the library, and finally her weekly book club. He, on the other hand, spent the day unsuccessfully trying not to think of Ava. The thoughts fell into three categories. When he would see her again, how she was dealing with what happened, and whether she'd get hurt investigating on her own. It was the third that troubled him the most. Especially since they didn't know whether Ava was on the killer's radar.

The fact that Patrick was shot from inside his vehicle suggested he knew his killer or at least let him into the car. Had he been followed to Ava's house, or did the killer know who Ava was? Marcus had seen nothing to suggest a bullet exited the SUV, which meant it was probably lodged somewhere in the car's frame. Hopefully, ballistics would yield some answers.

He put the truck in *drive*. "Tell me where to go."

"Head up to Commercial Boulevard, and we'll go from there."

A Fleetwood Mac song came on the radio, and his mother sang along. When was the last time he'd heard his mother sing? He tapped his fingers against the steering wheel, trying to recall. *Never.* He'd never seen her behave like this.

The volume of her voice increased as she swayed with the beat. She looked happy—happier than he'd seen her look in quite some time. But it was more than happiness. She looked...carefree.

The song ended.

They were near the restaurant where Ava worked. Somehow, nearly every thought he had led to that woman. A date with his mom should have been a distraction. Hell, he'd rather talk about Freddy than think about how he might never see Ava again. "How was your day?"

"Wonderful." She held out her wrist and rolled a beaded bracelet with her fingers. "This is what I made in jewelry class."

He glanced at the red and orange trinket, then back to the road. "Reminds me of the paintings at the museum the other night."

"That's why I picked these colors." She smiled at her creation. "It's nice."

"My friend Dot found these oblong beads in the box, so for her bracelet, she alternated hers with spheres. Did the whole thing in purple. The librarian said they looked like eggplants."

Marcus took a sip from his water bottle. At least Mom didn't seem to know the symbolism associated with the plum-colored vegetable.

"We said it looked like a dick and balls."

He spat water all over the dash.

"You okay?" She looked at him with concern. "Did it go down the wrong pipe?"

"Something like that." He pulled a microfiber cloth from the center console and mopped up as much of the mess as he could while driving.

"Turn into the parking lot on the right."

Marcus stared at the sign. On a Roll. "No. Pick something else."

"Why? Don't you want to see her again?"

"I do," he admitted, turning into the lot because he didn't know where else to go. "But I also don't want to look like a creep."

"Have you spoken to her today?"

Spoken to her? No, thought about her? Constantly. "I thought she might want some space after what happened."

"Did she tell you that?"

"No, but I will forever be the guy she was with when she discovered her friend's body."

"You should call her. Especially after what you went through together. I'm sure she needs a friend." His mother unbuckled her seatbelt and opened the door. Looked like they'd be eating here after all.

Marcus climbed out of the truck and went to the passenger side to help his mom down. The chance of Ava coming to work so soon after Patrick's death seemed low. But everyone was different. "You didn't call ahead to see if she was working, did you?"

Mom shook her head. "That's not the sort of information they give out over the telephone."

Had she always been this shameless?

The restaurant was quiet, which wasn't a surprise given it was mid-afternoon. They stepped to the hostess stand, and Marcus held up two fingers.

"Bar or dining room?" the hostess asked.

"The bar would be great." His mom shot him a smug grin.

They followed the young woman to the room off the main dining room. "Sit anywhere you'd like."

The first thing he did was glance at the bar. No Ava. He wasn't sure whether he felt disappointed or relieved. Rather than dwell on it, he followed his mother to the same booth they'd sat in the night Marcus arrived. Back when learning his mother had a new boyfriend was the worst thing that had happened.

He picked up his menu. "What are you thinking?"

Of course, he was asking about her food preferences, but she interpreted the question differently.

"I think we need to talk about Freddy." She stretched across the table and squeezed his hand. "I know seeing me with someone who isn't your father has been a shock."

Marcus let his menu drop to the table. "Do we have to do this now?"

"Putting it off won't make it go away. If you're ever going to be comfortable with the situation, we need to have it out. But I also want to be clear that you don't get to decide who and what is good for me."

He rubbed his hand across his brow. "I wish you'd told me you were seeing people."

"Not people. Freddy."

"Fine. I wish you'd told me you were seeing *Freddy*." The passive look on her face sparked his anger. "You're living with the man, for fuck's sake."

The flinch of hurt that crossed her face was almost enough to make Marcus tell her what she wanted to hear. Then he thought of his dad. A hard-working family man. Dad would never have moved on so quickly.

"Freddy stays over some, but he doesn't live with me."

That was splitting hairs as far as Marcus was concerned. He stared for a beat, then asked the real question, the one that had nagged him since seeing Freddy in his underwear.

"Did Dad mean anything to you?" Had everything he believed about their family been a lie?

"Darling, of course I loved your father. I think about him every day."

An indignant snort climbed up his throat, but he managed to stuff it back down. "Then how could you move on so quickly?" His strained voice broadcast pain he'd not meant to reveal.

"Your father was my world. To the point that I absorbed everything about him. His interests. His hobbies. I didn't look beyond him."

"That wasn't his fault."

"It wasn't. Not at all." She offered a sad smile. "But when he died, I realized I didn't want to play trivia. Or go to craft breweries. Or sailing. For the first time since becoming a wife, I had to figure out who I wanted to be."

A pang of sadness washed over Marcus. How much of herself had she sacrificed over the years?

"And then I came here, to a place where no one knows your father, and I'm free to make new friends and be whomever I want." She beamed. "It's fucking fantastic."

He felt his mouth tug up at the corner. He'd never viewed Mom as anything other than a mother. Hell, he'd never considered she might want more. But now, hearing her compare her life from before to her life now, he saw her as a full person, F-word and all. "Then I'm happy for you."

"I don't know if anything will happen with Freddy, but for the time being, he offers friendship and companionship, and that's enough." She waggled her eyebrows. "He's not bad in the sack either."

"Mom!" There was a limit to what he was willing to put up with, and listening to his mom talk about sex was a hard no. "If Freddy makes you happy, then I'm happy, but please, for the love of God, stop referencing your sex life."

"Fair enough. Besides, we have your love life to think about now."

She waved at the other side of the bar. Marcus twisted in his seat. His breath caught.

Ava.

He'd not prepared himself for how he would feel when he saw her again. It was like having the wind knocked out of him. She walked their way. He stood to greet her, running through everything he might say. *How are you doing? Did you get any sleep last night? Are you okay?* But when she reached their table, he could offer nothing but a nod.

Mom watched the exchange, then jumped to her feet, drawing Ava in for a quick hug. "Hello dear. It's nice to see you again."

Ava turned to look at Marcus, a question in her eyes. She was undoubtedly wondering if this was a ploy to see her again.

Mom spoke before he could figure out what to say. "I enjoyed the chicken sandwich so much I insisted Marcus bring me here for another."

"That's my favorite too." Ava smiled.

Marcus stood still, suddenly feeling out of his depth. Sure, he knew the protocol for informing families on the loss of a loved one, and he understood the emotional trauma associated with discovering a murder victim, but he didn't know what to say when the person who'd found her friend's body in her front yard was someone he found physically attractive. Someone he'd kissed and hoped to do more with.

"How are you doing?"

She sighed. "It was a rough morning. I went into the office, but didn't stay for very long. It was too difficult."

He shifted on his feet and rubbed the back of his neck. "I thought about calling, but I wasn't sure if you wanted me to bother you."

"It wouldn't have been a bother." Her face softened. "I thought about calling you too."

A vulnerability in Ava's expression tugged at Marcus, and he couldn't look away.

She gazed back for a beat, then shook herself free. "I should get to work." She motioned with her thumb over her shoulder and offered a shy smile. "I'm glad you came in today. It was good to see you again."

Before he knew it, she spun on her toes and was heading back to the bar.

"Ava, sweetie," his mom called after her.

What was she up to now?

Ava pivoted back in their direction. "Can I get you something?"

"Would you like to have dinner with us? Tomorrow night at my house?"

She chewed on her lip and, for a moment, Marcus wanted to climb under the table like he'd done when he was a boy.

"Oh, that is so nice, but I wouldn't want you to go to any trouble."

"It's no trouble. I love to cook." She lifted her chin toward Marcus. "Besides, I owe him at least one home-cooked meal while he's here."

"She's a fantastic cook." It was the truth, though he guessed everyone thought that about their mom.

Ava looked at Marcus, as if confirming he wanted her to accept. "Okay, in that case, I'd be delighted to accept. Stop by before you leave to give me your address."

"Nonsense. Marcus knows where you live. He'll pick you up."

Marcus shook his head. Once again, Mom had maneuvered them all into doing exactly what she wanted. A pint-sized puppeteer in linen pants and a purple blouse.

Ava was staring up at him. "Does five o'clock work?"

"Perfect."

With a smile, she returned to the bar.

He watched her walk away, then turned to his mom. "Well played, Mother."

She smacked him on the arm. "What did I tell you? I knew she'd want to talk to you." She pinched his cheek. "How could she not?"

Chapter 11

Photographs and mementos littered every surface of Violet Anderson's sitting room. Ava bent to inspect the picture of Marcus in an inflatable canoe with a young girl.

She picked up the frame. "Is this your sister?"

He nodded. "Melanie. She and her husband are in the military. Currently stationed in Germany."

"How exciting." Ava had always longed for adventure, but finding Patrick's body was not what she'd had in mind.

"She's three years older than me. I haven't seen her since my dad's funeral." He shoved his hands into his pants pockets.

"That was almost two years ago?"

He nodded.

"Is your family close?"

"I thought so," came the somewhat cryptic response.

The clanking of pans and dishes sounded from the kitchen, where Freddy was assisting with the dinner prep. Marcus let out an audible sigh. "I texted her when I first met Freddy."

Expecting him to elaborate, Ava waited. "And?"

"And she thought it was great. Told me I was being a baby."

Violet's laughter carried over the noise of the kitchen. "She seems happy."

"I can't argue with that."

She moved on, picking up one of Marcus's school pictures. He was missing a front tooth and looked adorable. "You were quite the looker." And still was. Dressed in jeans, a concert T-shirt and skate shoes, he was undeniably handsome.

He snorted. "I think you and my mom are the only ones who would say that."

She tilted the picture for him to see. "Look at that smile. And the freckles. I'm sure you drove the girls wild."

"Hardly."

Violet stepped into the room. "It's almost ready. Marcus, will you set the table?"

"On it."

He crossed to the dining room and removed a stack of plates from the shiny polished-wood cabinet. When he turned back to retrieve the silverware—which, if she had to guess, was actual silver—Ava spread out the placemats and distributed the plates. The process only took a minute, but there was something comfortable and companionable about setting the table together. An easy domestic ritual, and for a moment, Ava let herself pretend this was something they did every day.

Oh, but she was being silly. Marcus didn't live here. He had a career in Philadelphia. Some kissing, meeting his mother, discovering a dead body, and all of a sudden, she wanted him to drop everything to be with her? Ridiculous.

Violet bustled into the room with a steaming casserole dish. "When Marcus was a teenager, he could eat half of this all by himself. That's why he's so strong and handsome now."

An endearing flush rose to his cheeks. "You're laying it on a little thick."

His mother gave a dismissive wave. "Come on. Let's eat."

They took their seats, with Freddy and Marcus at the ends of the table.

"Go ahead. Help yourself." Marcus's mother pushed the casserole dish toward Ava.

She scooped a heaping spoonful, then turned to Freddy. "Can I get you some?"

He passed her his plate. She dished a similar-sized serving and then added a second spoonful when Freddy waved his fingers and said, "A bit more than that."

Next, she served Vi and finally Marcus. They ate in silence for a few moments.

The casserole was delicious. Some sort of cheesy tuna and pasta concoction. There was a heartiness to it, and Ava could imagine having it as a weekly family dinner. Not her family, of course. Her mother would never cook this. In truth, her mother rarely cooked at all, instead preferring to rely on her private chef. Salmon, whole grains, spinach salad. Those were the dishes in the Montoya household. She could almost see her mother's pinched face of disapproval if someone suggested she eat macaroni and tuna. Marcus's mom and her own couldn't have been more different.

Almost as though she could read Ava's mind, Vi said, "Where does your family live?"

"Chicago."

"And what brought you to Fort Lauderdale?"

"My nana lived in Wilton Manors. I spent summers with her when I was a kid. When she died, she left me her house. Moving here was a way to feel close to her."

"And your parents? What do they do?"

"Mom." Marcus's voice cut through the conversation like a knife. "You don't need to give her the third degree."

His mother looked offended. "Well, I didn't realize I was. She's our guest. I'm trying to get to know her."

"It's fine," Ava assured her, while squeezing Marcus's knee beneath the table. "My dad is an oncologist and my mom is a partner at an accounting firm."

"Your family sounds very driven."

"They are. My sister is a pediatric surgeon." Ava swallowed a gulp of water. "I'm the only do-nothing in the bunch."

She'd kept her words light, but judging by the way everyone stopped eating and stared, she'd misjudged her tone. Great. The last thing she wanted to do tonight was inspire pity. "At least I'm pretty." She forced a laugh. "That's what my mom says."

Again, more silence. She bent over her plate and shoved a forkful of casserole into her mouth. What was wrong with her? After swallowing her food, she chanced a glance at the table. Marcus's mother's stare locked onto her like a homing beacon.

"Oh, honey." Violet's soft, sad gaze penetrated in a way that made Ava squirm. She could feel the tears welling in her eyes.

A warm hand fell on her bare leg just below the hem of her skirt and gave a squeeze. She shot Marcus a grateful look, but her breath stuck in her throat when she saw the look on his face. Compassion mixed with concern mixed with—affection?

When was the last time she'd had someone in her corner? Patrick maybe, but no one else. Not since Nana.

Freddy grabbed a dinner roll, buttered it, crammed it into his mouth, then spoke with his mouth full. "I'd hardly call working two jobs being a do-nothing."

"My parents measure success in terms of salary or prestige. Attorney, doctor, engineer, architect." She shrugged. "Any of those jobs would have been acceptable, but I wasn't good enough at school to do anything like that."

"You got a degree in journalism," Violet argued.

She shrugged and rattled off her mother's words almost verbatim. "You don't have to be a genius to listen to people talk and repeat what they say."

A fork clanked against the plate. "There's more to it than that." Marcus's tone carried a heavy dose of disapproval.

"That's true," Ava conceded. "But I'm not good at the other parts."

"Ian Vanderbrook thought you were."

"I doubt that was about my journalistic integrity." She spoke through gritted teeth, not wanting to say the words aloud.

"You should exploit it." Marcus's voice was tense.

"Excuse me?"

"Use people's presumptions to your advantage. Catch them off guard. Give yourself some credit."

She considered that. Surprising Vanderbrook with some hard-hitting questions wasn't a bad idea. That was something Patrick would have wanted her to do.

The smile Marcus offered was sweet and sincere. It drew her attention to his mouth, which conjured some not-so-sweet memories. The bristle of his jaw against her skin. The press of his erection on her leg.

Her face warmed. They'd not kissed since the night in his hotel room, but she'd thought about it many times since. This was the last place she should have these thoughts.

Freddy cleared his throat. "Would you mind giving me another scoop?"

Ava took his plate, relieved to have something else to focus on, and served him another heaping spoonful of casserole. "I heard you're connected to the museum?"

"You heard correctly. Have been for several years." He swept up a large helping of macaroni and shoveled it into his mouth.

"What is your involvement? Do you work with Mr. Gerou?"

He wiped his mouth with his napkin. "These days, I'm on the board of directors, which doesn't do much, to be honest. George is kind enough to pretend we have a say, but we all know who runs the place."

"And how did you get involved?"

"Almost ten years ago, I oversaw the planning and building of the current facility. When that was done, George offered me a spot on the board. I was nearing retirement, and thought, 'Why not?'"

"Oversaw how?"

"General contractor." Freddy leaned back in his chair and patted his stomach. "That's what I did in my later years after I sold my dry-cleaning business. Had a company in Queens for twenty years. Sold that, moved to Florida and opened another, smaller firm."

"Can I ask you a question about something else I'm working on? Construction related?"

"Shoot."

"Are you familiar with the proposed Beachside at Seaside development on A1A?"

"I've heard bits and pieces."

"I'm wondering what the big deal is. One of our city commissioners has basically discredited everything he claimed to believe by supporting the project. I'm trying to understand why."

"Do you know whether they've commissioned any economic impact studies?"

"Not that I've heard of."

Freddy stroked his chin. "Hmm. If they had, I'm sure you'd know about it. That's the kind of thing they'd want to publicize to generate support. Economic growth and infrastructure enhancement are the two main reasons cities get behind new commercial development."

"That's very helpful." Ava made a mental note to ask Martin Singh about it. Chewing her last bite of casserole, she considered Freddy's connection to George Gerou. "Were you associated with the museum before the new building?"

"I've known George for almost three decades. He's got real estate interests, and we crossed paths over the years."

"Do you know how long he's been involved with the museum?"

"Since the 1980s, I think. You'd need to ask him, of course, but if I remember correctly, his father sent him here to get a feel for the international side of their business. They're in shipping."

Though she knew this wasn't an interview, she couldn't help but wish she had a pen and paper. Memorization had never been a strong suit, but she'd just have to do her best and write it down the first chance she got.

"The museum must be doing well to attract an artist like Ian Vanderbrook."

Violet rose to collect their dishes. She turned to Freddy. "Didn't you tell me that George and Ian went way back?"

"Let me help." Freddy stood and took the dishes from Violet. He kept talking from the kitchen. "George used his connections to get Vanderbrook into some galleries and shows when he was a kid. To hear George tell it, he is entirely responsible for Vanderbrook's success."

Ian had said nothing about having a relationship with the museum director. Perhaps that was an angle for her article.

"Who's ready for dessert?" Violet shot Marcus a loving look. "It's your favorite."

He'd been quiet for much of the conversation with Freddy. She'd been so focused on trying to commit to memory all the details Freddy shared, she'd not paid Marcus much attention. But now she couldn't look away. The look he gave his mother was pure affection.

"Thanks, Mom. You didn't have to do that."

She looked at Ava. "You don't have a nut allergy, do you?"

Ava shook her head, and Violet hurried to the kitchen. Marcus turned to Ava. "My mom makes the best pecan pie. You're going to love it."

She didn't doubt it. There were already so many things to love about this evening.

Marcus had lost track of the conversation. Not that it mattered. Right now, he saw nothing—thought of nothing—other than the woman seated to his left.

From his spot at the end of the table, he watched Ava interact with his mom and Freddy, both of whom appeared completely enchanted. And how could they not be?

Her laugh. Her smile. The way she leaned forward to show she was listening.

It was amazing how quickly she'd slotted into his life. And how easy it would be to get used to it. His mother's not-so-subtle throat clearing dragged Marcus from his Ava-filled stupor.

"As I was saying..." She gave him a pointed look. "Freddy and I have some theater tickets for next weekend. We aren't going to make it."

Confusion etched Freddy's features. "We're not?"

"No, we're not." Mom gritted out the words in a way so obvious it was comical. "Remember?"

"Oh...uh... Sure."

Marcus's gaze found Ava, who was clearly amused by the interaction. He winked in response. Then he stilled. Winked? Really? He wasn't a winker. What had gotten into him?

"Have you ever been to the Center for the Performing Arts?" Mercifully, his mother drew Ava's attention away from him and his overly confident eyelid.

"My grandmother took me a few times when I was younger, but not since I moved here. Patrick had tickets to that comedy musical that's coming through next month." Her eyes shimmered with moisture. "I guess that won't be happening."

"Darling, I'm so sorry." His mother's tone was soft, soothing, and familiar, the inflection identical to the voice she'd used to coax him through every disappointment he encountered. His chest filled with gratitude for the way she'd always been there for him and pride that she could be there for Ava now.

Marcus gathered the dessert plates.

"Oh, honey, don't trouble yourself." His mom rose and took the stack of dinnerware. "It's still early. Why don't you two go have some fun?"

He found Ava's hand under the table, and their gazes met. "Are you ready to go?"

"I think so."

Everyone stood and wandered toward the front door.

Ava turned to his mother. "Dinner was delicious. Thank you for the invite."

"You are welcome anytime."

Ava's eyes misted again when his mom pulled her in for a hug. Released, she turned to Freddy. "Thank you for the information about the museum and the Beachside project. It'll be very helpful when I work on my stories."

Freddy beamed, and Marcus had to admit, he wasn't the Casanova he'd first assumed. The man stuck out his hand, and Marcus shook it . "Good to see you, son."

Marcus startled a little at the word *son*, but knew Freddy meant it only as a term of affection and nothing more. He turned to say goodbye to his mom, and she yanked him down and planted a kiss on his cheek. "Why don't you kids stop at Riverwalk on your way home? Take a stroll to walk off dinner?"

Marcus pressed his hand into the small of Ava's back and steered her past his mother. "We'll talk about it. Thank you for dinner, and maybe we can get together for a coffee tomorrow afternoon."

"Sounds great." She waggled her eyebrows. "And then you can fill me in on the rest of your date."

Would she ever stop embarrassing him? Probably not. He guessed that was okay. "Goodnight, Mom."

His mother stood in the doorway, watching them make their way to his truck. He opened the passenger door and waited for Ava to climb inside. The way her skirt rode up made his mouth go dry. He'd had his hands on those legs once before... *Get a grip, man.*

He shut the door and made his way around to the driver's side. Once inside, he turned to Ava. "I swear I don't tell my mom about my dates." He heard the word *date* leave his mouth and had to stifle a moan. This wasn't a date. Was it? His mother had invited Ava to dinner, not him. "I mean...uh..."

She laughed, then leaned over and gave him a quick kiss on the cheek. "We don't have to label it, but if you want to call it a date, that's okay with me."

He started his truck and navigated out of his mom's neighborhood. "Does a date come with a goodnight kiss?"

"I just gave you a kiss." The cheeky smile she offered was both adorable and suggestive.

He practically growled his response. "Not the kind of kiss I'm talking about."

"You mean an air kiss?"

"Not even close."

"A kiss on the forehead?"

"I won't dignify that with a response."

"A half kiss?"

"I don't even know what that is."

"You know, you kiss my bottom lip, I kiss your top lip."

The thought of Ava's plump lip between his teeth was all the encouragement his body needed. He shifted in his seat, hoping to lessen his growing arousal. "Getting closer."

"Maybe something long and slow? Parted lips? Bodies pushed together?"

His cells buzzed, little prickles of desire shooting up and down his skin. Good God, this woman. "Something like that would be acceptable."

"So, we're calling it a date?"

He didn't trust himself to speak and grunted his agreement.

They drove for a few minutes in silence, then Ava pulled out her phone. "I want to take some notes on the things Freddy told me about George Gerou and the museum."

"Can I help?"

She breathed out a sigh of relief. "That would be great. Remembering things is not a strength. It's one reason I was terrible at school."

More self-recrimination. He wished she would stop doing that. "We studied memory at the academy. Mostly for interrogation, but I learned some strategies for myself. Might help you as well."

"Like what?"

"Creating associations, for one thing. The first time you hear something, try to associate it with something you already know. Or create a visual image and then take a mental snapshot of it. I like to use a combination."

"Can you give me an example?"

"I might say to myself, 'Gerou got galleries,' and then imagine George Gerou and Ian Vanderbrook at an art museum."

"I like the alliteration."

"Things like that make it easier to remember."

They went back and forth for a few more minutes, listing off tidbits.

"That wasn't so bad." She smiled at her phone. "Do you think Gerou is holding something over Vanderbrook's head?"

He shrugged. "I try not to speculate, but the first thing I'd do is verify what Freddy told us."

"Right." She tucked her bottom lip under her teeth. "Gerou seems like the type who'd want his benevolence recognized. Maybe I can find some old newspaper articles."

"That sounds like a perfect place to start."

Two more blocks before he needed to decide. Turn left to take Ava home. Turn right to go into downtown. He wasn't ready for the night to be over, and his mom's suggestions had worked so far. "Did you want to go to Riverwalk?"

"I do, but not tonight."

The hope he'd been holding in his chest plummeted into his stomach. He drifted into the left-turn lane. "Don't forget, we agreed this was a date. I'm still counting on that kiss."

"Is that all you want?"

Chapter 12

Ava was horny. By the time they got to her front door, she was ready to jump Marcus and have her way with him right there on the porch. Unfortunately, getting busy in the front yard was feeling like a real possibility. Why the stupid key wouldn't slide into the lock, she had no idea. She tried again.

"Is everything all right?" Marcus's deep voice rumbled against her ear as he leaned over her shoulder to see.

Not yet, but it would be once they were inside and his hands were all over her. "This lock can be tricky."

"Something wrong with it?" His voice had an edge. Gruff, firm, authoritative.

Here she was too turned on to function, and he was worried about security. Her abdomen pulsed. She fumbled the key again. "Just something that happens sometimes." Did she sound breathless? Sure, it had been a while since she'd been with a man, but panting like a dog was not a good look. *Pull yourself together, Montoya.*

Miraculously, the key slid into the keyhole and she turned the knob, resisting the urge to shout.

He extended a hand over her shoulder, pressed the door open and peered inside. She twisted to look at him and was struck by his closeness. Leaning in, she inhaled fruity notes of apple and citrus. Her eyes tracked from his broad chest to his parted lips and hungry eyes. She ran the fingertips of her right hand along the stubble on his jaw, imagining how it would feel between her legs.

She pushed onto her toes and stretched until her mouth met his. Considering he'd been the one to bring up the topic of a goodnight kiss, she had little worry he wouldn't reciprocate. And boy did he, meeting her halfway, the touch of his mouth hitting her like a heat wave—and that was saying something. This was Florida.

They stumbled into the house, lips still locked, his kiss the stuff of romance novels. Greedy, yet tender. Deferential, but possessive.

Waving her hand behind her back, she groped for the door. Then, without breaking their kiss, Marcus reached out and pushed it shut. Before she knew what had happened, he'd backed her up and pressed his body into hers. His growing erection bumped into her belly, and she moaned into his mouth. For a wonderful moment, everything other than Marcus ceased to exist. Focusing only on the sensation of his lips and tongue and hands liberated her from the way-too-shitty reality of her life.

He tugged on her ear with his teeth. "Tonight, I'm going to worship you. Take care of you."

That was the best idea she'd ever heard. She needed this, deserved it, and she wanted nothing more than to forget everything for just one night. Though if she was honest, this was already more than a single evening of pleasure.

She tried to speak, but instead, a needy groan erupted from her lips. He apparently got the message because, the next thing she knew, her skirt was gathered around her waist and her panties were shoved to the side.

His mouth returned to hers at the same moment his fingers found her slick entrance. She rolled her hips and hissed with the pressure of his thumb circling her clit. *Yes, more.* He could fuck her against the front door, and that would be just fine. She kind of hoped he would. He trailed rough kisses down her neck, and she grappled for the waistband of his pants.

Claws scraped the tile floor. A wet nose rubbed her calf. *Shit.* Ava tore her mouth from Marcus. She gasped like she'd lost her only source of oxygen.

He let out a startled laugh and ran a hand through his messy hair. "Wow."

"Yeah, that was…" She didn't know how to describe it. Passionate for sure. But there was something else there too. A closeness. A feeling of rightness. "I should let Bailey out and give these guys their dinner."

"How can I help?"

The cat appeared from the bedroom, stalked across the foyer and sat in front of his empty bowl, staring with a look of utter disdain.

"Let the dog out while I feed Mr. Belvedere? That'll give him a chance to eat in peace." If she made this quick, they could get back to what they were doing. She stepped toward the kitchen, but didn't get very far before he grasped her hand and hauled her back against him. The kiss was long and slow and intimate, and she understood it was more than lust. It felt like a promise.

Beagle Bailey squeezed through the sliding glass door as soon as Marcus opened it. He followed the dog into the small backyard, and Ava was grateful to have a moment to herself. Her pulse still raced from their encounter, though she suspected there was more to it than raw passion. Deep down, she knew that falling for Marcus would be easy. In fact, she'd already started the plunge.

She scooped a quarter of the cat food from the can and plopped it into Mr. Belvedere's bowl.

No, she was getting ahead of herself. She had no reason to believe he had feelings for her. He lived in a different city, in a different part of the country. He had his own life—a life that didn't include her.

The cat meowed, expressing its displeasure. She bent to put his food on the floor, then gave the black-and-white feline a scratch between his ears. With his nose already in the bowl, he didn't pay her any attention.

She straightened to look out the window. Marcus stood on the grass, throwing Bailey's toy rabbit across the yard. The dog took off after the toy, then trotted back to Marcus, who'd do it again.

Watching the backyard duo, a pang of guilt hit her in the chest. She'd not had the time or the energy to give Bailey the attention he deserved.

She slid the door open and stepped into the humid night. "Mr. Belvedere is done. I can feed Bailey and then we can…" Her voice trailed off. What were they going to do exactly? Have sex? Make love? Say goodnight? Her face heated. Thank God for the darkness.

Bailey bounded across the grass and onto the patio, dropping his slobber-soaked toy at her feet. She let out a defeated sigh.

"Is everything okay?" Concern marred Marcus's face as he stepped onto the concrete.

Why did she always have to feel like such a failure? "Tonight was wonderful..."

"But?"

"But I barely thought about Patrick. What kind of friend does that make me? And then I get home and realize I've neglected his dog." She almost sobbed the word *dog*. "Other than work, Patrick took Bailey almost everywhere. And I can't even find the time to take him for a walk."

"You have a yard for him to play in. Patrick didn't have that." Marcus dragged her against him. "I think you're too hard on yourself. You have a life of your own . You can't expect Patrick to be the only thing on your mind. There's more to mourning than thinking about the person who died and being sad."

She wiped a tear from the corner of her eye. "Like what?"

"Taking care of yourself. Cutting yourself some slack." Marcus picked up Beagle Bailey and scratched him behind the ear. "Will there be a memorial service? When my dad died, that was kind of a turning point."

"Only if I organize it." That was another thing. By now, Patrick's family had received notification. Other than a younger brother in jail, Patrick hadn't liked to talk about his upbringing, and she knew little about the circumstances of his estrangement. "A few people at work are waiting for me to put something together."

He brushed a strand of hair from her face. "Doesn't seem like something you should have to do alone. Maybe his girlfriend would help."

Amanda planned events for a living, and while she and Patrick hadn't even dated for three months, things had been getting serious. She very well might want to offer some input. "I'll ask the next time I speak to her."

He kissed her on the top of the head, and there was something so comfortable about his presence. Somehow, he knew how to strike the perfect balance of compassion and encouragement. The lustful energy from earlier had evaporated, but she didn't care. She was just glad he was here.

The dog pawed at the door and whined at the smug-looking cat on the other side of the glass.

"How are they getting along?" Marcus tugged open the door, and Bailey bounded into the house. The dog greeted Mr. Belvedere and received a swat on the nose. "I guess that answers that question."

"I wouldn't call them friends. Still, it could be worse." She stepped inside, with Marcus following.

He leaned against her kitchen peninsula while she prepared the dog's dinner. Once he was lapping at his kibble, Marcus looked around the room as though unsure what to do with himself.

She could sympathize, and as much as she wanted to pick up where they left off, the moment had passed.

"Do you want me to go?" He motioned with his thumb over his shoulder.

"No." She spoke a little too quickly. "I mean, not unless you want to."

"There's nothing waiting for me back at the hotel."

A wave of relief broke over her. "We could watch some television."

He smiled. "I think that's a great idea."

There must be something wrong with him. No respectable man would enjoy this quite so much. Because God help him, there was nowhere Marcus wanted to be more than here on Ava's couch with her snuggled against him watching a nineties rom-com.

He enjoyed being the one to soothe her anxiety, the one she went to when she was upset or feeling sad. Unfortunately, whatever he felt was irrelevant. Impossible even. He lived in another city. Besides, he was only here for three weeks. One of which was gone already.

Something tightened in his chest. He'd leave. Of course he would. That had never been a question.

But what if it was? The FBI had offices all over the country. Mom would love to have him close, especially with Melanie so far away. Would getting a transfer be difficult? He didn't know—it wasn't something he'd ever thought about.

Again, he was making assumptions. Ava had given him zero reason to think this might be more. And even if she did, a long-distance relationship made much more sense. At least to start.

Unfortunately, no amount of realism or rationalization was going to change the way he felt. He hauled her closer, gave her a quick kiss, and focused on the movie.

A task that became impossible when her hand slipped beneath his shirt. He tensed and heaved in a ragged breath as her fingertips skimmed along his stomach. Need and want gathered beneath her gentle caress, multiplying until his entire being radiated desire. She trailed up his stomach, tracing muscle and sinew, and when she plucked at his nipple, he nearly hissed.

"I hope you know what you're starting." His words came out as a growl.

She climbed onto his lap and slid her body down his. "I think I have a pretty good idea."

"Are you sure?"

"Hundred percent."

That was all he needed to hear. His hand knitted into her hair, and he pressed his mouth to hers. He forced himself to go slow, to be tender, but his body was a pressure cooker, and he was nearing his boiling point.

Her mouth was full and soft and begging to be bitten. He sucked her bottom lip between his teeth, and a moan rumbled from her throat. Shoving his hands into the back of her pants, he pulled her to him, dragging her against his arousal.

"Can you feel what you do to me?"

She answered with her body, grinding into him.

The landline trilled.

She moaned in frustration. Her chest heaved, and with her swollen lips and messy hair, he didn't think she'd ever looked better. The phone rang again. Her eyes darted to the cordless receiver on the table behind the couch.

"You should get that."

"Who would call now?"

He didn't care who it was, but her anxiety was evident. "Could it be work?"

"Maybe." Still straddling him, she reached over his shoulder and grabbed her phone off the sofa table. "Hello?"

With brows furrowed, she listened to the person on the other end of the line. "What kind of questions?"

"Did something happen?" Marcus couldn't shake the feeling that something wasn't right.

"Detective Kelly," she mouthed, then pulled the device from her face and turned on the speakerphone.

A deep baritone sounded over the line. It was the voice of someone who felt obligated to extend a courtesy. "...best we figure, Mr. O'Donnell was meeting a dealer and something went wrong."

Ava's body stiffened. Marcus rubbed circles on her back. If he had to guess, the detective chose the late hour for his call, hoping he could avoid a long conversation. Unfortunately for him, he was going to be disappointed.

"I already told you, Patrick didn't do drugs."

"Everyone says that. The longer I'm on this job, the more I realize everyone lies and everyone keeps secrets."

There were agents at the Bureau—usually the older ones—with a similar outlook, and Marcus understood where the detective was coming from. The more time you spent with the worst of humanity, the more you saw it everywhere you looked.

"I'm sorry that's your outlook on life, but Patrick wasn't like that."

She gave Marcus an imploring look, and while he hadn't wanted the detective to know he was listening, he couldn't stand the look of defeat in her eyes.

He cleared his throat. "Detective, this is Agent Anderson. Is there anything you can share regarding your investigation?"

The detective responded with a loud sigh. "Without saying too much, I can tell you there was residue found in the car, as well as a bag of cocaine under the driver's seat. We don't know if that's where he stashed it or if it fell during an altercation."

"What if someone planted it? Or maybe he was meeting someone about an article and that person dropped it." Ava would not be dissuaded.

"Was he working on anything drug-related?" The detective was placating her. That was obvious. Speaking to Patrick's editor would have been one of the first things he'd do.

Her voice was small, dejected. "Not that I know of."

"I understand you're frustrated, but we've looked for witnesses and we're coming up empty. We found a shell casing on the floor of the car, but it's clean."

"You think a drug dealer would bother thinking about fingerprints?" This time when Ava spoke, her voice was strident, angry.

The detective continued unfazed. "I get that you're disappointed, but you need to prepare yourself for the most likely outcome."

"That you'll decide it's unsolvable and stop looking for his killer."

The conversation was on the verge of antagonism, and Marcus suspected neither Ava nor Detective Kelly would retreat. "What about the postmortem?" he interrupted.

"Autopsy is done. Cause of death was pretty clear cut. Nine-millimeter to the head at close range."

Ava winced, and Marcus almost regretted the question. He'd not expected the detective to be quite so blunt. "Toxicology?"

"Yeah, those are running. Gonna take some time. You know how it goes. The more drugs in the system, the longer it takes to get the results."

Ava opened her mouth, most likely to protest.

Marcus spoke first. "Ballistics?"

"Yes, *agent*." The emphasis on Marcus's job title revealed the detective's growing impatience. "We recovered a bullet from the pillar behind the driver's seat. Like toxicology, ballistics takes time."

Marcus couldn't blame the guy, but he wouldn't back down to ease the detective's annoyance. He'd do anything to soothe Ava's frustration and grief. "Just gathering as much information as possible. To know where things stand."

"One more thing. I spoke to Patrick's mother."

"And?" There was a slight quaver in Ava's voice.

"She'd prefer Patrick's friends take care of things."

Detective Kelly's words hung in the air like a bad odor, but he pressed ahead, no doubt eager to get the conversation over with. "Assuming that is you, cremation will be the least expensive option, and if it helps, I might be able to call in a favor with a local funeral home."

Marcus half expected Ava to sag under the revelation, but instead, he saw her harden herself to the news. When she spoke again, her tone was formal and clipped. "Thank you, detective. Let me know when the medical examiner finishes, and I'll take responsibility for making the decisions."

After disconnecting and tossing her phone to the other end of the couch, Ava started to get off Marcus's lap, but he grasped her cheeks and forced her to look at him. "It's going to be okay."

"I know it will because I'm going to figure out who did this." She leveled a stare in his direction.

This wasn't the first time she'd said something like this, though there was a conviction in her tone that concerned him. "If the police can't figure it out, it's unlikely it will be any easier for you." It was a hard truth, but one she needed to hear. Besides, he couldn't bear her putting herself in danger.

"Maybe not, but the police don't see the big picture, and they don't care about Patrick the way I do."

He hadn't known Ava for long, but he knew her well enough to know she wouldn't let this go. He wrapped his arms around her and hauled her against him. "Tell me what I can do to help."

He held in a sigh. Just his luck. Rather than getting laid, he was agreeing to assist with a murder investigation.

Chapter 13

Not long after she'd hung up with the detective, exhaustion hit Ava like an eighteen-wheeler. "I don't think I can talk about this anymore."

Marcus still wore the concerned expression he'd wielded since the detective's call. Normally, Ava would reassure him that everything was fine, but she was too tired. Besides, everything was not fine. Far from fine.

The police were restricting their investigation and might never solve Patrick's murder. On top of that, she'd accepted responsibility for what to do with Patrick's remains.

The one good thing about all of this was that she wasn't alone. Marcus said he'd help with her investigation, and she couldn't be more grateful to have someone who knew their way around a criminal inquiry. When was the last time it hadn't felt like Ava against the world? Not since her Nana had been alive, that was for sure, and she intended to hold on to Marcus and his offer. At least until he left.

"I think I should go to bed."

Marcus stood. "Yeah, that makes sense."

There was an awkward moment of silence.

"I'll call you in the morning?" He shoved his truck keys into his pants pocket, his eyes tight with concern.

Her throat constricted. Right now, the thought of being alone was about as appealing as being left in a dark room with a candle and no match. "Actually, do you think you could stay?" She let her gaze drift up to meet his eyes. "I could use the company."

His expression relaxed, and she realized he'd not wanted to leave, either. "Of course."

Would he expect to pick up where they had left off earlier? After two interruptions, it seemed the universe was telling them it wasn't going to happen.

"I'll use the bathroom first." She bounced on her toes. "I'll be quick."

"Sounds good." He sat back down on the couch to remove his shoes. Ava watched. Something about having him here felt familiar. The idea struck her that this could become a regular thing. Dinner at his mom's house, then back to hers to watch television and go to bed.

Shaking herself from thoughts of a road they wouldn't be traveling, she changed into a pajama set, brushed her teeth, and washed her face.

"I found a toothbrush for you." She stuck her head into the living room and waved the package at Marcus, sitting on the couch, doing something on his phone.

He leaned back and looked at her. "Thanks."

"I'll leave it on the counter. There's a washcloth for you too."

He stood, and something in his eyes flared. She crossed from the bathroom to her bedroom, suddenly feeling bare in the pink tank and tiny pajama shorts.

When he spoke, his voice was rough. "Where do you want me to sleep?"

Apparently, she'd not been clear about her desire to have him near. "With me?" The words were a question, soft and uncertain. What if he preferred the couch?

He responded with a smile. "I'll just be a minute."

Ava made her way to the bedroom and, filled with unexpected nerves, hurried to throw her dirty clothes into a laundry basket. She drew down the covers and fluffed the pillows. Should she get into bed? Wait for him to return from the bathroom?

He cleared his throat from over her shoulder.

She spun. "Which side do you prefer? I sleep in the middle, so I don't care. You pick."

"The one closest to the door."

"To make a quick escape?" An insecure laugh bubbled out.

His gaze, hard and serious, locked onto her and held. "To be a buffer if someone breaks in."

Well, that wasn't sexy. Not at all. She swallowed, then squeaked out, "Works for me."

She rounded the foot of the bed and climbed in, pulling the covers to her chin. Marcus unzipped his pants, slid them down, and kicked them to the side.

So, he was a boxer-brief man. She stared as he lifted his shirt over his head. Well-defined chest muscles. The ridges of his abdomen. Dark chest hair she longed to run her fingers through.

He climbed into bed and propped himself on his elbow. "Much better views than the bed at the hotel."

Rolling onto her side, she mimicked his pose, resting her head in her hand. "I'll do my best not to kick you or steal the covers."

He cocked an amused eyebrow. "Should I be concerned?"

"Not if you stay on your side."

"Hmmm...that seems unlikely."

She swallowed the lump clogging her throat.

He must've sensed her uncertainty. "You ready to go to sleep?"

"I don't know how well I'm going to sleep..." Though she suspected having him beside her would help. "But I should try." She stretched her hand to her nightstand, clicked off the lamp and rolled onto her back.

He lifted himself up so that his face hovered above hers. She could just make out his features in the dark room. His kiss was a caress, soft and warm and gentle.

Then he embraced her, towing her into him so that her back pressed against his chest. He kissed her again, this time on the side of her face.

"Goodnight."

The word tickled her skin and made her shiver. She snuggled in, reveling in the warmth of his body, and before long, she heard his steady breathing. God, she was a goner for this guy.

Ava nestled against him, and though she tried to find contentment in the moment, their relationship had an expiration date, and that made her anxious. Because not only was she attracted to him, she was addicted to his strength and support.

She gritted her teeth. There were so few people in her life she could rely on. Could she withstand watching one more leave?

She closed her eyes. There was nothing she needed more than sleep, but her thoughts drifted to her investigation. She didn't know where to start, but Patrick would have backed up his work somewhere safe, and tomorrow morning, as soon as she got to the office, she'd try to access his folder on the server. Besides, she needed to start somewhere. She ran through some passwords until her eyes grew heavy and closed.

Stirring awake, she felt something hard pressed against her buttocks and a man's arm slung around her waist. Warmth rippled through her, both from the man stretched behind her, but also the feeling of satisfaction at waking up with him at her side.

Light crept into the room around the edges of her blinds, and Marcus snored lightly into her hair. It stirred something deep and demanding within her. Unable to help it, she wiggled into his length.

"Hello." He growled into her neck, his voice groggy. "This is one hell of a wake up."

She rolled over to say good morning, but the words stuck in her throat when she saw him. Eyes not quite open, hair messy, that lazy, contented grin. And despite the sleepy-eyed demeanor, something told her he'd fuck her into tomorrow if she asked him to.

"I agree." She rubbed her fingers against the bristles on his jaw, and her stomach clenched. Good God. Why did she find his facial hair so damn sexy?

Feeling very self-conscious of her morning appearance, her hand shot up to the bird's nest on the top of her head.

He tugged her hand away and interlaced their fingers. "You look amazing."

Then, he leaned over to kiss her and she forgot herself. Morning breath be damned. There was something almost magical in his ability to make her forget about everything in the world other than him and the way he made her feel.

He gathered her to him. At the same time, his tongue skimmed between her lips. She opened for him with a breathy moan. Their kisses turned greedy. His hand slipped beneath her tank top and glided up her ribcage to palm her breast.

The pulse between her legs grew heady and insistent, and she rubbed herself against him. Teeth scraping her lips, his hand slid into her pajama shorts. By the time his fingers dipped inside, she was electrified, a current of desire surging through her, lighting her up from head to toe. His thumb circled her clit, and she thought she might burst into flames.

With every other lover, she hadn't liked to feel exposed during sex, preferring modesty to stark nakedness. Marcus was different. He left her feeling worshiped and beautiful in a way she'd never experienced before—a way that was about more than physical attraction. Curling his fingers inside her, he landed on the spot that drove her crazy. And that was it. Her body arched forward. A cry tore from her lips. She shook with release.

Sweaty and sated, she brought her hands to her head. "Motherfucker," she mumbled.

He laughed and kissed her with tenderness, maybe even affection. The rhythm of her heart went from indie rock to heavy metal. Already, she couldn't imagine giving this man up, but she had to be realistic. He was temporary. Someone who'd come into her life when she needed him and would be gone before she knew it.

He rubbed the back of his hand against her cheek. "Everything okay?"

Telling him how she felt was out of the question. These feelings—whatever they were—needed to stay inside her head, because if they got out, she'd only sound desperate. And then he'd leave even sooner.

"Never better." She pasted on a smile she hoped looked convincing and dipped into his shorts to cup his hardness. He hissed when she rubbed her thumb across his slick tip.

"When...work?" He jerked into her grasp.

His grunted words made her smile.

"Are you asking if I have time?" She found the vein on the underside of his cock and rolled it beneath her thumb.

Wrapping her hand around him, she squeezed the base of his erection and pumped. He jerked and moaned, gripping her ass beneath her shorts.

She smiled smugly. "I'll take that as a yes."

Knowing she could reduce this strong, sexy man to groans and grunts made her feel like she could do anything. She was a warrior princess, a goddess, a superhero.

She made a show of lifting her head to look at the clock. In truth, as long as she fulfilled her weekly article obligation and showed up for editorial meetings, no one cared when she arrived or when she left. But he didn't need to know that. She tightened her grip ever so slightly. "I think I can squeeze you in."

Chapter 14

Driving to the office, Ava felt lighter than she'd felt in a long time. And happy. There was a warmth in her chest that hadn't been there since...well, ever.

Marcus hadn't made it easy to get out of bed, but when she finally emerged from the shower, he had a pot of coffee ready. He'd also made breakfast—a cheese omelet they cut in half and a toasted English muffin for each of them. They ate and chatted, keeping the conversation light. No talk of Patrick or her investigation or their feelings. With Marcus's imminent departure, she guessed it wasn't a conversation he wanted to have right now. Maybe never would.

He filled a travel mug with coffee for her, and they stepped into the South Florida morning sauna at the same time. When she turned back from locking her front door, he took her hand, and they walked to her Camaro, where he pressed her against the car door and delivered a panty-melting kiss that nearly made her knees buckle.

"See you tonight?" He said with his forehead still pressed to hers.

She wet her lips. Coherent words were more than she could manage. "Uh huh."

He gifted her with one more quick kiss, then climbed into his truck. "I'll call you."

She'd stood there, glued to the side of her car like a barnacle until he drove away. Her heart swelled. Marcus was unlike any man she'd ever been with, and she could imagine mornings like this becoming part of her daily routine.

Now she was two blocks from the office, and she couldn't stop smiling. What would everyone think if a week after Patrick's death she showed up to work grinning like she'd won the lottery? Oh, who cared? They'd think what they wanted anyway.

She waited for an opening in traffic before turning left off of Oakland Park Boulevard. The office, which backed up to the interstate, was around the next bend, but her smile faded when the building came into view. At least a dozen police cars lined the street. Her heartbeat kicked up. There were a few other buildings in the area, but the cruisers were centered around the newspaper. Had someone else been hurt? Or worse?

Hands shaking, she guided her car to the side and parked on the grass, then got out and walked to where some of her colleagues stood in a cluster.

"What's going on?" Her voice wobbled.

Evan Pearson, the entertainment editor, and someone Patrick had encouraged her to befriend, spoke first. "Someone broke into the office. Heard they took a bunch of computers."

A prickle of unease raced up Ava's spine. "Who discovered it?"

"One of the circulation guys."

Lisa, a reporter who knew everyone, turned her attention from the police officers streaming in and out of the building back to the group. "I heard from a distributor that the place was trashed."

The conversation continued, but Ava wasn't listening. First, Patrick's laptop went missing, and now computers were stolen from the office. It couldn't be a coincidence.

She surveyed the scene, looking for Detective Kelly, and found herself staring at the managing editor, standing away from the group and talking on the phone. His gaze met hers and held. After a moment, he disconnected and walked her way.

He motioned for her to step aside. "Have you been working on anything sensitive?"

As if he had to ask. Ava was the queen of basic, at least as far as journalism went. "Not really. My two most recent articles were about a zoning meeting and the refurbishment of the water treatment plant. There's the Beachside at Seaside development, but I haven't even started working on that. Why?"

"Seems your computer was one of the ones taken. Also, your desk drawers were dumped onto the floor." Joe ran a hand through his messy hair. "Once they let us back inside, you'll need to look to see if anything is missing."

She stared into the distance, focusing on nothing in particular. Why was this happening?

"There's something else." Joe cleared his throat as though giving her an opportunity to prepare herself for whatever crap-tastic news he had yet to deliver. "They also trashed Patrick's desk."

She wasn't surprised.

"Don't get me wrong," Joe continued. "Plenty of other desks were rummaged, but the detective I talked to thought your desk and Patrick's desks were specifically targeted. The rest was for show."

Something bothered Ava. Producing a daily paper was a huge undertaking. "Shouldn't someone have been here when the break-in happened?"

Joe sighed. "We've scaled back the printing operation in the last couple of years, especially with so many subscribers going digital, so there's no longer a twenty-four-hour presence. At the time of the break-in, there were two employees in the printing room, but they use a separate entrance at the back of the building and have their own security system. Plus, the machinery is loud."

"Is there an alarm? What about cameras?"

"No alarm, and a buddy at the sheriff's department told me whoever it was disabled our security cameras using lasers."

He put a hand on her shoulder and steered her back toward the group of reporters.

"Listen up, people." The chatter and speculation died down. Everyone turned to look at Joe. "We will not be allowed back inside for at least a couple of hours. Some of you have deadlines to meet, so work from home for the rest of the day. Be advised, you might be called back later to make a list of missing items for police."

Ava milled around for a few minutes, hoping to spot Detective Kelly. She wanted to talk to him about Patrick's case, but didn't see him. Even if she had, what would she say? He'd already proved he didn't care to hear her opinion.

She made her way through the still-swarming crowd and headed toward her car. There was only one person she wanted to talk to. Marcus would listen, and he'd have an idea where she should look next.

She'd just gotten back into her Camaro and turned the ignition when her phone rang. Amanda. They hadn't talked for a few days. Had she heard about the break-in? And if so, how?

Amanda spoke the moment Ava answered the phone. "I've got that brochure."

A vague recollection of a conversation teased at Ava's subconscious. She searched her brain but came up empty. "Brochure?"

"The one about the exhibit Patrick had asked about."

A surge of excitement shot through Ava. "You found it?"

"Yes, I've put it aside. The painting he was most interested in was called *Mon Enfant*. Done by a French painter in the 1800s. Was only here for a short time as part of a Nineteenth-Century Western Art exhibit."

"Can I come by and look at it?"

"You can have it. I've got an entire box of these things."

After so many disappointments, Ava felt energized. "Fantastic. I'll be there soon."

She disconnected. Finally, a lead. Maybe this would be a clue, something to point her in the right direction.

Police cars blocked the street ahead. Ava made a U-turn and headed back to the main road. She drove past a gray sedan that must've had the same idea. The guy mimicked her turnaround and slid in behind her in the turn lane.

She merged onto the interstate, tapping out an anxious beat on the steering wheel. Brake lights indicated a slowdown ahead. Awesome. Just what she needed.

Traffic moved slowly with cars speeding up, tailgating, and braking. Ava did her best to roll along at a slow but steady pace. Glancing in the rearview mirror, she noticed the same gray sedan one lane over and a few cars behind. Strange. She didn't recognize the car. Of course, that meant nothing. There were people coming and going from the office at all hours. She didn't know all of them, and she definitely didn't pay attention to the make and model of everyone's car.

The highway was at a standstill now, which meant she had time to think about Patrick and his story. Her initial enthusiasm about Amanda's call faded. Sure, she knew the name of the painting Patrick had been interested in, and would get some basic information about it, but what was that going to do? Without any context, would she be any further along than she was before?

She shook off the negativity. Any clue that might lead to answers had to be treated as important.

Finally, she exited the highway and made her way toward downtown. She pulled into a metered parking spot on the side of the road. Before getting out of the car, she checked her hair and lipstick in the visor mirror and saw the gray sedan turn down a side street. *Shit.* She had no idea what she should do. Continue driving? Or go about her day? She twisted to look out the window. Even though she didn't see the car, she knew it was there. She climbed out of her Camaro and raced across the street.

Inside the lobby, Ava stepped to the information desk and told the clerk, an older man wearing a name tag that said Barney, that she was meeting Amanda Soto. The man picked up the phone and spoke in a soft tone. "Yes, of course. I'll bring her up." He turned back to Ava. "Ms. Soto has a meeting in fifteen minutes. She's asked me to escort you upstairs."

"Thank you."

Ava followed Barney down a hallway on the opposite side of the exhibit hall. They arrived at an elevator. Stepping out onto the second floor, Ava was struck by the plushness of the office. Gray textured wallpaper, solid-wood furniture, and floor-to-ceiling windows overlooking the city. Seemed luxurious for such a small museum.

"This way, miss."

They walked past a reception desk and around the corner, and coming from the opposite direction was a short man carrying a portfolio case. He walked with his head down, but mumbled an obligatory greeting as he passed.

Did he speak with an accent? Ava's head twisted to verify her suspicions. Ponytail. She recalled the conversation she and Marcus had overheard in the hallway at the gala.

"Here you go." Barney motioned with his hand toward an office.

Ava stepped through the open door, then thanked her escort.

He motioned as though tipping an imaginary hat, then spun on his heels and was gone.

Amanda came around her desk and drew Ava into a hug. "Sorry I couldn't meet you downstairs, but Mr. Gerou called a surprise meeting with almost no notice. Here is the pamphlet from the event. I don't know if it'll be of any use."

"I don't know either, but I appreciate you taking the time to find it."

"Anything I can do to help." Amanda's expression softened, and her eyes glistened with unshed tears. "I miss him."

"I do too." Ava felt a little guilty saying the words, knowing that her focus these last few days had been elsewhere. But at least she was sticking to her plan to figure out what Patrick had been working on.

Amanda gathered items from her desk—a tablet, a stylus, and a folder full of papers. "Was there something else? I hate to cut this short—"

Ava needed to hurry if she was going to get any more information. "I saw a man with a ponytail in the office. He looked familiar. I think I might have seen him the night of the exhibit opening."

"That's Henrick. He's a restorationist."

Ava turned the word over in her head. She could guess the meaning, but didn't want to jump to any conclusions. "What does that mean?"

"He touches up damage, usually wear and tear."

"Does he work for the museum?"

"We contract with him on a piece-by-piece basis. He's a pretty decent artist in his own right, though from what I've heard he's had a hard time gaining any traction."

"I imagine that's frustrating."

Amanda shrugged. "Some of the best artists never become successful. It's a business filled with gatekeepers and rejection."

"Sounds brutal."

"It can be." She stared at Ava, clearly eager for her to leave.

An idea struck, but Ava needed to be careful. Amanda worked for the museum, after all. "Would you happen to have the contact information for the winning bidders at the Vanderbrook show? I'm thinking about writing an article about buying art at auction and what to expect afterwards."

Amanda grabbed a pad of paper and scribbled down a note. "Most likely yes, but I'll have to check the paperwork to see whether they signed the media release. They almost always do. Most people want the recognition. But once I've verified that it's okay, I'll email you their contact information. I'll try to do it when I'm out of this meeting."

"That would be great." Ava fished a business card out of her bag and handed it to Amanda. She held up the brochure. "Again, thank you. I appreciate it."

"Not a problem." Amanda scooted her out of the office and shut the door. "I wish I could walk you out—"

"That's okay. I know my way."

Ava ambled back the way she'd come to the elevator. She stared at the brochure in her hand. Perhaps additional research on the painting might shed some light on what had interested Patrick. Once back in the lobby, she waved to Barney and stepped outside.

The library was only a block down the street, and since she couldn't go back to the office, perhaps she'd start some research. Decision made, she turned to cross the street, but something in her periphery caught her eye.

A gray sedan.

Chapter 15

The first thing Marcus did when he left Ava's house was call his mom and set a lunch date, realizing how easy it would be to forget why he came to Florida. Now he stood outside the small cafe wedged between a tourist shop and a wine bar on A1A waiting for his mom but thinking about Ava.

There was something about her. She was sweet and funny and smart—despite the self-deprecating jabs about her abilities and intelligence. And waking with her in his arms? He knew the moment he felt her warm body pressed against him he wanted to repeat the experience. Many times over.

But that was the problem, wasn't it? He was already a third of the way through his vacation, and while he was certain he wanted more than a vacation fling, it wasn't anything they'd discussed.

"Darling!" His mother came bustling down the street in white pants and a flowy blue top. She looked stylish and happy, and while he hated to admit it, she'd never had that sort of glow when his dad had been alive.

"Hi Mom."

She grasped his face and pulled him closer, bracelets clanking. He bent to receive a kiss on the cheek.

His mom shaded her eyes and appeared to scan the footpath on the other side of the street. "I thought after lunch maybe we'd take a walk along the beach."

The humidity had officially reached ten thousand percent this afternoon, and his jeans and t-shirt were already plastered to his skin, but sure, why not? "Sounds great."

He held the door, and she swept past him into the small but busy restaurant. The hostess seated them at a booth beside the window where they could watch shoppers and beachgoers walking up and down the street.

They studied the menu for a moment. His mom flipped hers over, dropped it on the table, and folded her hands. "So..." A look of glee spread across her face. "What did you and Ava get up to last night?"

"You're a master of subtlety," he joked, not wanting to answer her question. He'd just started to process his feelings and wasn't sure he could handle Mom's incessant comments and advice.

"Subtlety is for the under sixty crowd," came her response. "Now spill it."

"Mom." Whether he wanted it there or not, there was an edge to his tone.

"At least tell me if you went to Riverwalk."

"We did not. I took her home, and she fed her animals." He left out the part where he'd pinned her against the door and nearly devoured her.

A server set glasses of water in front of them, but didn't stop to take their order.

"And how is her work going?"

This was a topic he wouldn't mind some advice on. "She's convinced her friend was killed because of a story he was working on. She's decided she wants to figure out what it was."

"That sounds dangerous."

"I've asked her to be careful, but she's certain the police are looking in the wrong place. She wants justice, and she doesn't think anyone else is going to get it."

"Do you think she's right? About the police?"

Though he hated to criticize another investigator, it looked that way. "I don't think it's intentional. All they can do is follow the evidence."

"But Ava doesn't believe the evidence?"

"Because she knew Patrick, she's convinced someone planted it."

Mom appeared to mull this over. "If she's right, and this story got him killed, she could get hurt." Her face paled. "Or worse."

"That's what I'm worried about."

"Well, what are you going to do?"

Ah, the million-dollar question. "I told her I would help if I could."

"That's my boy." His mom beamed. "Always looking out for those you care about."

He started to protest, but the server appeared at their table, chomping on a piece of gum. "Do you need more time, or are you ready?"

"I think we're—" His phone rang.

The server stuck her pencil behind her ear. "I'll give you a minute."

Marcus pulled his phone from his pocket. Ava. His heart filled with something he couldn't describe.

"Is it her?" his mom asked.

He waved her off and answered.

"Are you busy?" The sound of Ava's voice, combined with the implication she wanted to see him, filled him with happiness.

"At lunch with my mom. What's up?"

His mother tapped him on the hand. He ignored her and focused on the call.

"I've had an interesting day so far. Wanted to run some things by you."

"Interesting good or interesting bad?"

"A little of both." There was a note of concern in her voice. He glanced at his mother, wondering how upset she would be if he bailed on lunch.

"Ask her if she wants to join us," Mom stage whispered.

He smiled at his mother's insistence and returned his attention to the phone conversation. "Do you want to meet us for lunch? We haven't ordered yet."

"Yeah, sounds great."

He gave her the name and location of the restaurant.

"I'll see you in ten."

He disconnected and looked at his mother. "She's coming, so be on your best behavior."

"Really, Marcus, you act as though I have no self-control."

"Do you?"

His mom harrumphed, but she was clearly thrilled he'd found someone he enjoyed spending time with.

The server returned. "So, what'll it be?"

"Turns out one more person will be joining us."

The woman let out a sigh. "Let me know when you're ready."

Marcus turned to his mom. She opened her mouth, and while he didn't know what she'd say, he was pretty sure he didn't want to hear it.

"How are things with Freddy?" The deflecting question rolled off his tongue before he could reconsider it.

Her face registered surprise. "It's going well."

"Does he have kids?"

His mom took a sip of water. "Three. All grown. All living in New York. His two oldest are about the same age as you and Melanie, but his youngest is in her early twenties. A later-in-life surprise."

Marcus tried to picture Freddy with a family, and despite his initial assumption that the man was a scoundrel, it wasn't hard to imagine.

"You know, Freddy's been around criminals. Maybe he could help with Ava's investigation."

Marcus inhaled his water. He coughed. "Excuse me? Criminals?"

"Well, he owned a construction company in New York City. Of course, he knew made guys."

"Made guys?" The words shot from his mouth like a bullet. He leaned forward and tried to modulate his tone. "And you're not the least bit concerned about this?"

Mom waved her hand dismissively. "It was a long time ago. Besides, that's why he moved to South Florida."

Was this what George Gerou meant when he said Freddy's connections helped to get the museum built? Marcus opened his mouth, preparing a rapid-fire interrogation, but his brain sputtered to a stop when Ava stepped through the door. She was gorgeous. Wind-blown hair, eyes sparkling, a huge smile on her face.

Standing to greet Ava, he pointed a finger at his mom. "This conversation is not over."

Ava approached. Should he kiss her? Mom would never let him hear the end of it, although right now, he wasn't sure he cared. When she reached the table, she leaned in for a hug and kissed him on the cheek.

She slid into the booth next to his mother. "Good to see you again, Vi."

His mom returned Ava's hug, then made a show of realizing she had something else to do. "Oh, my goodness, is today Wednesday?" She looked at her watch. "I forgot. I have canasta at the senior center in thirty minutes. If I leave now, I can get there just before they start. Dot will kill me if I'm late."

Ava stood, and his mom scooted out of the booth. "You two have a nice lunch." She looked at Marcus and winked. "Freddy and I have dinner plans tonight." She winked again. "I'll talk to you tomorrow."

Ava's eyes lit with amusement as they watched his mom exit the restaurant but then stop to look at them through the window. "Do you think she knows we can see her?"

He shrugged. "I'm sorry about that," he said, though he really wasn't. Mom was going to be Mom. She'd always been a bit silly, but South Florida had amplified her playful streak.

Ava gave him a warm smile. "No worries. She's fun."

Marcus nudged his mom's glass to the edge of the table, and when the server returned, they placed their order.

"So, you said you had some good news and some bad news?"

She inhaled deeply, then described the newspaper office break-in. "Either they didn't find what they were looking for on Patrick's laptop or they were checking for a backup copy." She sipped her iced tea. "But wouldn't they have guessed the police already have Patrick's computer?"

"You'd think so." Patrick's desk may have been rifled, but that wasn't what concerned Marcus. His concern was that the break-in targeted Ava, not Patrick. "Was there anything on your computer about any of this? Any notes or anything?"

She shook her head. "Just last night after the detective called, I decided I'd try to log into the server using Patrick's credentials, thinking maybe he saved something there."

"Do you know Patrick's login?"

"No, but his username would be his employee number, which is part of his email, and I thought he might have used Beagle Bailey for his password. Although now that I'm saying it aloud, I realize he would have chosen something more secure." She sagged into her seat.

"Okay, so office break-in, bad." Really bad, in his opinion, but he wasn't going to say that. Not yet, anyway. "What else happened?"

"Amanda called. She found the pamphlet for the exhibit Patrick asked about. He was interested in a painting called *Mon Enfant*. It was an early example of romanticism and depicts Mary and the Baby Jesus." She yanked a glossy brochure from her bag, opened it up, and spun it around so he could see. "After I left the museum, I popped into the library, where I did some research. Turns out there was a scandal with this painting a few years back when the owner tried to sell it."

Their food arrived. Marcus squeezed ketchup onto his plate and dipped a fry. "What type of scandal?"

"It was a fake." Her cheeks flushed, and her eyes sparkled at the revelation. "The seller's father purchased the painting over forty years ago. He inherited it as part of his father's estate, and after some business troubles, decided to sell it."

People were killed over things like this, especially when organized crime was involved. Marcus's brain went to the paintings at Mickey the Fish's place. Erickson was running the investigation, and while it had barely been more than a week, maybe he could offer some insight into the marketplace for forged art.

Ava continued. "The buyer asked to have the craquelure analyzed, and that analysis revealed that the painting was counterfeit." She took a bite of her hamburger, chewed and swallowed.

"Surely the seller wouldn't have agreed to the test if he'd known the artwork was fake. What happened?"

"The buyer pressed charges for fraud, but because the piece had been in the man's family for so many years, there was no way to determine when or how he came into possession of the forgery."

"And this painting was on display at Fort Lauderdale?" More reason for him to reach out to Erickson—maybe even alert the local field office.

"Yep." Ava looked pleased. "This has to be what Patrick was researching."

Marcus hated to state the obvious, but felt it needed to be said. "It could also be what got him killed."

"I know." The words were so soft, he could barely hear them. "But we need to figure out what happened. For Patrick."

"Does it have to be you?"

"If not me, who?"

Marcus leaned back in his seat, pretty sure that even though he'd been starving thirty minutes ago, he was done eating. The thought of Ava putting herself in danger was a surefire appetite suppressant. He rubbed his brow. "Is that everything?" He almost dreaded the answer.

"Well, no..."

His heart swan dived into his stomach.

"Amanda gave me the contact information for the winning auction bidders. I called the guy who purchased *Masai Mara Reserve* and set up a meeting for tomorrow morning."

A cement block dragged his heart further into the depths. "And you're thinking it might be a forgery too?"

She finished chewing, her appetite apparently unaffected. "Makes sense, doesn't it?"

It did. Unfortunately.

"You're going to this guy's house? Tomorrow?"

"Yes. He lives on Key Biscayne. I was thinking maybe you'd come with me and we could find something to do down there afterwards."

If she hadn't suggested it, he'd have insisted she let him accompany her. "Sure. I'd love to."

She slurped her tea down to the ice and gave him a grateful smile that nearly broke his heart.

"Anything else?"

"I saw the guy with the ponytail again. The one we saw at the gala? Turns out he works as an art restorer."

He considered this. "He could be our forger."

"Right, but maybe also Patrick's source. Remember the person we overheard at the gala said he had nothing to lose?"

"He could also be the killer."

"I'm going to see if I can get his contact information and then reach out to see if he wants to meet."

For someone who considered herself a not-very-good journalist, she'd uncovered quite a bit in a matter of hours. The thought gave him pause. How much more would she know twenty-four hours from now, and how much more danger would she be in then?

"There's one more thing..."

Someone get a defibrillator. These revelations were going to kill him.

"I think someone was following me today."

He gripped the tabletop nearly ripping it off its base. "Explain."

She described a gray sedan she saw outside the newspaper office, on the interstate, and again outside the museum.

"Did you get a license plate?"

"I only saw the car when it was behind me."

Damn Florida's single-plate system.

"If someone is keeping tabs on you, we need to limit your movements."

"I get that, but I have things I need to do." She started ticking off tasks on her fingers. "I have to go by the office to make a list of anything taken in the break-in. Then, I have a meeting scheduled at the Seaside City Hall. Tonight, I have a shift at On a Roll."

"Promise me you'll be careful and pay attention to your surroundings."

"I'll be fine. Don't worry." She squeezed his hand.

Don't worry? He almost laughed at the ridiculous statement. Though there was at least one thing he could do to ease his apprehension.

Chapter 16

A va had many things to worry about. And yet, the only thing she could think of was Marcus's fingers laced with hers as he walked her from the restaurant to her car.

They arrived at the public lot where she'd parked. She couldn't get enough of this man and didn't think she ever would. She'd spent the night with him, had lunch with him, and she planned to see him later today. And still, she didn't want to say goodbye—a fact that loomed in her brain and in her heart. In less than two weeks, they'd be sharing a more permanent goodbye. How much more attached would she be then?

Marcus released her hand and cupped her face. "See you tonight?"

"Hope so. I work until nine."

With her face still in his hands, he kissed her, then drew back, letting her see the sincerity in his eyes. "Be careful."

Her stomach did a somersault. She couldn't speak past the lump of emotion climbing up her throat. Finally, she managed a nod.

He kissed her again, then opened her car door and waited for her to get inside. When he leaned down, one hand on the top of the door and one on the Camaro's roof, she thought for a moment he might be about to confess his feelings. Instead, he repeated a different version of the same directions he'd given her earlier. "Don't look at your phone when you're in public. Pay attention to who's nearby."

"Got it." She resisted the urge to salute, knowing that the instinct to make a joke came from a need to lessen her own anxiety. Maybe he was right. Maybe she'd involved herself in something beyond her abilities. Who was she kidding? Of course, he was right. She was a junior reporter working the city beat for a tiny community filled with retirees, and she was following an investigative lead that may have gotten her friend killed. Didn't seem like such a stellar idea when she thought of it like that.

He shut her door and stepped away as she backed out of her parking spot. Pulling out of the lot and turning onto a side street, she glimpsed him crossing to his truck parked at a meter on A1A.

Again, she made a mental tally of everything she needed to do before getting herself to On a Roll for the evening shift. According to Joe, the police department wouldn't release the building to staff until they checked all affected workspaces—including hers. The managing editor was eager to get back to business, so that was at the top of her to-do list. Before that, she wanted to go by her house to check on Beagle Bailey. Mr. Belvedere was pretty self-sufficient, but having a dog was going to take some getting used to.

The first thing she noticed when she got home was the disemboweled sofa cushion that had been dragged onto the floor. Mr. Belvedere stared from the back of the couch, his eyes saying, "I told you so."

"Oh, shut up," she said to the smug cat. This was the last thing she needed right now. "He's adjusting." And while she knew it to be the truth, to her knowledge, Bailey had never destroyed any of Patrick's furniture.

She called his name and heard the frantic scuffle of claws against the tile. Bailey came running, tongue lolling to the side and tail wagging.

Dammit if it wasn't impossible to stay mad with a greeting like that. She bent and scratched the dog behind its ears. "Are we having some growing pains?"

The dog ran in circles in response. He followed her to the back door, and while Bailey ran around and did his business, she gathered stuffing pieces from the floor and inspected the cushion. Hopefully, it could be patched. Maybe Marcus's mom would have some ideas on an inexpensive fix.

Ava's shoulders sagged. There she went again, assuming Marcus and his mom were going to be a part of her life. She needed to get real and stop fantasizing about things that would never be.

After several minutes, Bailey wanted back inside. She opened the door, and the dog ran to his bed in the corner of the living room. She glanced at the clock. Time to go.

"I'm watching you." She pointed to each of the animals. "Be good."

The stop at the office was quick. Joe met her in the lobby, and a police officer escorted her to her desk. She thumbed through the contents of the drawer and couldn't think of anything that might be missing.

She arrived at City Hall with a few minutes to spare. At the reception desk on the third floor, Ava showed her press pass, and the administrative assistant directed her to a conference room. She peeked her head inside, noting the dark hair of Martin Singh and several others seated in the plush leather chairs situated around the large table with a 3-D model at its center.

Singh jumped to his feet and shook her hand. "So glad you could make it." The man was about the same height as Ava. He grinned, his white teeth a striking contrast to his russet complexion. "I'm sure you recognize Jared Meeks from our community meeting a couple of weeks back."

Meeks was tall and broad and had the droopy jowls of a bloodhound. There was a toughness about him that was a little unsettling. He leaned forward to shake her hand. "Pleased to get an official introduction."

Her last introduction was of someone else she recognized—George Gerou.

"A friend of Amanda's, right? Nice to see you again." The museum executive was a handsome man of about sixty. He had short silver hair and looked trim in a navy-blue suit. "I hope you enjoyed the gala."

"I did. It was lovely."

"Always happy to lend a hand for charity." He let out a satisfied chuckle. "The publicity for the museum wasn't too bad, either."

Despite his words, Ava had a hard time believing philanthropy was Gerou's primary motivation. He seemed like one of those people who did good things, not out of the goodness of his heart, but because he enjoyed the attention.

"Are you involved with the project?" Ava motioned to the model in the middle of the table.

He shook his head. "Jared is an old friend. He invited me to ease my mind that this project won't negatively affect my property."

"Are you opposed?" Criticism from a prominent figure like George Gerou could certainly derail development.

"I wouldn't say that, but I am concerned about increased traffic and lower property values."

Martin Singh cleared his throat. "Shall we begin?"

Ava glanced at Gerou. Would she have time to speak with him after the presentation? She'd love an opportunity to ask about *Mon Enfant*. She took her seat and pulled out her tablet to take notes.

Ava listened as the men discussed project timelines, operating costs, and parking. Money and logistics appeared to be the primary focus. No one asked about the people. She waited for the talk to die down and thought about some comments she'd been hearing. "How do you plan to appease resident concerns that Beachside at Seaside will impact their way of life? Many are concerned about crime and disorderly conduct."

A slight smirk played on Meeks's lips, almost as though he were only humoring her by answering. "This is going to be an upscale shopping district, not an outlet mall."

"The development will bring shoppers to our city. Everyone will benefit from increased business." Singh motioned to the artist's rendering, which showed a crowded common area. "What else would you like to know?"

"Has there been an economic impact report?"

Singh's responding laugh was high-pitched and a little shrill. "Why do you ask?"

"Your opinions about the growth of Seaside were very different during the campaign. I'm wondering if there's something about the project that justifies your change of heart."

"I've seen the projections, and I believe in this project."

"So there is a report? Can I see it?"

The commissioner had the desperate look of a trapped animal.

"Of course there's a report—" Meeks interrupted. "But we went outside the normal city channels, and Martin is worried about bending the rules. I'd be happy to have my secretary make a copy and send it over to you."

"Thank you. I'd appreciate it." Ava watched Martin Singh, currently dabbing a folded-up tissue against his forehead. Why would they need to subvert the normal process? To speed up the timeline? It all seemed suspicious, as did the perspiring man suddenly anxious to end the meeting.

"Thank you all for coming. I will reach out soon regarding the next steps." The commissioner bolted from the room.

Ava took her time putting her tablet into its sleeve and then tucking it into her bag. The other men filed out of the room, leaving Jared Meeks and George Gerou.

She stood, lifted her bag to her shoulder, and tried to channel her inner Patrick. He'd always believed in her. She could do this. "Mr. Gerou?" She cursed the wobble in her voice.

He turned and regarded her with a placating look on his face. "Did you need something?"

"I don't know if you recall Amanda saying that I might be working on a story about the museum?"

His posture stiffened ever so slightly. "I remember."

"Since Patrick's death—he was the reporter killed the night of the exhibit opening—I've learned he was interested in a painting titled *Mon Enfant*. Are you familiar with it?"

"We had it on display some time back."

"Were you aware that it was a fake?"

His expression went from neutral to irate. "I believe if you check your facts, you'll learn that the forgery was not revealed until after it had been displayed in Fort Lauderdale." His voice rose with indignation. "Do you honestly think I would have included it in the exhibit if I'd known?"

"I didn't mean to imply—" Ava stammered. "I was curious whether there are any checks on loaned art."

He relaxed, but was clearly still on guard. "We require provenance for any artwork we display. I don't remember the specific documentation provided with *Mon Enfant*, but whatever it was, we would have used that to determine authenticity."

Ava wanted to ask if they kept a record of provenance, but decided she'd rather not press her luck. She could always just talk to Amanda. Besides, she had another job to get to, and the sooner she finished her three-hour shift tending bar, the sooner she could be in Marcus's arms.

⁓

Marcus had never felt like a bigger creep. *It's for her own good.* That was the mantra he told himself when the guilt seeped in.

Somehow, extenuating circumstances didn't seem like enough to justify tailing a girlfriend—a descriptor that seemed inappropriate given the short length of their relationship but also its failure to capture the depth of his feelings.

All afternoon, he'd kept his vehicle out of sight and followed at a considerable distance, parking in secluded spots where he could watch her come and go without her knowing he was there.

The guy in the gray sedan must've been a complete amateur. Or he wanted Ava to know she was being followed. A more troubling prospect as far as Marcus was concerned.

For his part, Marcus had seen no sign of the gray sedan or any other indication anyone was tailing her. Himself excluded.

Now here he was, backed into a spot at On a Roll with a clear view of the entrance. He considered going in, sitting at the bar, and telling her he missed her. It would've been the truth, but also an opportunity to scope out the clientele, see if anyone paid her any interest.

She had another hour left to her shift, and it would feel good to stretch his legs. He cut the engine and opened the door.

His phone rang. Erickson. Thank God. He'd called the other agent earlier in the day and left a message saying he had some questions about the stolen art market. "Eric, thanks for getting back to me."

"Aren't you supposed to be on vacation?"

"It's complicated."

"So, it's a woman?"

"What?" Even to his own ears, Marcus sounded like a suspect caught off guard.

Eric laughed. "Tell me what's going on."

Marcus explained meeting Ava at the gala, discovering Patrick's body and her theory that Patrick's murder was connected to a story he was working on.

After he finished, Eric was quiet for a moment. "Sounds like there's a good chance she's right."

"I agree." Unfortunately. "She's learned her reporter friend had been looking into a painting that was on loan at the museum about five years ago. She dug into it and learned that a couple of years later, it was discovered to be a forgery."

Eric had obviously gotten a crash course in stolen art in the last week. "It's not as uncommon as you might think. Some estimates put the number of fakes on the art market at nearly fifteen percent. Some say higher. Many museum and gallery collections contain forgeries."

"Sounds like you know a bit about it."

"Some I know from previous cases, and some are related to the Mickey the Fish murder."

"That's why I reached out. Last time we talked, we were in the fence's house, standing in front of a wall of artwork."

"Mostly real, by the way. Some had been reported stolen, but there were a couple where the owners didn't even know that the piece hanging in their home was a fake."

Just like *Mon Enfant*. "So, how does this forgery stuff work?"

"To start with, they can be hard to detect because experts don't always agree on authenticity. That's one reason so many forgeries end up in reputable museums."

"So, showing a forgery at Fort Lauderdale is not all that remarkable?"

"Not really, no."

"What else can you tell me?"

"The artwork itself often isn't the only forgery. Fake provenance is part of this as well. Forgers will go to great lengths to create an origin story for their pieces."

Marcus mulled this over. An idea was niggling at his subconscious, but it wasn't there yet. He put it aside for now. There was something else he needed to know. "Is any of this dangerous?"

"Probably depends on how big the operation is and how much money is involved."

This was what he expected, but not what he wanted to hear.

Marcus ended the call with Eric and was about to get out of his truck when there was a knock on the window. The one person he wanted to see most in the world.

"What are you doing here?" Ava looked delighted. He couldn't help but think she might feel differently if she knew just how long he'd been sitting there.

"Wanted to see you. Was about to go inside when I got a call from a buddy at the FBI."

"Are they calling you back to work?" A look of disappointment settled on her face.

He bit back a smile. Just knowing she cared about whether he left sent a shot of warmth through his veins. "I reached out to ask about art forgeries. He gave me some interesting information."

"Like what?"

"How 'bout I tell you when you're done with work and we're back at your place?"

"I'm done now. Things were pretty slow tonight. Why don't we order in for dinner?" A mischievous grin lit up her face. "And maybe another sleepover?"

That was the best idea Marcus had heard in a while.

Chapter 17

Ava's heart swelled when Marcus stepped inside her house, his large frame seeming to expand beyond its proportions until it filled the room and he was the only thing she saw. She caught herself staring and shook it off.

"I was thinking we could do Chinese food for dinner." She handed him a couple of takeout menus. "Then maybe we can talk about the investigation. I want to have a plan for my visit with Mr. Klein tomorrow."

Marcus stiffened slightly at her mention of the trip to Key Biscayne, but didn't look up from the menus. He didn't approve of her plan to finish Patrick's research—she knew that—but that didn't mean she was going to stop. It was like that old saying. He was either with her or against her.

Though, to be fair, she looked forward to having him against her. On top of her. Underneath her. Inside her.

"I know what I want." His voice broke the trance. He handed back the menus and pointed to the one on top. "Number six."

Ava used the landline—Nana's phone number for over thirty years—to call in the order. Marcus shoved his credit card at her.

"You sure?"

He nodded and took a seat on the couch with Mr. Belvedere, who was sitting on the damaged cushion she'd flipped over to hide the laceration. Beagle Bailey appeared at his feet. He bent to scratch the dog on the head.

"Should be about twenty minutes," she said after disconnecting, then turned to look at him. "What do you want to do in the meantime?"

His gaze drilled into her. When he spoke, his voice was raspy. "Twenty minutes isn't very long."

She dampened her lips, stared back and swallowed. He was right. Twenty minutes wasn't much, but there were certainly things that could be done with the time.

Bailey whined, and Marcus turned his attention back to the little dog. The heaviness of the moment evaporated like water in the desert. Just as well. The last thing they needed was another interruption.

"We could watch some TV." She joined him on the couch and lifted Bailey to her lap, ruffling the dog's ears and scratching his head. "I need to do a better job of taking care of this little guy."

Marcus watched her and the canine for a moment. "You're doing fine."

"No, I've been neglectful. He's used to getting a lot more attention than I've been giving." She moved Mr. Belvedere to the back of the couch and pulled out the cushion. She turned it over so he could see Beagle Bailey's handiwork. "He never did this to Patrick's furniture."

Marcus rubbed a hand over the torn cloth. "Don't be too hard on yourself. You're having to adjust your life around something you hadn't planned for."

"But am I? I'm hardly accommodating my lifestyle for him."

"Didn't you stop by in the middle of the day to check on him?"

Ava continued her scratching, but then stopped. She hugged Beagle Bailey against her and turned to face Marcus. Despite an initial flinch, he held her gaze. She spoke slowly, desperate to believe her suspicions were wrong. "How do you know I came to the house this afternoon?"

He didn't answer with words, but the way he stared back, his glare intense and unwavering, said plenty.

"Did you follow me?" A ripple of indignation replaced the warmth she'd felt for him only moments before. "Were you even going to tell me?"

"I wasn't planning on it, but I wasn't hiding it either." He didn't even have the decency to apologize.

"I told you I was fine."

He shrugged as though his transgression had been justified. "I needed to see for myself that you were safe. And if the gray sedan showed up, I wanted to be there."

"You didn't *need* to do anything. You made a choice. A choice to invade my privacy."

"And?" Though his expression remained impassive, she sensed his agitation rising.

"You had no right."

"I had no right to make sure you were safe?" He stood and faced her, frustration clear in his pulsing jaw. "Somebody needed to keep an eye on you."

There was that word again. *Need.* "I didn't ask you to do that."

"No, you just want my help with your investigation. But you don't have any idea how much danger you're in."

Her heart sped up at the condescension in his voice. "What do you know about it? You spent...what, five minutes with Patrick?"

"I know you're in over your head."

Just as she'd feared. He didn't take her seriously. "Patrick was my friend. He believed in me, and I owe it to him to figure this out. He'd want me to look into it."

"Would he want you to get yourself killed?" His voice rose again, as though more volume would make his point. "You're not a detective."

"Just because I don't have a badge doesn't mean I can't investigate. Reporters do it all the time."

"For fuck's sake, you don't know what you're doing!" He paced away from her, his shoulders stiff, hands clasped on the back of his head. Then he let his arms drop and turned to stare at her.

Her anger grew like a viral social media post. "There it is." She plunked Bailey onto the floor and stood. "I thought you were different. I thought you believed in me." She shook her head and backed away. "But you're like everyone else. Poor stupid Ava." Saying aloud the words she'd thought so many times was like being crushed by a wave, dragged under and swept away. Tears pricked her eyes. Oh God. She didn't want to cry. Not now. Not with him.

An assortment of emotions—concern, exasperation, defeat—flittered across his face until settling into the last thing she wanted to see. Pity.

"Ava..." His voice was soft. He came toward her. "Sweetheart."

Hurt feelings transformed into resentment. Another feeling she'd become acquainted with over the years. "Don't touch me."

"I didn't mean to suggest—"

Ding dong. Thank God. Dinner.

She wiped her eyes with the back of her hand, then opened the door, took the food, and shoved a ten-dollar tip at the delivery guy. She kicked the door closed and set the bag on the linoleum peninsula in her tiny kitchen.

Marcus said nothing, just stood there watching.

Not yet ready to look at him—to see the judgment she was certain she'd see in his face—she averted her gaze and busied herself with removing containers from the brown paper bag. She tossed a fork onto the counter next to his meal.

"Let's eat."

He didn't move. "I think we should talk about this."

"Nothing to talk about." She let her shoulders sag, releasing the tension she held there. "You don't think I can do it."

"I never said that."

"You think I'm not a good enough reporter to get justice for Patrick."

"You know that's not true." His annoyance returned. She saw it in his crossed arms and angry scowl.

She squared off, mimicking his stance. "Do I? Because it sure sounded like you think I need a babysitter."

"That's not what I said, and it's not what I meant." He ran an agitated hand through his hair. "I think you're a fantastic reporter. Following you was as much for me as it was for you."

Her outrage faltered. His words—and their sincerity—caught her off guard. "How so?"

"If I knew what you were doing, I wouldn't have to wonder whether you were okay." A bewildered expression flashed across his features, as though the admission surprised him.

She reached up to touch his cheek but dropped her hand to her side. He'd said what he'd said. She wouldn't let herself be fooled.

"I don't think you're incapable of anything." He tipped her chin so she had to look him in the eyes. "When you went over all the things you discovered just this morning, I nearly died."

"What do you mean?" Her voice was low and raspy.

"How do you not see it?" He kissed her on the forehead. "We've not known each other long, but I care for you. I'd lose my mind if something happened to you."

He cupped her face and rubbed her cheek with his thumb. Closing her eyes, she leaned into his touch. His hands were warm and rough, and there was a rightness to it she'd never felt before.

One of his thumbs traced the contours of her mouth. "Look at me."

There was longing in his voice, and when she opened her eyes, his pupils flared. They'd already kissed. Hell, they'd done a lot more than that, but there was an added intimacy to this moment. Something about it felt heavy, important. This was more than a vacation fling, and they both knew it.

She stretched up on her toes at the same moment he leaned forward. The initial touch of lips was just a brush, but it ignited something within. Her mouth glided against his, desperate to communicate what she wanted. He sucked her bottom lip between his teeth and a warm ache throbbed between her thighs.

She groaned. "I want you."

"You sure?" He drew back, searching her eyes and stroking along her jaw. "A minute ago, you were ready to tell me to fuck off."

"Yeah, well now I just want you to fuck me."

His hands shot to her waist, and he hoisted her up. She wrapped her legs around his middle, and he carried her into the bedroom. When they arrived at their destination, he released her, and she slid down, skimming his erection.

He took her mouth again, and she responded with enthusiasm. Her feelings for this man grew exponentially, and since words were inadequate, she poured her emotions into the kiss.

Again, he nipped her lip ever so lightly. Marcus rubbed her earlobe between his fingers before dipping his head to trail kisses up her neck. Heat bloomed in her abdomen.

She angled her head to the side to give him better access. At the same time, his hands found the curve of her hips beneath the waistband of her pants, and his thumbs began a rhythmic caress. Back and forth. Back and forth.

Something about his hands on her bare skin—

She groaned and gasped. How could she already be so turned on? Her sex pulsed a hard, steady rhythm, like a beacon sending out its signal. *Find me. Fuck me.*

Marcus dragged his nose across her face. He claimed her mouth in a demanding kiss. His fingers skimmed higher. Her breath hitched.

"Are you sensitive here?" He stroked along her ribs, just beneath her bra.

Sensation spiraled through her. She let out a moan.

"What about here?" His voice rumbled against her mouth as his hands slid around her hips to cup her ass.

Her breathing increased in both speed and volume. Had she ever been this turned on? Surely not.

"We're just getting started."

"Is that a warning or a promise?" she asked, though in truth, a part of her longed to believe it was a statement about a more permanent arrangement.

He looked at her, eyes hooded and heavy with lust. "Maybe both."

"Give it to me." She stripped off her T-shirt and threw it onto the floor.

His eyes flared with appreciation. But then he swept her into his arms and lowered her onto the neatly made bedspread. Pressing his body into hers, he kissed her again. His hand found its way to the front clasp of her bra and clicked it open. "Beautiful."

She slipped her arms from the undergarment and threw it across the room. Lying back, she watched the emotions flitter across Marcus's face. Appreciation. Reverence. Tenderness. Never had a man looked at her like that, in a way that suggested he wanted more from her than a roll in the sack. It unnerved her. And excited her.

"I'm so fucking lucky." He cupped her breast in his hand and stroked his thumb over her nipple before dropping his head to the other one and sucking it into his mouth. The devotion with which he worshipped her was a bigger turn on than the little nips of pleasure he coaxed.

Her hands traced the powerful muscles of his back, then found their way into his boxer briefs. She grabbed a cheek with each hand and tugged him against her, shamelessly rubbing her sex against the rough fabric of his jeans.

She found the button of his pants and popped it open, then glided the zipper down and cupped his erection. He lifted away from her.

"Nope. We're doing you right now."

"But I want to touch you." She skimmed her fingers up his length, still tucked inside his underwear. "I want to get you off."

"Very glad to hear it." He drew her hand away and placed it above her head. "But I promise we'll both be satisfied when this is over."

She bit her lip and nodded. "Carry on."

"Thank you," he said, sliding his hand down her stomach and into her underwear, his fingers finding her soft curls. "Let me see. Where was I?"

He dragged his fingers along her opening, his touch tearing a gasp from her lips.

"You like that?" he asked, doing it again.

"Gold star." She panted her approval.

Next, he swept his finger along the underside of her entrance, lingering before pressing inside of her. Her stomach muscles tensed, clenching around him. He skimmed his finger against the wall of her entrance and slid back out. She whined at his withdrawal, but then he repeated the process with two fingers, simultaneously pressing his thumb against her clitoris. A sharp burst of pleasure shot through her. Her body jerked, and before she knew it, she was writhing against him.

Good lord. It had never been like this before. Even this morning, while amazing, hadn't been *this*.

He withdrew his fingers again and circled her sensitive bud, alternating pressure and motion.

Whatever the explanation, she didn't care. She just wanted more.

"So good," she breathed, bucking into his hand, rubbing herself against him with abandon. A complete and utter lack of restraint.

"I want to make you come," he murmured, his breath feathering her ear. "And I want the satisfaction of knowing it was me who did it."

Something about those words...Her legs shook. Her pelvis lifted. "OhGodohGodohGod."

He clamped his mouth over hers. And that was it. The orgasm ripped through her, with Marcus kissing and cajoling the entire time. Gasping, she fell onto the bed, her arm resting on the pillow above her head. "Give me a minute and I'll return the favor."

"This is only the beginning," he said, as though she'd been silly to expect otherwise.

"It is?"

He flashed a wicked grin and slid down her body.

"You don't have to do that." She tugged on his arm, hoping he'd reverse direction. "I can't...I mean, I've never..."

"You've also never done it with me." He sat up and tugged off her pants.

"Seriously, don't waste your time."

His gaze lifted and locked onto her. "I want to taste you."

The man clearly knew what he was doing, and the thought of him down there, sucking and licking and getting her off, produced an involuntary moan.

"Is that a yes?"

She nodded. "But if it takes forever, you can stop."

"However long it takes, I'll keep going."

She gulped and nodded. This guy was too much.

He fit himself between her legs and planted a soft kiss on her inner thigh. With his thumb, he manipulated her nub through her underwear, then kissed her there as well. Her eyes rolled back with pleasure.

Good lord. If she were kindling, he was the arsonist. Lighting her up. Setting her on fire.

He sat and pulled down her panties, then returned to his spot between her legs. Placing a feather-light kiss on her sex, just below her slit, he licked her from bottom to top. Her body quivered in response.

He'd just started and already she was closer to an orgasm than ever before.

"Better than I imagined."

Before she could respond, he was back at it, circling her gently with his tongue, then pressing down on the sensitive bundle of nerves. She shuddered again.

"You're so beautiful." He pressed a finger to the delicate skin beneath her entrance and licked her again. A restless tension twisted within her, intense and exhilarating, wicked and wonderful.

She whimpered and wriggled, but he took his time. Another slow lick that stopped short of the place she needed him most. "But braver than anyone I've ever known."

Doubtful. But before she could say as much, he continued with a series of short, quick flickers. It was torture. A terrible, wonderful torture.

Her hips rocked against him, her sex searching for his tongue. Some sort of keening cry she'd never made before slipped from her lips.

"Is this what you want?" He blew on her arousal, and somehow, the barely there sensation was like a shot of dopamine. She panted a string of unintelligible syllables.

"Or do you want this?" He ran a finger along the soft skin just above her most sensitive spot.

"Lower...please."

"Not yet."

Her hands clenched the bedspread in her fists. She whimpered in desperation.

His finger slid down the length of her opening and then dipped inside. He licked her again, but this time he pressed down on her clit with his tongue. Her arousal built until it filled her, and then he curled the finger inside her, and the orgasm exploded. He stayed with his tongue pressed against her, letting her ride it out, as she pushed and ground against him.

Her chest heaved. "Oh. My. God."

He climbed up and kissed her. "I told you I'd stay for as long as it took."

"That was—" Her blissed-out brain struggled to find the words. "I'm speechless."

"Happy to be of service." He rolled over, rifled through his pants pocket and pulled out a condom. "You got any more in you?"

"I think I can manage." It was the least she could do, considering he'd just given her the two best orgasms of her life. She took the condom and waited for him to tug off his shirt and slide out of his pants. She rolled the latex down his length, then pressed him back onto the bed. "Let me do the work this time."

Straddling him, she placed his tip at her entrance. While he stared at his cock disappearing inside of her, she memorized the emotions flittering across his face.

She rocked, thinking about how profoundly he'd changed her life. He'd protected her, believed in her. Saw beyond the pretty face to the woman she was beneath, imperfections and all. And still, he wanted her.

Strong hands gripped her hips. Marcus thrust into her, urging her faster. "You feel so good." His voice was thick with desire.

She leaned down to kiss him, and the change of angle was exactly what she needed. His breaths became less rhythmic, more ragged as he thrust into her again and again. Faster and harder.

Her arousal grew, gathering and pulsing, until it crested and broke, rolling through her in wave after wave. Her muscles spasmed around him, and he slammed into her one more time. They cried out, climaxing as one, and the entire time, she held his gaze, staring into his eyes, desperate to convey the depth of her feelings. The gratitude. The affection. The utter devotion.

She rode out his orgasm, then collapsed in a heap on top of him.

"I've never felt like this before," he said, stroking her cheek.

"I know what you mean." What would she have done without him this week? She couldn't even imagine trying to navigate any of this alone. And now that she had him, she didn't want to let him go. And after three orgasms, she owed him the truth.

She gulped down the voice telling her she wasn't enough and never would be, and said the words she'd been too chicken to admit aloud. "I don't want this to end. I don't want you to leave."

He hugged her tight. "Me either."

Chapter 18

Ava pasted Mr. Klein's address into her navigation app, then pulled her tablet from her bag to review her notes. Last night, after the most fantastic night of sex she'd ever had, she and Marcus ate Chinese food and went over everything they knew about Patrick's investigation.

Now, she sat at a table in the lobby of Marcus's hotel, staring at the elevator and waiting for him to return. She'd asked him to come along for the interview and suggested they have lunch at one of the sidewalk cafes in Coconut Grove afterwards. Marcus wanted to stop by his hotel for a shower, change of clothes, and to retrieve the firearm he'd stashed in his room safe.

The fact that he thought he might need a gun gave her pause. When he first mentioned it, she'd wanted to argue that it was unnecessary, but then she considered everything that had happened—Patrick's murder, the gray sedan, the office break-in—and snapped her mouth shut. Having him at her side made her feel safe. It gave her confidence, and as much as she wanted to deny it, he was right. This plan to investigate Patrick's murder was dangerous.

Acknowledging that—and the fact that Marcus's criticisms were coming from a place of concern—had allowed them to reach a mutual understanding. It had been something they needed to get through. It brought them closer, and the intimacy they shared last night went beyond the physical. It was intense in a way she'd never experienced before or realized was even possible.

As ridiculous as it seemed given the short time she'd known him, she couldn't deny her feelings. Nor did she want to. She was tumbling hard and fast, head over heels for this man, and she felt no desire to slow her descent. And he felt the same. She couldn't believe it.

Everything about the experience was wonderful. Also, over-whelming. Which was why she'd opted to stay in the lobby rather than tag along to his room. She had a lot to think about, and though they'd not discussed what the relationship would look like—whether he'd still go back to Philadelphia—they'd agreed to talk about it.

While she believed he'd stay by her side, at least for the rest of his vacation, what would she do if he left? How far was she willing to take this investigation on her own? At the very least, she should come out of this with a handful of articles about the South Florida art world. Would that be enough?

The elevator doors opened, and she sucked in a surprised breath. Marcus emerged wearing faded jeans, a blue T-shirt and black skate shoes. His hair, still damp from showering, had a messy, towel-dried look. She wanted to grab it, tug on it, run her fingers through it. A visceral need to ravish him suddenly replaced every thought about work and her investigation.

She swallowed her desire and stuffed her tablet into her bag. He approached with a lazy smile.

"I hope I didn't take too long."

"Not at all," she squeaked. "We've got plenty of time to get down there."

Dragging her gaze from his face, she noticed for the first time the slight bulge on his hip where his shirt concealed his weapon. Right. Danger.

"Ready?" he asked.

"Think so."

He laid a hand on the small of her back, guiding her toward the door. Her body pulsed with a desperate awareness of his touch. Good Lord. She needed to get a grip. What was happening to her?

When they got to his pickup, he opened the passenger door and waited for her to climb inside. Then, he rounded the hood of the truck, unclipped the gun and holster from his waist and shut it into the center console.

They headed south on Interstate 95, speeding past buildings and billboards of Broward and then Miami-Dade counties. She closed her eyes and saw Patrick, blue and bloody, slumped against the window.

She must've gasped at the image, because Marcus put a hand on her knee. He gave her an uncertain smile. "You okay?"

"Thinking about Patrick."

"You don't have to do this, you know? If it's too much—"

"I'm fine. Guess I needed to remind myself what this is all about."

At the intersection of Rickenbacker and South Miami Avenue, Ava noted signs directing visitors south towards the Vizcaya Museum and Gardens, and the Miami Science Museum.

She'd only been in the area a few times with her nana, but those had been trips to the beach. There were several other attractions in the area she hoped to visit, especially now that she had a companion.

Marcus paid the toll and headed onto Rickenbacker Causeway while Ava stared at Biscayne Bay. The water looked calm, the exact opposite of the chop churning her insides. Uncertainty over the interview, worry that she was putting herself and Marcus in danger, plus her rapidly developing feelings for the man sitting next to her.

The road tipped upward. One thing that made Rickenbacker Causeway so memorable was the enormous bridge that connected the island of Virginia Key to mainland Miami. They passed a line of cyclists fighting their way up the bridge.

Miami Seaquarium went by on the right, and then they crossed a much smaller bridge to Key Biscayne. Once on the island, Ava monitored her GPS. She'd studied the map last night, and had a pretty good idea of where they were going.

"Take the next right," she told Marcus. "Second turn at the traffic circle."

They drove a couple of blocks before turning into a neighborhood containing beautiful houses of differing architectural styles. Lush tropical plants, along with tall stone walls, shielded the homes from view.

Marcus slowed and pulled into the driveway of red-stamped concrete leading to a cream-colored home with a Spanish-tile roof. He followed the circular drive past the front of the house, stopping so that he was facing the street. "You can do this."

"I know."

"And I'll be out here if you need anything."

She nodded. They decided last night that Marcus would wait in the car. For one thing, she didn't want to look like she needed a sitter. For another, Marcus wanted to keep an eye on the road.

She opened the door, but before she could get out, he tugged on her hand and drew her in for a kiss. Though just a brief sweep of his lips, it had the effect of an electrical current. He sucked her bottom lip between his teeth, and her entire body buzzed to life.

"Good luck."

Nodding and uncertain whether her legs would hold her, she climbed from the car and made her way to the front door. After a brief wait, the door opened to reveal a trim, middle-aged white man whose dark hair was graying at the temples.

"You must be Ava. Welcome." He held the door wide.

Ava stepped over the threshold and followed him through the entryway and into a short hallway.

"It's right in here." They passed through an arched entrance into a living room, and somehow, Ava held in a gasp. The back wall of the room was floor-to-ceiling glass. Through the enormous window, she saw a patio, a pool, and a fantastic view of the bay.

"Your home is lovely."

"Thank you." His smile was genuine. They gazed at the water for a moment, and then he motioned to another wall and the painting. "Here it is."

The bold colors were a striking addition to the elegant, though almost entirely beige room. In any other room, this painting would unquestionably be the star. Here, she wasn't sure what was more impressive: the Vanderbrook or the bay. "It looks amazing."

Mr. Hughes stared at the piece, but didn't respond.

"Do you mind if I record our conversation?"

"Oh sure. Go ahead." He motioned toward the couch positioned across from the artwork.

She pressed the record button on her transcription app, took a seat and pulled out her tablet. "What prompted you to go to the auction?"

"I like to support local galleries and museums. I rarely go into Fort Lauderdale, but when I heard Ian Vanderbrook planned to auction pieces from his personal collection, I didn't want to miss it."

"Did you bid on any of the other pieces?"

He shook his head. "When I saw the three works, I knew this was the one I wanted."

"Why this one?"

"The subject matter, for one thing. I've been to Africa several times. I have other African pieces in my collection, but part of what interested me was that this was an American interpretation."

"Do you own any other Vanderbrooks?"

He shook his head again. "Vanderbrook does a lot of landscapes, which isn't my primary interest. But he's popular right now, and while I know they say you shouldn't buy art as an investment, I can't help but hope the value will increase."

Ava returned her attention to the tablet balanced on her leg. She scrolled through her questions. "What documentation did they give you with the piece?"

"There's a certificate of authenticity signed by Vanderbrook, and on the back of the painting is an exhibition sticker." He paused to think. "I've got the exhibit catalog, of course, and the insurance company did an appraisal, so I've got the paperwork on that. I'd also love to get a copy of your article."

Cocking her head, Ava studied the piece. Something wasn't right. "Were you able to examine the artwork before bidding?"

"I did. Everyone who registered as a bidder could see the art beforehand."

"Can I take a picture of you with the painting?" Ava could put in a request to send a photojournalist down to take photos, but didn't want to inconvenience Mr. Klein a second time.

He stood beside the painting and smiled. Using her phone, she snapped a few pictures with Mr. Klein and several of just the painting, then stepped back to absorb the artwork.

"Are you satisfied with the purchase?"

"It's a brilliant piece of art…"

"But?"

"But it just doesn't look as impressive as it did at the museum." Clasping his hands behind his back and pressing his lips into a thin line, he watched her expectantly. "Please don't print that."

Ava looked from him to the painting and back at him. "I don't have to include that in my story, but can you tell me why?"

"It looked more majestic at the museum, don't you think?"

While she didn't respond, she had to agree.

"Don't get me wrong, it's a beautiful piece of art, but hanging here in my living room, it just doesn't seem to pop like it did the other night."

She studied the picture, walking from side to side, looking at it from different angles. There was a shimmer, but it didn't seem as radiant as it had the other night.

"I'm happy to have been able to help out a charity, but I'm also a little disappointed. I suppose it's kind of like buying a diamond. You'll never see it sparkle the way it did in the jewelry store."

Ava considered the comment. The diamond comparison was quite perfect. At the auction, it had a definite sparkle. Here? Not so much. Surely, the museum would know how to use lighting to make the pieces dazzle.

"What about the delivery process? How did that work?"

"I think one of the fellows who delivered it gave me a business card. I left it on the table in the foyer." Mr. Klein turned and headed back toward the front entrance with Ava following. He plucked a card off an antique-looking table. "Here it is. Gentle Hands Fine Art Movers."

"May I keep this?"

He nodded, and Ava tucked the card into her bag along with her tablet.

"How did scheduling the delivery work?"

"Funny you should ask. The piece should have arrived on Monday, but someone from the museum called and said they needed to reschedule."

A tingle slithered up Ava's spine. "Do you know who you spoke to?"

"I'm certain he told me his name, but I don't remember what it was."

"But it was a *he*?"

"Yes."

"Did he speak with an accent by any chance?"

"Not that I recall."

She was missing something. "Were you given a reason for the delay?"

"The insurance appraisal. The appraiser had a scheduling conflict and wasn't able to get over to see the painting until later in the week."

"Who arranged for the appraisal? You or the museum?"

"The museum."

"And that's normal?"

"For the most part, yes. I could have provided my own person, but they offered to make all the arrangements, so I took them up on it."

Ava couldn't think of anything else to ask, and she was eager to get back to Marcus to talk through the new information. She extended her hand. "Thank you so much for your time. This has been a tremendous help."

"You're welcome. It's been a pleasure to meet you."

"If I have any follow-up questions, would it be okay for me to reach out again?"

"Absolutely." He held open the door for her. "And please don't forget to send me a few copies of your article once it's printed."

Ava stepped through the doorway, but then turned back. "I agree with you about the painting, but it's a fantastic piece, and it looks beautiful in your home."

And she meant it. Still, she couldn't help but wonder...was it the real thing?

Chapter 19

Marcus alternated between staring in the rearview mirror and watching the street for people and cars displaying an unusual interest in the house.

Ava had been inside for over thirty minutes. He didn't know how long an interview should take, but another fifteen and he was going to be banging on the door to see that she was okay.

He'd been working for the FBI for ten years, and never had he felt so inadequate. Much of it was that he'd never had to protect someone he cared about, and Ava's insistence on putting herself in danger didn't help. There was only so much he could do for someone determined to chase every lead regardless of consequence.

And this was the thought that kept him awake last night. Long after they'd made love for the second time, he'd lain in bed imagining possible scenarios, each one worse than the last. When he finally fell asleep, he dreamed it was Ava face down in the kitchen at Mickey the Fish's place. He'd startled awake, heart racing, and covered in sweat.

Movement in the mirror caught his attention. The front door opened, and Ava bounded out. She climbed into the car, an excited gleam in her eye.

Just seeing her made his heart swell. He wanted to kiss her, but could see she had things to share. "Go well?"

"Great." Her smile was radiant. "Learned some interesting things."

"Such as?" He needed to show enthusiasm, wanted to be supportive, but he also dreaded where this new bit of information would lead them next. He put the truck in *drive* and started rolling down the long driveway.

"First, the delivery of the painting was delayed two days. The museum blamed it on the insurance adjuster, who, according to them, had a scheduling conflict."

Marcus didn't respond. On the surface, a scheduling conflict didn't seem significant, and as far as excuses went, was plausible. Of course, if someone had manufactured the delay, then the question became why and by whom? "Any thoughts on what it might mean?"

"Well, no, not yet, but it's something to file away for later."

Marcus navigated through the neighborhood, negotiating speed bumps, observing the twenty mile-per-hour speed limit, and watching for suspicious vehicles.

"Mr. Klein gave me a card for the delivery company. I thought I might reach out to them this afternoon."

So far, he'd heard nothing that made his heart palpitate. He considered that a good thing. "Was that it? Or was there something else?"

"The other thing was more of an observation."

"Oh?" He waited for traffic before turning left on Crandon Boulevard. A car entered the traffic circle behind him. He glanced in the rearview mirror. Gray. His training kicked in, and he instinctively slowed his breathing, inhaling through his nose and exhaling through his mouth.

"Remember the shimmery sunset in the paintings?"

He lifted his eyes to the mirror again, careful not to alert Ava that anything was wrong. "Of course. That was the most impressive thing I saw all night."

"The painting in Mr. Klein's living room has a sheen, but it's different."

"Could it be the way the light was hitting it?"

"I considered that, but I don't think so. I'm going to ask Amanda about the lighting at the museum."

The car in front of them slowed. Apprehension prickled at the back of Marcus's neck. Could there be something on the road? Or maybe the person driving was a sightseer enjoying the views? He kept his focus ahead and his senses alert. "Did you say anything to Klein about your suspicions?"

"No, but he was the one who brought it up, so I'm not the only one who noticed."

He exhaled a sigh of relief.

She took out her phone and started flipping through pictures, pinching her fingers across the screen to enlarge different parts of the image.

Another glance in the rearview revealed the gray car coming up quickly from behind.

They were nearing the bridge between Virginia Key and Key Biscayne, with a car in front and one behind. If this was what he thought it was, the other cars were preparing a trap formation. He retrieved his gun from the center console, still in its holster, and dropped it between his legs.

Ava stopped fiddling with her phone and stiffened. "What's happening?"

"Hopefully nothing." He eased into the left lane, but an older model SUV with windows so dark he couldn't see inside appeared beside him.

Shit. Exactly what he'd been afraid of. They were boxed in. Cars on three sides, a bike lane, and a concrete partition on the other. How could he be so stupid? Why hadn't he done a better job watching for a tail? The what-if game would have to wait until later. Right now, he needed to make it to the end of the bridge.

With two fingers, he repositioned the map on his digital display. Looked like there might be a turnoff into a park after they crossed onto Virginia Key.

Ava twisted in her seat. "That's the gray sedan. Behind us."

Without taking his eyes off the road, he laid a hand on her leg and squeezed. "Everything will be okay." He wanted to believe that was true, but recognized their limited options.

"Once we clear the bridge, I want you to hold on. Do you understand?" When she didn't respond, he tried again. "I need to know you're going to be ready for this."

She still said nothing, so he allowed himself a quick glance. With one hand, she gripped the oh-shit handle above the passenger window. The other clung to the seatbelt. Her eyes were wide, and her chest heaved, but she nodded.

That would have to do.

They neared the end of the bridge. He scanned the roadway, considering his options. There weren't many. The concrete partition in the center of the road continued, separating one direction of traffic from the other. Not ideal, but traffic was light, which meant there was less chance of any bystanders getting hurt. No cyclists or pedestrians either. Thank God.

He saw his opportunity ahead. "Hang on." As soon as the turn lane appeared, he careened into it and slowed. The SUV came over at the same time. When Marcus's front fender was even with the back tire of the SUV, he surged to the left, making contact with the other vehicle's back end. *Wait for it... Wait for it...* He yanked the wheel to the left and slammed his foot into the accelerator. The SUV lost traction and spun across the front of Marcus's pickup, ending up backwards in the turn lane.

Ava craned her neck to look at the disabled vehicle. "What was that?"

"Tactical maneuver." He took a sharp right into the park on the southeastern portion of the island. "I've never done it before. Wasn't sure it would work."

"What?" she screeched, her tone high-pitched and filled with disbelief.

"I'll explain later." At least he hoped so, assuming they got out of this unscathed. The remaining two cars were behind them—the gray sedan and a souped-up import. His heart thumped hard and heavy against his chest. He tightened his grip on the steering wheel.

Tires screeched as he steered toward the park entrance, looking for anywhere his four-wheel drive could take them that the cars couldn't follow.

A little guardhouse came into view. No gate or mechanical arm. Marcus pressed the accelerator and slammed his hand onto the horn. One long, loud warning honk. The last thing he needed was some park employee to step into the street.

They tore past the entrance, one car on his bumper, the other a few car lengths behind. Time to lose these assholes. "Keep your eyes open for a dirt road, gravel, or a beach."

"I'm looking." Her voice was sharp and tense.

At the last minute, he veered into the parking lot. The vehicle on his bumper continued straight, though he was under no illusion he'd lost him. The parking lot had a handful of cars, but few pedestrians. He put his hand on the horn again, hoping to alert anyone who might be nearby.

Just as he expected, the little race car came in the opposite end of the parking lot and sped straight for them.

Marcus cut the wheel, driving over the curb and between two trees. His suspension bounced. He pressed his foot harder on the accelerator and continued to honk. His breath was quick and shallow. A quick glance in the rearview. The gray sedan made it over the curb, but the bumper on the import was way too low. Two cars down, one to go. *Get to the beach. Get to the beach.* In truth, he wasn't sure how the truck would do on sand, but he was pretty sure he'd have a better shot than the car behind him.

Ava squeaked as they rocketed over uneven ground toward the ocean. While he regretted causing her discomfort, he couldn't spare any attention. Not right now.

A thick line of trees blocked direct access to the beach. Shit.

"There's a path." Ava pointed ahead.

Sure enough, a dirt footpath cut through the trees. He veered to the left. A woman and a dog stood beneath a tree. Dear

God. *Please don't step onto the path.* He leaned on the horn. She startled, but when she saw them coming, dragged her dog around the back of the tree and gave them the finger.

Here and there, pockets of sand peeked through patches of grass. They neared the beach. *Please let this work.* Driving over a low embankment, they hit the sand. The truck lost traction, the backend swaying to the right, then to the left. But then his tires dug in and shot them forward.

Marcus looked in the mirror the minute he hit the gas. The gray sedan followed, but had slowed.

Beachgoers turned to watch, but thankfully they all stayed where they were.

Ava let out a relieved sigh. "Is it over?"

Good question. The chase had lasted only minutes, but felt like a lifetime. In his periphery, he glimpsed Ava with her hands braced on the dash.

Another quick look in the mirror revealed the gray sedan had stopped, its front bumper burrowed into the sand. "I hope so."

Had the little import given up, or was it still out there? Someone must have called the police by now. If the other drivers were smart, they would have hightailed it out of here, just like he was about to do.

They arrived at the edge of the beach, drove onto the grass and then back into the parking lot. Marcus turned onto the main road and made his way back to the park entrance and onto Rickenbacker.

He didn't allow himself a single breath of relief until they crossed the big bridge and were back on the mainland.

"What do we do now?" Ava's voice was small and scared. Marcus hated himself for finding comfort in that fact, but maybe now she'd take everything he said more seriously.

He clenched his jaw. The stakes had just gone up. They were going to keep coming for her, and there was only one thing to do now.

"Figure out who's after you."

Chapter 20

Despite the immense sense of relief at having eluded the other vehicles, Ava's heart hadn't returned to normal. It beat against her ribs like an animal trying to escape its cage. Reality swirled around her like a thick fog. They could have been killed.

"Do you think your truck was damaged?"

Marcus responded with a nonchalant shrug. "Don't know. I'll look when we stop."

"What about the car chase? Will you get into trouble with the FBI?"

He shook his head. "But we need to call Detective Kelly."

Ava nodded and slumped into her seat. What had Patrick gotten himself into? And now she'd involved herself in the same thing. She should have listened when Marcus told her to be careful. Nothing like a good-old-fashioned car chase to clarify the oh-my-fuckness of the situation.

At a stoplight, he popped open the center console and stowed away his firearm. She had no idea what she would have done if she'd come down here on her own. She never could have driven like that or would have even known what to do. A sick feeling settled in her stomach.

They merged onto the highway. She was both relieved and disappointed to realize the afternoon in Coconut Grove was off the table. Though she'd looked forward to spending time with Marcus in a setting and with a purpose that had nothing to do with Patrick's death, they had other things to think about.

Marcus must've sensed her roiling emotions. He squeezed her hand. "None of this is your fault."

The words were a balm to her frazzled ego, and she appreciated the sentiment. But he was wrong. It was all her fault. "You warned me that this was more dangerous than I realized, but I wouldn't listen."

He pursed his lips, and she could see him forming his rebuttal.

She continued, not letting him speak. "I can't believe I got you involved in all of this. I never should have started—"

"Hey." His tone was decisive. "I wouldn't have wanted to be anywhere else. I certainly don't want you to get hurt."

Her heart melted a little, the warmth of his sincerity spreading through her chest. "Still, I'm done. No more investigating."

Much to her surprise, he shook his head. "Too late for that now."

"What? Why?"

"That stunt back there? Surrounding us like that? That wasn't just a message to back off. They planned to force us off the road, most likely direct us to a secluded spot where they could either abduct or kill us."

A hitched breath stuck in her throat. Sure, she was scared during the chase, but it hadn't occurred to her that their pursuers planned to kill her. "All the more reason to stop."

"We can't. Our only option now is to figure out what they're protecting."

Ava's stomach churned. She swallowed back the rising apprehension. "What do you propose?"

"We work together. Try to figure out who is after you and why."

She took a fortifying breath, resolving to see her investigation through. Once again, she thanked God she didn't have to deal with this alone. "And find out why Patrick was killed."

"Exactly."

They passed into Broward County, and another unpleasant thought settled upon her. "But you're leaving. What if it's not resolved by the time you need to go back to Philly?"

He reached over and squeezed her hand again. "I don't know yet, but I won't leave you unprotected. We'll worry about that when the time comes."

The tension in her muscles released just a fraction. She didn't know why, but she wasn't ready to go home. "Want to stop to get something to eat?"

"What do you have in mind?"

"Diner near my house?" Her hands shook with unspent adrenaline.

"Works for me." Though his demeanor seemed relaxed, his clenched jaw told her otherwise. "Maybe we can go over what we know, see if we can make any sense of it."

She directed him to a strip mall on Oakland Park Boulevard. JoJo's Diner was located between a hair salon and a comic book store. A hostess seated them in a booth and gave them menus. When the server returned with waters, Marcus ordered a patty melt, and Ava ordered a short stack with a side of scrambled eggs. Breakfast for dinner was her favorite thing about diner food.

Sighing, she took her tablet and stylus from her bag and opened a blank document. After what happened with the car chase this afternoon, the last thing she wanted to do was talk about the investigation. What she really wanted was to pretend it never happened.

She wrote and underlined the words *What We Know* on the tablet. "Okay, so we know Patrick had a lead on a story related to the museum. He left the gala to meet a source." She drew a question mark after the word *source*. She looked at Marcus. "Should we brainstorm who it might have been?" Even to her own ears, her voice sounded flat, defeated.

"No, leave that for later. For now, let's just focus on known quantities."

"Patrick didn't return, and for some reason, he went to my house where he was—" The word was a lump in her throat. "Killed."

Marcus gave her a sympathetic smile, but didn't suggest stopping like she'd hoped he would. "Drugs of unknown origin were found in the car."

She wrote it down and added, "Patrick's condo was broken into and his personal laptop is missing."

"All of which implies someone is looking for something, most likely information."

Ava wrote *Information?* on her tablet and circled it. "Patrick had been interested in the painting *Mon Enfant*, which turned out to be a forgery." The name of the painting went onto her tablet.

Marcus rattled off several other things for Ava to add to her list. "Henrick, the newspaper break-in, delayed delivery of the painting."

"We're forgetting something." A thought floated just out of reach. She stared at the list, looking for a connection. Then it hit her. "The overheard conversation." She jotted a note. "The voice said, 'I need more time.' Then, the delivery of the painting was delayed. What if that was what they were talking about? The artist wanted more time to finish the forgery?"

"Makes sense."

Their food arrived. Ava stowed her tablet and unrolled the fork and knife from the napkin. She smeared butter between the pancakes and also on the top, then doused the flapjacks with syrup.

She cut off a bite, crammed it in her mouth, and chewed. "We know Henrick works as a restorer for the museum. Maybe he was Patrick's source."

"Does Henrick speak with an accent?" Marcus bit into his sandwich and chewed.

Stupid. She'd forgotten to ask. "I'm not sure."

He seemed to sense her internal criticism. "It's okay. We'll figure it out."

"So what's next?" She wedged a huge piece of pancake into her mouth.

"We should contact Henrick, see if he'll talk to us." He dunked a French fry in ketchup. "Of course, he could be the killer. We'll want to do it on our terms, make sure we're in a controlled environment."

Ava sopped up the remaining syrup with the last bit of pancake. She took a bite of the eggs, then pushed her plates to the edge of the table. Though still scared, having a plan and a partner made her feel better. "I'll see if I can get Amanda to pass him my information."

After paying at the counter, they were on their way back to Ava's house, which was only a few blocks away. It was late afternoon when Marcus parked his truck in the driveway behind her car. He clipped the holster with his gun onto his belt. They got out of the truck and started for the house.

Crunch. Something cracked beneath Ava's feet. She looked down. Glass. Her brain didn't register what she was seeing, but then her gaze landed on the broken car window. "What the—"

"Stay behind me." Marcus had his gun out and pointed at the ground. He stepped quietly to the gaping front door and tapped it open.

Trashed. Just like Patrick's place.

Marcus motioned for her to stay at the door as he advanced through the house, checking for intruders. Her gaze swept her living room. Furniture turned over and ripped. Drawers pulled out and dumped. Sugar and flour emptied onto the counter and onto the floor. She didn't see Mr. Belvedere or Beagle Bailey.

She stepped past the carnage, hoping they hadn't gotten out. Or worse.

When they found Beagle Bailey at Patrick's place, he'd been shut in the pantry. Ava made her way toward the kitchen and flung open the pantry door. Not there. Next, she checked the hall closet. The banging started the moment she turned the doorknob, and the little dog rammed through the opening and bounded into her arms.

Thank God. Now to find Mr. Belvedere.

Marcus stepped out of the bedroom, tucking his gun back in its holster. "Looks like they're gone. The cat is under the bed."

A mixture of relief that the animals were safe and a large dose of hopelessness descended upon her. She stood in the center of the room, hands on hips, surveying the damage.

"Anything missing?" He stepped over a pile of old newspapers and notebooks thrown on the floor.

"Laptop."

Her bottom lip trembled. She sucked it between her teeth and blinked back tears. Fortunately, Marcus was there, standing in front of her.

He drew her into an embrace, stroked her hair and murmured in her ear. "It's okay. I'm here."

And then, for the first time since this began, she couldn't hold it together anymore. She let herself cry.

ee

Marcus could think of nothing to do other than hold Ava and hope it would be enough. He rested the side of his face on the top of her head and gripped her tight.

With a deep breath, she wiped a knuckle across her face. "I'm sorry."

He tilted her chin until she was looking into his eyes. "You have nothing to apologize for."

She nodded. "I guess we need to clean this place up?"

"Probably want to call the police first. Do you still have Detective Kelly's card?"

Ava wiped her nose and plucked the card off the kitchen counter.

Marcus dialed the detective's number. He answered on the second ring.

"Detective, this is Marcus Anderson. I was with Ava Montoya when she discovered Patrick O'Donnell's body."

"I remember." His voice was deep and rough. "Something happen?"

"A couple of things, actually." Marcus put the overturned cushions back on the couch.

A resigned sigh traveled through the phone line. "I'm listening."

"Ava and I went to Key Biscayne earlier today and were accosted by three cars on our way back to the mainland. We lost them in Virginia Key Beach Park."

A barely audible *fuck* sounded on the other end of the line. "They put out an APB on a truck and three cars involved in a vehicle pursuit earlier today. That was you?"

"Unfortunately."

"Thanks for letting me know. I'll reach out to the Miami PD."

"Do they have any leads? Did anyone get a license plate?"

"Nothing other than make, model and color."

Marcus wasn't surprised. "There's something else."

"More?" No doubt, the detective was eager for all this to end.

"When we got back here, the place had been tossed."

"Fuck." This time, the word came out loud and clear. "I'll send over a unit. I need to wrap a few things up, but I shouldn't be far behind."

"Thank you."

Marcus ended the call and turned to Ava. "The police are coming. Detective Kelly is also going to stop by."

She sagged beside him on the couch and ran her hand over the slashed cushion. "Kind of makes the damage done by the dog look inconsequential."

He wrapped an arm around her shoulder and tugged her against him. "It seems impossible now, but we'll get through this."

She let her head fall onto his chest. "I like that you used the word *we*."

He kissed the top of her head.

They sat like that for several minutes. Finally, there was a loud knock on the door. "Sheriff's Office."

Marcus rose and answered the door to find a patrolman.

"Come in." He stepped to the side, then closed the door behind the officer.

The man produced a little notebook and got down to business. "Was anyone home at the time of the burglary?"

"We went to Miami and were gone for several hours."

"Who was the last person to leave the house and when?"

"We left together," Marcus answered. "I'd say mid-morning."

"Windows and doors? Locked?"

"Yes." Ava looked stricken, and Marcus wondered if the shock of the car chase and finding her home broken into was subsiding.

The officer asked a few other questions, wrote a case number, and said he was going to interview the neighbors to see if anyone saw anything.

Ava let out a defeated sigh. "Seems kind of bold to break into someone's house in broad daylight."

The police officer shook his head. "It's not that uncommon. Most burglaries take place around ten o'clock in the morning after people have left for work."

She responded with a weary nod.

Marcus turned to the officer. "If there's nothing else, I think we want to clean up."

He handed each of them a card. "When you've finished, email me the list of damaged and missing items."

Other than the laptop Ava identified as missing almost immediately, determining if anything else was taken would take some time.

Marcus shut the door and turned to find Ava staring at the business card.

"I've gathered more police contact information in the last few days than I have in my entire career as a reporter."

Her cynicism was understandable. He wasn't about to tell her how to feel. Distracting her was a different matter, however. "Where are your big garbage bags?"

"Garage. On the shelf above the washer and dryer."

"I'll grab a couple so we can pick this place up. You get something to write on."

She trudged to her home office, a small nook meant to be a dining room, and scooped a notebook and pen from the floor.

Marcus stepped into the garage, grabbed two bags, and returned to the main room.

They worked like that for some time, adding broken items of value to Ava's list, throwing away anything that wasn't salvageable, and putting everything else where it belonged.

Still dressed in the slacks and blouse she'd worn for her interview earlier in the day, she moved with a defeated heaviness, as though every motion required a massive effort. Marcus hated to see her like this, to know she was afraid, and while he wished they could wipe their hands of the whole mess, turn the investigation over to the police, that didn't seem possible.

"Do you think they'll leave me alone now that they've taken my computer and torn my house apart?"

How he longed to be able to tell her what she wanted to hear. "I doubt it."

She frowned, and before he could explain his reasoning, a knock came from the door. Ava froze, questions filling her wide eyes.

"It's probably the detective." Marcus strode to the door and cracked it open. Sure enough, Detective Kelly stood on the other side.

"May I come in?"

Marcus nodded, and the detective stepped inside, his gaze sweeping the room—which, while a big improvement from before they started cleaning, was still a mess. "Seems you've kind of been through the wringer."

"Sure feels like it," Ava said.

"Tell me what happened in Miami this afternoon."

When Ava didn't start talking, the detective turned his attention to Marcus, who recounted everything that had happened since they arrived at William Klein's house on Key Biscayne.

"Did you recognize anyone in any of the cars that chased you?"

"Dark tinted windows. Couldn't see anything," Marcus said. "Ava recognized one of the cars. She thought it might have been following her the other day."

Detective Kelly turned to Ava. "It would be helpful if you could describe the vehicle for me."

"I didn't see much, but it was a gray sedan."

"Make and model?"

She shook her head. "I'm not sure."

The detective turned to Marcus.

"Definitely a Chevy," he said. "Maybe a Malibu. Guessing between ten and fifteen years old."

The detective wrote the information down in his notebook. "Anything else you want to share?"

Ava shook her head.

"In that case, there's something I need to tell you." He leveled his stare at Ava. "The toxicology came back on your friend. There were no signs of drugs or alcohol in his system."

Ava perked up. "What does that mean?"

"Means we're back at square one."

"So you think someone planted the drugs?" Her entire demeanor changed. She'd gone from overwrought to exhilarated in nothing flat.

"Either planted or dropped by the perpetrator."

"Are you going to investigate the story he was working on?"

"We'll look into all aspects of his life."

Ava released a sigh of relief so big, Marcus wondered how long she'd been holding it in. Maybe since they discovered Patrick's body.

"Contact me if anything else comes up." Detective Kelly moved toward the door, and Marcus followed him outside.

He was about to share his concerns, but the detective spoke first. "She's in over her head."

Marcus bristled. Ava put all of this together with nothing to go on but an exhibit brochure and a painting bought at auction. "If anything, she's too astute for her own good."

"Okay, okay. I meant no offense." The detective chuckled. "You want me to send a patrol car by the house every so often? Maybe the newspaper, too?"

Marcus felt the tension in his chest ease, grateful the detective could put aside his dislike to see that Ava was taken care of. "That would make me feel better, thank you."

"Consider it done." The detective turned toward his unmarked car, but then stopped and looked at Marcus. "A patrol car can only do so much."

"I know. I'll keep an eye on her."

He wouldn't be letting her out of his sight.

Chapter 21

Today had been the longest day of Ava's life.

She changed into her pajamas and pulled down the covers. Though how she'd be able to sleep after what happened, she had no idea.

"What are you doing?" Marcus appeared in the doorway.

Her nerves, already frayed, snapped a little tighter. "Getting ready for bed."

He stared for a beat, jaw pulsing. "Absolutely not."

"What? Why not?"

"Pack a bag. You're coming to my hotel."

Ava bristled. The arrogance of this man barking orders at her like she was some sort of helpless underling. "Excuse me?"

"You're not staying here." His tone was matter-of-fact. Not up for discussion.

Annoyance bubbled up inside her. "And who do you think you are?"

With two big steps, he closed the distance between them. "I'm the guy who will lose his mind if anything happens to you." His voice was low and raw and rich with emotion.

She studied his face, strained and serious, and her indignation faded away. He was right. But even though someone had invaded her home, leaving felt too much like running away. This was Nana's house. The only place she'd ever felt safe and loved.

He lifted his hand and stroked her jaw. "It's not safe. Not right now."

"What about Mr. Belvedere and Beagle Bailey?"

"They can come too."

"Can they? Do you know your hotel takes pets?"

"Well...no, but if not, we'll move to a different hotel."

"I don't want to be a burden." This entire mess was her fault, and it wouldn't be fair to impose on him like that. Even though they agreed they wanted the relationship to continue, they'd had zero discussions about what that might look like. She was better off not getting attached or becoming reliant on his protection. "You don't think it would be too disruptive—for you, for me, for the animals?"

"If you were at a hotel, there would always be someone around, cameras keeping track of who comes and goes."

"They already know I don't have whatever it is they're looking for. Why would they come back?"

"They have no way of knowing what you have up here." He tapped her on the head. "If they come back, this time it'll be to hurt you."

She swallowed a swell of despair. They were going to keep coming. A bead of sweat ran down her back. She understood what he'd meant when he said they couldn't stop. "I want this to end. Does that make me a horrible person?"

Marcus stared, his eyes searching. "Of course not. Why would you say that?"

"I should have stayed out of it."

"Too late for that now." His brows furrowed, and she realized she needed to spell it out.

"If I'd never gotten involved, no one would ever know what happened to Patrick." Her throat tightened as though trying to strangle the words. "And right now, I would prefer Patrick's murder to go unsolved to this."

Marcus wrapped his strong arms around her and hauled her against him. He didn't speak, simply held her. After a moment, he drew back. "I'll call the hotel and ask about pets. You'll get ready to go?"

She nodded. How had her life turned into this? "When can I come back?"

"We'll figure it out once I get a security system set up."

Ava watched Marcus step from the room, collected herself, and pulled a bag from the closet.

A warm body pressed against Ava's back. A possessive arm slung around her waist. The steady rhythm of Marcus's breath feathered her ear.

Ava sighed, inhaling blissful contentment. She wanted to stay like this forever. Then, an imaginary record scratch brought her back to reality. Her eyes popped open, and she remembered. Nothing was perfect. Or blissful. Or content.

Last night she'd packed a few days' worth of clothes and loaded the cat and dog and half of their belongings into Marcus's truck. When they got to his hotel room, Mr. Belvedere had anchored himself between the dresser and the desk while Beagle Bailey whined himself to sleep.

Marcus's arm tightened around her waist. "You okay?"

"Yeah, why?"

"You're huffing like a bull."

Great. As if morning breath wasn't bad enough. Another unattractive quality to worry about. "Sorry. I was remembering yesterday."

He rolled her over and gifted her with a slow, sweet kiss, then pulled away, taking her anxiety with him. Propping himself on an elbow, he stared down at her. "What are your plans for the day?"

"I need to stop by the paper, but then I'm going to go to the museum to see Amanda. I want to tell her about Patrick's toxicology report." And pump her for information on Henrick. "After that, I guess I'll go back to the office. I have a couple of stories to finish up, and I need a computer."

"I'll come with you."

"You'd be so bored." She could imagine Marcus standing around, growling at everyone like a guard dog. "You should spend some time with your mom."

He looked like he wanted to argue, but she didn't give him the chance. "There will be people around me all day long. Both the museum and the office have security."

His heavy stare of resignation bore into her. "I want you to check in every hour on the hour."

"You don't think that's a bit much?"

"After everything that's happened, do you think my needing to know you're okay is an overreaction?"

"No." The admission was strained. She should be grateful Marcus was here, and that he cared enough to keep tabs on her. "What will you do while I'm at work?"

"Probably touch base with my mom. Look into getting you a security system. At the very least, I can set up some cameras. Maybe get your car window fixed."

She'd never needed cameras before. Things were different now. Not to mention the look on Marcus's face—the honesty and distress—told her he needed to feel useful and protective. Something warm and unfamiliar grew in her chest. "Okay. I'd appreciate that."

That slow, sexy smile she couldn't resist spread across his face. She snaked her arms around his neck and dragged him closer. "Come here."

He cocked an eyebrow, then lowered himself until his mouth hovered just above hers. There was a gleam in his eyes that made her stomach clench. She'd been the recipient of appreciative looks from men for most of her life, but never had a man looked at her like this—like she mattered more than anything else in the world.

Emotion clogged her throat, and her voice hitched when she spoke. "What are you waiting for? An invitation?"

His mouth quirked. "Now that you mention it..."

She exaggerated clearing her throat. "You are cordially invited to take part in the ravishment of Ava Montoya. The event will take place in the very near future." She tried to keep a straight face. "Orgasms accepted in lieu of presents."

He laughed, his eyes crinkling at the corners. "I'll see what I can do." And then he dipped his head, leaving a trail of kisses up her neck. His warm breath brushed her skin and sent a tingle straight to her core.

She tugged his mouth to hers. Somehow, his lips managed to be both soft and firm, hungry and restrained. Her own control was teetering on the edge of a cliff, and she opened to him, letting herself topple over the side. Their kisses turned ravenous, raw. Insatiable.

And it wasn't enough. She needed more. More lips and tongue. More closeness.

More Marcus.

Her hands took over from her brain. Acting of their own accord, they migrated from his neck down his chest and into the waistband of his boxer briefs.

Marcus's palms skimmed her stomach and pushed up her tank top. Gathering her breasts in his large hands, he brought one to his mouth, sucking on a nipple, while rolling and pinching the other. Another lustful arrow found its mark. She arched involuntarily. An uninhibited moan slid from her throat.

The sensations she had when she was with Marcus differed from anything she'd experienced before. Why did this feel so good? So right?

She squeezed her eyes shut and batted the thought away, only to have it bounce right back. This time she held onto it, turning it over, looking for an explanation—any explanation—to justify the emotional attachment. Feelings didn't develop this quickly. Or this strongly.

But maybe when you found the right person, they did.

Marcus pressed soft kisses down her neck. His hands glided down her body, tracing her contours with his fingers. She shuddered, though whether the reaction was a result of his touch or the reminder she was falling for this man, she didn't know.

He let his fingers trail down her stomach and dip into her pajama shorts, lightly dragging over her entrance. Her legs fell open, and he rolled against her, his erection pressing into her leg.

His finger dipped inside while his thumb pressed into her clit.

"Please..." She'd been reduced to begging and wasn't the least bit embarrassed about it.

A happy growl rumbled from his chest as he kissed her again. "You're so wet."

She bit her lip and nodded. Words eluded her. Some writer she was.

He continued his slow, sensual exploration, seeming to enjoy her growing desperation. Finally, when she could take no more, his underwear was slid off and his large body climbed on top of hers. He positioned the head of his cock at her entrance, but before he slid inside, he clasped her hands, linking their fingers. A simple action, but one that made her feel safe and cherished. She wrapped her arms around him, held him tight, and decided she'd do whatever it took to never let him go.

Chapter 22

They pulled into the driveway at Ava's house, where her car and its broken window waited. She handed Marcus her keys. He'd offered to get her window fixed, and since she declined having him as a tag-along, he'd insisted she share her GPS location so he'd know where she was—just until the danger had passed.

"Be safe," he said, and her insides melted like ice cream under hot caramel.

She'd not realized how good it would feel to be cared for, and then the flip side of that—to adore someone else to distraction. "Tell your mom I said hi."

He gave her a lopsided smile. "She's going to have a lot of questions about this."

"Tell her I can't get enough." She gave him a quick kiss on the lips, then ran for his pickup, which he insisted she take. "See you later."

His truck was several years newer than her Camaro, and she enjoyed driving it. Some of it was the height and being able to see over other vehicles. Some of it was the hum of the engine. But most of it was the fact that Marcus trusted her with it. She let out a contented sigh. It was almost enough to make her forget the current shitstorm.

Smiling the entire way, she drove straight to the museum. The smart thing would have been to call first, but she couldn't take the chance Amanda would put her off. She parked Marcus's truck near the library and waited for a break in traffic to cross the street.

She pushed through a glass door into the lobby of the museum, pausing to appreciate the impressive space. For some reason, she'd not paid attention to the details the other times she was here. White walls adorned with colorful artwork, a polished marble floor, and high ceilings. She glanced upward, curious about the lighting, and her breath caught when she noticed a glass-tile sculpture in the center of the ceiling, winding and curving and catching the sun from the nearby skylights.

After a moment, she composed herself and made her way to Barney and the concierge desk. He tipped his imaginary hat as she approached. "Miss Montoya."

"How's it going?"

"Oh, can't complain." Something in his smile told her the comment was sincere, not just a standard, run-of-the-mill response. Here was someone who enjoyed life.

"What's your secret?" she asked. "To being happy?"

He scratched his head. "I guess it's living in the moment, not worrying about the past or fretting about the future. Caring about people, accepting them—and ourselves—as we are."

Ava considered this for a moment. "Something to aspire to."

"What can I do for you today?"

"I was hoping I could speak to Ms. Soto for a few minutes."

"Do you have an appointment?"

"Afraid not. Inspiration struck, and I wanted to talk to her before it disappeared."

He held up a knobby finger. "Give me a minute."

Ava wandered around the lobby, glancing at the artwork. She recalled her conversation with Ian Vanderbrook—something else she had yet to follow up on—and what he'd said about much of the art being loaned. She saw nothing on the placards that indicated these pieces didn't belong to the museum.

Barney beckoned her over. "She'll be down to speak with you in a few minutes."

Apparently, Amanda wanted to keep this quick. Probably shouldn't read too much into it. Could just be that she was busy and Ava's visit had been unplanned.

About fifteen minutes later, she heard the echo of heels clicking across the smooth floor. She turned and saw Amanda coming her way.

"Ava." Amanda's voice, though friendly, did not convey the usual warmth. "I wish you'd scheduled some time on my calendar. I have a busy day."

Exactly the reason she hadn't called ahead. "I'm sorry, but I will be quick, I promise."

"Is this about a story?"

"Partly, but first, I wanted to give you an update on Patrick's case. I spoke to the detective yesterday. He said the toxicology report showed there were no drugs in Patrick's system, so they are shifting away from the drug deal angle."

"Oh, thank God." Amanda squeezed Ava's hands. "I tried telling them Patrick didn't do drugs, but they seemed determined to prove otherwise."

"Detective Kelly said they don't have any new leads, so we'll see what happens now."

Amanda's expression was wistful and pensive. But then she took a deep breath, seeming to reset herself, and it was back to business as usual. "Was there something else?"

Ava dug into her bag and found the business card on which she'd written her personal cell phone number. "Would you be able to get this to Henrick? Tell him I'm interested in speaking with him? I'm not sure how to get in touch."

Amanda tucked the card into the pocket of her blazer. "I'll see what I can do."

"I appreciate it." She paused for a moment, recalling the night of the gala and the argument she and Marcus had overheard. "Also, does Henrick speak with an accent?"

"He's French. Why?"

"Just a hunch."

"Anything else?" Amanda checked her watch.

Ava glanced at the painting behind Barney's desk and couldn't help but think about how different the Vanderbrook painting looked in William Klein's living room than it had at the gala. "Does the museum use a special type of lighting to enhance the artwork?"

"Not really, no. We try to let the art speak for itself." Amanda glanced at the glass sculpture on the ceiling. "In the exhibits, we mostly use white light, but natural light is always preferable.

That's why the museum was constructed with so many windows."

Now that she was looking, Ava noticed light streaming into the spaces, including the exhibit hall, which she could only just glimpse from their location in the lobby. "I assumed there were all kinds of fancy tricks you used."

"Nope." A gleam flared in Amanda's eyes. "I mean, wattage and beam angles are taken into consideration, and we never use bulbs stronger than seventy watts."

Knowing the museum did nothing special to light its pieces, and considering that William Klein had lots of natural light, the painting should have looked the same in the Klein living room as it did at the gala.

"I need to dash." Amanda actually looked regretful, but then added, "We should get drinks sometime."

Ava nodded, hope blooming in her chest. Patrick cared a great deal for Amanda. He would have wanted them to become friends.

***

Marcus's mother's sedan careened into the parking lot of the glass repair shop. Ava's car wouldn't be ready for a couple of hours, so he'd asked her to pick him up so they could go to lunch.

The car screeched to a stop. He stepped off the curb and opened the passenger door.

"Don't get in," his mom said. "You're driving." She threw open her door and climbed out.

He didn't argue. Mom had never been the most attentive driver. Drove his dad nuts. Marcus stepped around the front of the car while she went around the back.

Once they were both seated and had their seatbelts on, she leaned over and patted his cheek. "I'm so proud of you."

"For what?" He brushed away her hand and adjusted the rearview mirror.

"For helping Ava with her car and letting her use yours. So polite and thoughtful."

Marcus swallowed, remembering Ava's soft moans and the way she writhed beneath him only hours ago. He'd been anything but polite then, sinking into her, claiming her as his own. The mere memory made him hard. Good Lord, it was like he'd reverted into a teenage boy, driving Mom's car after getting his learner's permit and thinking about sex. He cleared his throat and shifted into *drive*. "Not a big deal. Seemed like it made the most sense."

"It may seem that way to you, but I assure you Ava feels differently."

Did she? He liked the idea of being her go-to person.

"I take it things are going well? You obviously spent the night together."

Marcus's gaze shot to his mom. "How do you know that?"

"It doesn't take a genius to puzzle it out considering your pickup was available for her to take to work."

She'd deduced all that based on the fact he let Ava borrow his truck?

Smug satisfaction spread across his mother's face. "You know, you're not the only one in this family who can make infer-

ences. Where do you think you got your investigative skills?"
She snorted. "Certainly not your father."

"As a matter of fact, I drove to her place this morning." It
wasn't a lie.

"There's no reason to pretend. Just tell me the truth."

He wasn't much of an agent if he couldn't withstand an
interrogation from his mother. He clenched his teeth before
answering. "Fine. Yes. She spent the night with me at my hotel."

His mom clapped her hands together. "Marvelous, darling.
I'm so happy for you."

Again, not the type of praise he needed from his mother.

"Just make sure you communicate, especially in terms of
what you like."

Marcus groaned again. "Please stop."

"I'm speaking from experience. Your father was a bit of a
one-trick pony. Don't get me wrong, it was enjoyable, but I
never asked for anything else. I suppose if I'm being honest, I
didn't know I could. But then I met Freddy—"

"Mom." Marcus held up his hand between them. "Stop."

"But honey, you've never been serious about anyone before,
and I have the experience of a long-term relationship. There are
plenty of things I'd do differently if given the chance."

He inhaled slowly, knowing he needed to be careful with
what he said next. The last thing he wanted was to hurt his
mother's feelings. "Don't you think I'm a bit old for the sex
talk?"

"Oh, I don't know—"

"That was rhetorical." He ground out the words, wanting to find a common ground, something that wouldn't offend Mom. "I will concede that I like Ava—"

"A lot."

"Yes, I like her a lot, and I will be honest with you about the things that are going on in my life, but in return, please stop talking about sex. I don't need to hear about you having sex, and I don't want to talk about my sex life, either."

"Sure. I can do that. I just got so excited. Ava is special, and I want things to be perfect."

"I appreciate that, but I need to figure this out on my own." They passed a shopping center on the right. "Where are we going?"

Rather than respond, his mom stared out the window, and he wondered if he'd upset her. After a long moment of silence, she turned and looked as though prepared to dole out another dose of wisdom. He braced himself for what came next.

"How does Thai food sound?"

Marcus swiped his credit card and took the bag of home security equipment from the clerk.

"More affordable than I would have guessed," his mom said as they made their way back to her car. "Makes me wonder if I need something like that."

"I wish you'd said something when we were in there. But if you're concerned, I can always set up a doorbell camera for you."

"I'll think about it."

They climbed into the car and headed toward the glass repair store. He'd gotten a text while they shopped that the window was finished.

"Thanks for tagging along today. I enjoyed the company." Things felt more normal now that he'd drawn a clear conversational line. Thank God he put an end to it before she started citing positions from the Kama Sutra.

"How about a double date tomorrow night? Somewhere nice. You and Ava and me and Freddy?"

"I'll ask." He bent to kiss his mom on the cheek. She fell into the driver's seat.

Once again behind the wheel, she peeled out of the parking lot and veered onto the roadway. Marcus went inside to get Ava's car.

He sent a text to let her know the car was done, then stopped by the hotel to pick up Beagle Bailey. When he got to her house, he let himself in with the key she'd given him. After playing fetch in the backyard, he got to work installing the security system. If he'd had time to do it properly, he would have contracted a security company, but given the short notice, he did the best he could, purchasing sensors for the windows and doors. Since Ava lived in a one-story house, that meant a sensor for every entry point. He added glass-break detectors in her bedroom, living room, and bathroom.

He installed motion-activated lights on all outdoor fixtures, and finally, he fitted wireless cameras around her property. One above the front door, one beside the garage door, one next to the sliding glass door in the backyard. The cameras connected to

Wi-Fi, which meant that if the internet was out, they wouldn't record, but they were better than nothing.

When he had everything installed, he let the dog into the house and sat on the couch. The items he'd purchased came with a three-month home monitoring trial. He could leave that to her to set up, but he wanted to make sure he had access to the system, at least until this was over.

Or until they were over.

They needed to discuss expectations. Did she think a relationship meant keeping in touch and seeing each other when he visited his mom? Or that they'd travel to and from each other's cities to spend time together? Maybe she wanted him to move to Fort Lauderdale. He didn't know. On top of that, he worried her feelings were nothing but leftover adrenaline and would evaporate as soon as Patrick's murder was solved.

His stomach clenched. Mom was right. He was serious about Ava. And he'd not even known her two full weeks. How could he be in so deep in such a short time?

The front door opened, and there she was. She had that look of unbridled excitement—similar to the way her eyes glistened with desire when they were in bed—but this look told him she'd found another clue.

He was off the couch and tugging her to him before he realized what he was doing. Wrapping an arm around her waist, he drew her in for a kiss. The moment their lips touched, all of his anxiety about their relationship abated. There was no one else, and there never would be. How he knew this, he had no idea, but the jolt zinging through his body told him it was true.

He pulled away, delighted by the flush in her cheeks. "Good day?"

"It is now." She melted against him and stretched onto her toes to kiss him again. "Thank you, by the way, for taking care of my car."

Satisfaction at having pleased her filled him. "I was happy to do it."

"Well, it means a lot."

Apparently, Mom was right again.

"Did you get any leads today?"

"Nothing major. I learned Henrick has a French accent. I also learned that the museum does nothing special with the lighting."

Marcus considered this. He wanted to keep his response measured. "Still not proof, but it's looking like William Klein's painting is a forgery."

"My thought too."

"So, what's next?"

"I've set up an appointment for a tour of Gentle Hands, the moving company the museum used for its deliveries. I'm going to do that tomorrow." She averted her gaze, looking suddenly shy. "If you want to accompany me. I was thinking maybe this time you'd come along for the interview. Since we'll be talking about security, you might think of things that don't occur to me."

"My mom asked if we'd like to go to dinner tomorrow night, but otherwise, you are the only thing on my schedule."

She flashed a smile—a mixture of gratitude and affection, and it was like seeing a shooting star on a cloudless night.

"I've got the security system set up. Why don't I show you how it works? Then we can set up your account?"

Ava opened her mouth to answer, but then her phone pinged. She turned the screen over, and the corners of her mouth pulled down. Her complexion transitioned from rosy radiance to bloodless pallor.

His heart raced, as though fleeing whatever new clusterfuck had just revealed itself. "What is it?"

"A text message." She looked up, her eyes haunted. "From Patrick."

Chapter 23

Had he heard her correctly? Marcus stepped beside Ava to get a look at her phone. Yep, there it was. A text from Patrick. "He must've scheduled it before he died."

Like an untied balloon, air whooshed out of Marcus in a steady exhale. It was probably too much to hope the message contained a clue that would lead them to Patrick's killer. "What does it say?"

"Nothing really." She read aloud from the message. "'If something happens to me, please take care of Beagle Bailey. And whatever you do, don't lose his collar. It's important.'" The bewildered look on her face transformed into exasperation. "So, he knew he was in trouble, and this is what he sends? A text about a dog collar?"

"Does Bailey have a history of running off? Could he have been worried he'd get lost if he's not wearing his tags?"

"I don't know." She plopped onto the couch and groaned, the upturned phone resting loosely in her hand.

Marcus sat beside her. "May I see?"

She nodded and handed it over.

The message was as she said. Short and vague. Though there was one line at the end she'd not read aloud. *I believe in you.*

Geez. Guilt snaked its way through Marcus's insides. When he first met Patrick, he'd pegged him as a self-important doofus. But the guy genuinely wanted the best for Ava. He saw something in her she didn't see in herself—a feeling Marcus could relate to.

If only Patrick had included something regarding the danger he'd found himself in. Marcus glanced up to find Ava slumped into the cushions. "You going to be okay?"

"Maybe?" She shook her head in disbelief. "I just don't understand. A message from the grave and it says nothing."

"Could be he didn't have time to write more. Or maybe he got interrupted and sent what he had."

"But it's been a week since he died. Why now?"

"My guess is he knew he was in danger, but didn't know how imminent the threat was. There are lots of possibilities."

"He could have said something about what all of this had to do with me. He was at my house, for Christ's sake!"

He pulled her in for a hug. "It's not fair. But I hope we find some answers."

She sagged against him, burying her face in his neck. The sweet, and now-familiar floral scent of her shampoo drifted around him. Closing his eyes, he rested his cheek on the top of her head. If only he could do something to make all of this better.

They sat like that for a long time, so long he wondered if Ava had fallen asleep, but then she sat up and rubbed her eyes. "Can we stay here tonight? Since you installed the security system?"

"We'll have to get Mr. Belvedere, but I think that would be okay. Do you feel safe enough?"

"I do. Especially if you're here." She snuggled into his embrace. "Besides, this is my home."

Something about those words, said with her nestled beside him, dislodged something in his heart, carrying to the surface an accumulation of emotions he'd not known he possessed. Hope, wonder. Love.

He squeezed her closer, hoping to convey the words not yet formed.

"Are you still going to the moving company tomorrow?"

"Gentle Hands?" She nodded. "I have an appointment after lunch."

"Do you know what you want to talk about?"

"I have some ideas, but it wouldn't hurt to write some notes." She grabbed her tablet from her bag and sighed. "I guess I need to think about getting a new laptop one of these days."

He gave what he hoped was a sympathetic smile. "Want me to contact my friend at the Bureau? Ask him if he has any thoughts about what we should ask?"

"That would be great." Ava squeezed his hand and smiled. "I don't know what I'd do without you."

Hopefully, she'd still feel that way when all this settled down.

Gentle Hands Fine Art Movers was located in an unremarkable building in a warehouse district near the port. Ava wasn't sure what she'd expected, but it wasn't this.

"Are you ready?" Marcus glanced at her from the driver's seat of his pickup, and she was struck again by the fact his time with her was limited.

Regardless of what they decided about their relationship, in less than two weeks, he'd be heading back to his home and his life in Philadelphia. She refused to delude herself into thinking he'd leave his job to be with her, but didn't know what she would do without him. He'd been there for almost every horrible thing that had happened since the night of the museum gala. Even last night, she'd been thankful for his presence. Without him, a simple text message would have sent her spiraling. He provided comfort and stability. She'd be lost without him.

"Ava?"

Preoccupied with her thoughts, she'd forgotten to answer his question. "Let's go."

They got out of the pickup. Marcus met her at the tailgate and took her hand. "You're going to be great."

That remained to be seen, though she appreciated the encouragement. "I'll do my best, but I can't stop thinking that this should have been Patrick's interview."

Marcus took a deep breath, seeming to inhale her comment. "Maybe. Maybe not. You're your own person with your own ideas. You don't know he would have ended up here."

She considered this and realized it was likely true. Her investigation could be totally different from Patrick's.

She released Marcus's hand and smoothed her outfit. She wore a knee-length pencil skirt and blouse with a pair of low heels. Her usual work attire was much more casual, but clothing and appearance had always played an important role in her life.

It was a place from which she drew strength, and today she needed every bit of extra confidence she could get.

Marcus followed as she made her way to the front door. He pointed to a sign directing visitors to ring the bell.

A voice boomed through the speaker beside the door. "Can I help you?"

"Ava Montoya. I'm here to meet with Mr. Alvarez."

The door buzzed and popped open. Marcus took the handle and waited for Ava to enter.

The woman motioned to the small waiting area. "Mr. Alvarez will be out shortly."

Ava silenced her phone for the interview, then moved to the waiting area. She and Marcus had just taken a seat when a short, bearded man emerged from a hallway behind the receptionist. He approached with hand outstretched. "You must be Ava?"

She hurried to stand. "Yes, that's correct. Mr. Alvarez?"

"The one and only."

"Thank you for seeing me on such short notice." She gestured to Marcus, now standing beside her. "This is my colleague, Marcus Anderson."

Last night, they decided he would pose as a security consultant. Marcus shook the other man's hand. "Pleased to meet you."

"You're writing a story about art transport. Is that correct?" Mr. Alvarez raised a questioning brow.

"Kind of. I attended an auction and exhibit at the Fort Lauderdale Art Museum, and it made me curious to learn how these things work once someone invests in art." Not a complete lie. "Given the interest in the Vanderbrook exhibit, I thought it would make an interesting article." She removed her tablet from her bag.

"Let's start with the vehicle bay."

Ava and Marcus followed Mr. Alvarez down a hallway until they reached a garage filled with panel trucks.

"How did you get into the shipment and transportation of art?" she asked.

"Grew up working at my father's moving company. When he died, I inherited the business. Not long after, I decided I'd moved enough sofas, bedroom sets, and televisions to last a lifetime." He motioned toward Marcus. "I bet this guy knows what I'm talking about."

Marcus nodded. "I used to get asked to help people move all the time. These days, there's no amount of free pizza that would ever make it worth my while."

"Right? I was getting paid, and still didn't want to do it." Alvarez chuckled. "I've always been a bit of a collector, and the one part of the job I enjoyed was looking after our clients' personal treasures. I began designing special boxes to protect collections during transport. By the time Dad passed, I knew where I wanted the company to go."

They stopped next to a medium-sized cargo truck with the Gentle Hands logo painted on the side. "You're probably wondering what makes these trucks different from any other moving truck."

That had been her next question.

"Each one is hard-wired with a GPS transmitter that allows us to track deliveries in real time. The system we use is similar to what's in police cars."

Marcus tilted his head as though considering the information. "How accurate is the tracking?"

"The service we use guarantees accuracy within ten to forty feet."

"And what do the readings look like?"

"I'll show you when we get back to my office. It's basically a map with a delivery summary that shows how far the truck drove and the average speed of the trip."

They walked around the back of the truck. Alvarez threw open the back door and pressed a button. "Hydraulic liftgate. Our handlers push nothing up a ramp, and we limit the need to lift anything very high or very far." Once the gate contacted the ground, he stepped onto it and motioned for Ava and Marcus to do the same. "Holds up to forty-five hundred pounds."

They took a quick ride and stepped inside the truck.

"Every one of our trucks is climate controlled."

Ava wrote the words on her tablet. "I didn't realize there was a temperature for storing art."

"Between fifty and seventy degrees is ideal, but in humid regions like South Florida, we also want to keep the art ventilated because of the moisture." He pointed out bars along the ceiling, as well as grooved panels on the walls. "Once we crate and load the artwork for transport, we secure it with belts to the sides and ceiling of the truck."

"I wouldn't have guessed there was so much to it," Marcus said.

"As I like to tell my employees, 'We treat every item like it's going to the Smithsonian.'"

The three of them stepped back onto the liftgate and rode it to ground level.

"Over here is where we design our crates. The vast majority of our business includes creating custom containers and packing material. We design and build everything on site."

He reached for a roll of blue tape. "Once the boxes are sealed, we secure them with a strip of tape. This ensures a sense of security." He held up a long section of tape stamped with the company logo. "We sign it, date it, and write the time across it. This verifies for the recipient when the packing was completed and when it left for its final destination."

Ava made a note to ask Mr. Klein about the tape on his shipment. It probably wasn't relevant, but you never knew what a single question might reveal. "Who at the museum contacted you about the Vanderbrook auction?"

"We do a lot of work for the museum. Mr. Gerou is very particular. We were hired weeks prior to the auction."

"So, your company delivered all three of the Vanderbrook paintings?"

"That is correct." He motioned them toward the office located on the far side of the garage. "I can show you the GPS files for those particular deliveries.

He printed the summary files for each of the three paintings. Ava glanced at them, noted the dates and times, then passed them to Marcus.

"How far in advance does a delivery need to be scheduled?" she asked.

"At least seventy-two hours to allow time to make the packaging materials."

"What happens when a delivery needs to be changed at the last minute, like with the *African Sun* painting from the auction?"

"Depends on the circumstances and whether the delivery needs to be pushed up or moved back." He stroked his beard. "But your information about a delay with one of the Vanderbrook paintings is incorrect. All three deliveries happened on time, as scheduled."

"I heard there was some sort of insurance appraisal delay and the painting to William Hughes had to be rescheduled."

He shook his head, clearly not realizing the significance of what he'd just said. "Delivery dates were set approximately two weeks before we took possession of the artwork."

Mr. Alvarez herded them back toward the reception area. "I hope I've answered all of your questions?"

"This has been a tremendous help. Very enlightening." What an understatement.

Neither Ava nor Marcus said anything until they were inside his pickup. Marcus spoke first. "William Klein's painting was never delayed."

"Which means there was no issue with the insurance appraisal." Ava's mind reeled. "But why did they say it was coming on a different day than scheduled?"

"So, it appeared all the paintings were being treated the same? To avoid making one painting seem more important or different from the others?"

Absently, she took out her phone and noticed a missed call. She pressed the voicemail button. The speaker had a thick accent. "Meet me at Vista del Mar. Sixth floor, Unit B. Tonight. Sundown. Come alone."

She turned toward Marcus. "That was Henrick. He wants to meet."

Chapter 24

Marcus leaned against the counter in Ava's kitchen and ran a hand up and down his jaw. "You are not going in there alone." They'd discussed this nonstop since Ava had played Henrick's voicemail in the parking lot at Gentle Hands. Now they were back at her house, and Marcus couldn't seem to get through to her.

He rubbed a hand against his chest, unsure how much his heart could take. "You don't know whose side Henrick is on. And just because he said you should come alone doesn't mean he'll be alone."

"This was your idea. You said I should reach out."

"I also said we wanted to control the environment. Meeting at the time and place of his choosing is the opposite of controlled."

"I have to meet with him. What if he was Patrick's source? He'll know what Patrick was working on." She tucked her bottom lip between her teeth. "He may have been the last person to see Patrick alive."

"And he might have killed him." Marcus's voice rose with his frustration level. Why wasn't she getting this?

She shook her head. "I don't think he did."

"But you don't know." He ran an agitated hand through his hair. Why was she so determined to put herself in danger? "This morning you wanted to quit. Now you're determined to meet a possible killer?"

"Don't you get it? This might be my only chance to learn what Patrick discovered. I can't pass it up." Her eyes implored him to understand. "Weren't you the one who said I couldn't stop?"

"Yes, I said you couldn't stop. I didn't say go meet a potential killer by yourself!" He clenched and unclenched his fists. Keeping her safe was going to become a full-time job if she continued to make reckless decisions. "I understand you want to know about Patrick's death. But putting yourself in danger is not the answer."

"We don't know if I'll be in danger."

"Maybe not, but we can't rule it out." His voice was pleading. "Let me come with you."

"I can't. He said to come alone, and what if Henrick wants to blow the whistle on the forgery operation?"

"Suppose what you say is true? Let's say Henrick told Patrick all about it." He paused, hoping his words would finally sink in. "That information is probably why Patrick was murdered. He had to be silenced before he printed his story."

"Why not kill Henrick if he's the one dishing the secrets?"

Did she truly want to know what he thought? Probably not, but he was going to tell her, anyway. "Once they get what they want from Henrick—another painting or whatever—he's dead too."

"All the more reason for me to speak with him while I can."

She couldn't be serious. "Do you hear yourself? We're talking about a man—a criminal—being killed because of things he knows, and your biggest concern is talking to him before that happens?"

She stared back with a defiant lift to her chin. "Don't you dare put words in my mouth."

"I do this for a living. I understand the risks better than you ever could. If I can't keep you safe, why am I even here?"

"I thought you were here to help and because you care about me."

Marcus couldn't take any more. "Unless I'm with you, you're not going. I forbid it."

Her eyes flared, and she let out a humorless laugh. "You forbid it?" She jabbed her index finger in his direction. "I think you've forgotten that you don't get to tell me what I can and cannot do."

He held up his hands in surrender. "I don't want to fight. I'm just trying to protect you."

"I know." She stepped closer, reaching for his hand. "I appreciate it, but Henrick might be the only person who knows why Patrick was killed. I need to know what he has to say."

Her fingers grazed his. What would he do if something happened to her? The thought of losing her, of seeing her hurt—or worse—sent a searing pain through his chest. He couldn't speak.

She, however, suffered no such affliction. "You have to understand why I need to do this."

"I just—"

"I want your support, but if you can't give it to me, I understand."

"When will it end?" He didn't know if he was asking about the investigation or their relationship. Or both.

"When I figure out who killed Patrick."

"And what if you don't?"

"I'll never stop looking."

He was afraid that would be her answer. "In that case, I can't do this. I'm sorry."

"I'm not asking you to do anything." Her demeanor didn't change at all. "I can handle Henrick on my own."

"No, I mean, I can't do this." He motioned between them. "I can't continue watching you put yourself in danger. You mean too much to me."

She bit down on her bottom lip. "So that's it? We're done?"

Her question stole his wind like a punch to the gut, and for a disorienting moment, he forgot how to breathe. This wasn't how he wanted it to end.

Tears stung at the back of his eyes. Jesus. This woman. "Seems that way."

"This is the most important thing I've ever done. I won't skip out on a chance to get answers, ultimatum or not."

He couldn't continue to argue with her. She wouldn't change her mind, and neither would he. "I can't stand around and watch you get hurt."

Anger flared in her eyes. "You need to leave."

Marcus picked up his keys from the sofa table and stalked toward the door. He kept waiting for her to say something, to tell him not to go, to say she was wrong. His fingers grazed the doorknob.

"Marcus…"

His breath caught in his throat. He closed his eyes and turned back. "Yes?"

"Don't come back."

———ℓℓ———

Painfully aware of the pounding of her heart, Ava stared at the door long after it clicked shut. She listened for the sound of his truck starting. The rumble of the engine. And then nothing. He'd left. He fucking left. With heavy limbs, she sank onto the sofa.

He was her future—she'd been so certain of it, and then one little argument and he bailed. Of course, that wasn't entirely true. He'd not bailed so much as let her push him away. She'd been the one who acted like a jerk. But he had to understand. This was her friend's death they were talking about. A friend who had been killed while waiting to see her.

And she still didn't know why.

Which was more important? Talking to a source who may or may not have information about Patrick's death? Or the man who made her feel loved? The man who always knew what she needed?

God, she was such an idiot.

She didn't want to let Marcus go. A jolt of awareness had her on her feet. He said he cared for her. *Too much*. Those had been his words. He still had almost a week and a half before he'd need to head back to Philly. There was still time. This wasn't over.

It couldn't be.

She'd find him and tell him she wouldn't meet with Henrick. Not unless he was with her. She picked up her phone and dialed his number. Straight to voicemail.

He wasn't getting off that easily. They were going to sit down and talk this out. She grabbed her keys and bag and headed for the Camaro.

She drove for about fifteen minutes to his hotel. Surely this is where he would have gone? His truck wasn't here. She pulled into a parking space and hurried through the lobby to the elevator.

What if he'd checked out?

She mashed the elevator button several times as though that would make it arrive sooner. Finally, the door dinged open. She stepped inside and pressed the button for the second floor.

This had to be the slowest elevator in the universe. She paced the length of the small space.

Ding.

She sprinted down the hallway, skidded to a stop and rapped on his door. No answer.

Then she banged. When Marcus still didn't appear, ready to haul her into his arms, she pressed her ear to the door. Nothing.

With a self-loathing huff, she raced back to the elevator. This was all her fault. Why hadn't she told him how she felt?

Once back in the lobby, she stopped at the front desk.

"Excuse me," she said to the man behind the counter. "Are you able to tell me if a guest is still staying here?"

"I don't think I'm supposed to do that. Privacy and all."

"Please." She sounded desperate. Hell, she was desperate. "It's important."

"Uh..." He looked around as though someone would appear to tell him what to do. "I guess if I'm only confirming this person is a guest, it's probably fine."

She almost leaped over the counter to hug him. "His name is Marcus Anderson. He's staying in room two-fifteen."

The man clicked his mouse, then typed for a moment. He looked up and smiled. "Yes, Mr. Anderson is confirmed for seven more nights."

So he hadn't left. A relieved whoosh of air burst from her. She still had time.

"Thank you—" She checked the desk clerk's name tag. "Zayden, I can't tell you how much I appreciate your help."

He blushed. "Of course. Any time."

Ava hustled through the doors of the hotel and back into her Camaro. Maybe he went to his mom's house. She started up the car and peeled out of the lot.

⎯⎯ɛɛ⎯⎯

"Would you like something to drink?" Violet headed for the kitchen.

"That's okay. I was just wondering if Marcus was here." She followed the woman into the back of the house.

Marcus's mother sat at a round kitchen table, looking confused. "Is he supposed to be?"

"No. I had something to talk to him about, and I thought he might have come over to visit."

"I figured he'd be with you."

"He was." She dropped into the chair across from Vi. How much did she want to tell this woman? "We had an argument."

The woman squeezed Ava's hand. "Oh, I'm sorry. Was this about that article you're writing?"

"He told you?"

"He said you believed your friend's death was connected to something he'd been working on." She tilted her head sympathetically. "Marcus is worried you might get hurt."

"I know." How could she have been such a fool? "I got a call from one of Patrick's sources. He wants to meet tonight, but said I should come alone. Marcus didn't think it was a good idea. We got into a fight, and he left." She left out the part where she told him they were through.

Vi squeezed her hand again. "He's a bit of a hothead, but he almost always cools down and comes around. I'm sure everything will be fine."

"Do you think so?" She couldn't bear it if this was how things ended between them.

The older woman offered a knowing smile. "Absolutely."

"I hope so." Ava cleared her throat to cover the quiver in her voice, but suspected Vi had heard it, anyway.

"So, are you still planning to meet with this man?"

"I don't know. I hoped to talk to Marcus and have a more rational discussion about it."

"Please be careful. Marcus isn't the only one who cares about you."

Ava was touched by the sentiment. Other than her nana, she'd grown accustomed to being ignored and disregarded. It was nice to feel cherished, and so easy to imagine Marcus and his mother becoming a permanent part of her life.

She stood. "Thank you for the advice. If you see Marcus, will you tell him I'm looking for him?"

"It'll be the first thing I say. Not even hello." There was a tinge of sadness in Vi's smile.

"I appreciate it."

Vi walked her to the front door, and they said goodbye. Losing Marcus might be the worst thing that had ever happened to her, but losing his mother would also be a blow.

Once Ava was back in her car, she tried calling again. Voice mail. Rather than leave a message, she sent a text.

—*I'm sorry. Can we talk?*—

The sun was dipping toward the horizon. Sunset was only a couple of hours away. She'd go home, give Mr. Belvedere and Beagle Bailey their dinners, and wait for Marcus to call. If that didn't happen, she'd make a decision about meeting with Henrick.

Chapter 25

Marcus pulled up to Vista del Mar a half-hour before sunset. The anger and disappointment from their earlier argument had subsided. Now, his only concern was Ava's safety.

The place she planned to meet Henrick was a cinderblock dump covered in beige stucco. Whoever named this shithole must've had a sense of humor because, as far as Marcus could tell, the only water view was a dirty canal running behind the property.

And to think he'd almost let Ava do this on her own. As his mom would say, sometimes he could be a real asshole.

He was here now, and that was what mattered. Or at least he hoped she'd see it that way. Part of him wanted to believe she would decide not to come. But he knew Ava, and that seemed unlikely.

When she got here—and he expected she'd be right on time—he'd be waiting, ready to offer his support, as well as a bit of additional security.

Her refusal to see common sense had left him agitated, and when he walked out of her house after their fight, he'd been too frustrated to think and turned off his phone so he wouldn't have to think about the fact he might never hear from her again. Gradually, his anger cooled, and as he drove around, her words repeated themselves on a loop in his brain. *Don't come back.*

Though he didn't believe she meant it, he couldn't shake the idea this might be all they'd ever have, and there was one thing he knew for certain. They had no future if they couldn't be honest about their feelings.

Once that realization moved in and made itself at home, he headed to the nearest electronics store, where he purchased an audio transmitter. She didn't want him going into the meeting with her, but this way, he'd be able to listen in on the conversation. More importantly, he'd know if things got dangerous. A listening device wasn't his first choice, but it was the next best thing.

He stared up at the exterior walkway circling each floor of the building. With the little transmitter in hand, he got out of his truck and headed for the stairs. First, he'd do a quick reconnaissance of the sixth floor. He wanted to be nearby when Ava went in for the interview, but he also needed to be hidden.

His inspection of the property revealed a recessed niche near the elevator bay. The perfect hiding spot where he could get to her quickly if something happened.

A worst-case scenario. God, how he hated those.

Inhaling a deep breath, he used the weight of his gun on his belt to ground him. Ava was smart. He'd be here if she needed him. Everything would be fine.

Once he was back at ground level, he leaned against the wall beneath the first flight of stairs. He wanted to be in position before she arrived. The last thing he needed was for someone to see them together and think she'd set a trap.

Several minutes later, a yellow Camaro pulled into the lot.

Damn. He'd not realized how much he hoped she wouldn't show. But she had, and he wouldn't criticize her for it. There were two things he wanted: to keep her safe and to support her when she needed him most.

He wanted to run to her, but resisted, keeping himself hidden until she got out of her car and started in his direction.

When she reached the bottom of the stairs, she paused and looked around, almost as if she sensed he was there.

"Ava."

She jumped, and he stepped out of the shadows.

"I didn't mean to startle you."

"Oh, Marcus." She threw herself into his arms and buried her face in his chest.

He wrapped possessive arms around her and drew her close. "Hey, it's okay."

"I'm sorry. I regretted what I said as soon as you left." She pulled back, and he brushed away the tears brimming in her eyes.

"I said things I shouldn't have." He leaned in and gave her a soft kiss. "I'm sorry for making you think I wouldn't be there for you."

She smiled. "I don't have to do this. Not if you don't want me to."

"I don't want to be the reason you sacrifice getting information that might help us figure out who killed Patrick. But I do want to make sure you're safe." He removed the little microphone and a roll of medical tape from his pocket. "We're going to set up a listening device. That way, I don't have to be with you, but I'll still know what's going on."

She looked down at the cotton-swab shaped microphone. "I'm going to wear a wire?"

"Kind of." He flipped on the power button, ripped a strip of tape and positioned the audio transmitter to her skin beneath her collar.

He stepped back and inspected her shirt. If he hadn't just secured the mic to her body, he'd never have known it was there. He held out his hand. "Let me see your phone."

She handed over her mobile and pinched her shirt away from her body to stare at the device adhered beneath her collar bone. "Did you just get this?"

He nodded. "After I left your house, I realized I couldn't let you do this alone. I know you don't want me in the room with you, but I thought—hoped—you'd agree to let me listen in." Using Bluetooth, he connected her phone to the mic. Then fiddled with the call settings. "Now let's call my phone."

Once he verified the phones were connected, he tucked hers into her bag. "Keep that hidden. I'll be able to hear your conversation, and Henrick won't suspect a thing."

She gave a half-hearted nod, and he cupped her face in his hands. "Are you okay?"

"A little nervous, I guess."

"Don't worry, everything is going to be fine." God, how he hoped that was true. He pointed toward the walkway. "I'm going to ride to the sixth floor in the elevator. I'll stay out of sight, but you'll know I'm there." He kissed her again. "I'll see you when it's over."

She took a deep breath. "I'm ready."

The sound of a scuffle echoed from above.

"Stop! What are you doing?" The voice sounded panicked. And it had a thick French accent.

Ava turned wide, frightened eyes on Marcus. She grasped his hand.

"Please! Don't do this," the accented voice pleaded.

A second, lower and more menacing, voice responded. "You can't be trusted to keep your mouth shut."

"I won't say anything. I promise. Just don't—" The words were cut off by a bloodcurdling shriek.

<hr />

Thwack. Henrick's body—easily identified by the pony-tail—landed face-down in an empty parking spot about ten yards from where they stood. Ava's gaze shot up to the sixth-floor walkway, where a dark-haired man strode to the stairs at the other end of the building. She lunged forward, but Marcus pulled her back. What was he thinking? The guy was going to get away. "We have to go after him."

Marcus shook his head. He had his phone out and had already dialed 9-1-1. She slowly tuned in to what he was saying. "Vista del Mar off of Oakland Park Boulevard...A man was thrown off a balcony...Sixth floor."

The memory of finding Patrick's body slammed into her. This was just like that. Marcus taking charge, calling for help, while she stood around in shock, unsure what to do.

A moan drew her attention back to the man on the pavement. She lifted a hand to her mouth. "I...I think he's alive."

Marcus kept the phone connected to the 9-1-1 operator while approaching the unmoving man. Ava followed. He grasped Henrick's wrist and spoke into his phone again. "There's a pulse. It's beating rapidly."

Sirens sounded in the distance. She squeezed her eyes shut. Please let them be coming here.

Sure enough, an ambulance and a police car turned into the parking lot. She stared dumbfounded as paramedics surrounded the battered Henrick. There was a flurry of action, and in a flash, they had him in a cervical collar and strapped to a backboard. They ripped his shirt open and attached electrodes to his chest. The EMTs lifted him onto a gurney and boosted him into the ambulance.

Ava turned to Marcus. "What do we do now?"

"We witnessed a crime. We need to wait for the police to come talk to us." He wrapped an arm around her and tucked her against his side.

"What about the man who did this? He got away."

"Going after him would have been too dangerous. At least we can give a description."

Ava nodded and tried to remember the details. The man had brown hair. No, wait...black. He had black hair. Dark brown? At least she knew he was wearing a black short sleeved-button down. Or was it a T-shirt? She let out a frustrated growl. "I'm not sure what I saw."

Marcus squeezed her against him. "It's okay. It happened fast. I've got a rough idea of what he looked like."

A police cruiser and a dark sedan screeched into the parking lot. The door of the sedan swung open, and Detective Kelly climbed out. "Well, well, well. Why am I not surprised to see the two of you?"

Indignation swirled in Ava's belly.

"What are you doing here?" The detective took out his pocket notebook and flipped to a blank page. "At the scene of an attempted murder."

Thank God for Marcus. He threaded his fingers through hers and offered a reassuring squeeze. It was enough to calm her agitation and allow her to answer the detective's loaded question. "Henrick contacted me this afternoon saying he wanted to meet to talk about a story."

"A story about what?" The detective's tone was skeptical.

"He didn't say. I assumed he wanted to tell me what he knew about Patrick's murder."

"And why would you think he would have information about that?"

"I believe he may have been Patrick's source—the one he was meeting the night he was killed."

"If that's the case, he could have also been Patrick's killer."

She threw up her hands. "So everyone keeps telling me."

"How did you know it wasn't a setup?"

"I didn't, but I thought it was worth a shot."

Detective Kelly gave her the same incredulous look she'd seen on Marcus's face earlier in the day. He turned to Marcus. "Were you also going to be there?"

"No, but nearby."

Ava tugged on the collar of her shirt, revealing the microphone.

"I was planning to listen," Marcus said.

"That's good thinking, but you never should have done this on your own." Detective Kelly leveled his focus on Marcus. "I'd have thought you knew better."

Marcus didn't respond to the dig—didn't look the least bit bothered—but it annoyed Ava.

She ground her teeth. "Shall I inform you every time I schedule an interview?"

"If it involves an open case—" The detective's phone rang. He looked at the screen, then held up his hand. "Excuse me, I need to take this."

Once he turned his back and stepped away, Ava turned to Marcus. "Do you think they'll let us see Henrick? We need to see if he can tell us who did this and why."

Detective Kelly ended his call and returned to their conversation. "Unfortunately, Mr. Dubois didn't make it. He went into cardiac arrest in the ambulance on the way to the hospital." He flipped his notebook to a new page. "Let's start with a description of the person you saw leaving the scene."

A chill rippled up Ava's arms. Another murder. Another dead end.

Chapter 26

Ava flipped down the visor and checked her reflection. She looked as tired as she felt. Two nights had passed since Henrick's death, and she doubted she'd gotten a combined eight hours of sleep. Even having Marcus beside her hadn't stopped the tossing and turning. Until all of this was in the past—until she learned who killed Patrick and now Henrick—sleep was a luxury she couldn't afford.

She stared across the street at the museum, a place that not so long ago, she could scarcely imagine herself entering. Now, it seemed she was here every other day. She climbed out of her car, pulled her messenger bag with her tablet onto her shoulder, then jogged across the street and up the steps to the front entrance.

The tall glass doors whooshed open. She stepped inside the artificially cooled lobby.

"Miss Ava!" Barney called. "Good to see you again."

Reports of Henrick's death had appeared in the papers and on local TV news. Barney would have heard about it. As she stepped forward, Ava realized this might be an opportunity to find out what Henrick's coworkers were saying.

"Are you here to see Miss Soto?"

"I am." She shifted her bag to the other shoulder, unsure how to broach the topic. This was one thing she hated about being a reporter—asking people how they felt after someone had died. She considered the most delicate way to begin. "Um...how are things?"

Not her smoothest opening.

Barney's face fell. "You've heard about Mr. Dubois?"

Though she doubted Barney knew Henrick very well, she'd be surprised if he hadn't interacted with him from time to time. "I did. That's why I'm here." She let the man regain his composure. "Did you know him?"

"Only in passing. Funny man."

Ava straightened. This was new information. "Funny how?"

"Just the way he said things—very self-deprecating." He gave a half-laugh. "He had no filter. Could be inappropriate."

Again, information she'd not heard before.

"Inappropriate in terms of the jokes he told?"

"That, as well as the things he said. He liked women and often made comments that weren't proper by most standards." He shook his head in wonder. "Somehow, he always got away with it."

"Could he have crossed a line and ticked someone off?"

"Around here? No, I don't think so." He paused, and his eyes took on a faraway look. "It seemed as though something had changed recently. He was more subdued, distracted."

Ava nodded. "How recently?"

"I don't know, maybe the last couple of months."

Barney looked tired, and Ava didn't want to prod any further.

"Can you see if Amanda has a few minutes for me?"

He brightened and picked up the phone. "Absolutely."

While Barney called upstairs, Ava got out her tablet and stylus and jotted down some notes. She was about to put it away when a notification dinged. An email. From Martin Singh. She rolled her eyes. This guy did not give up.

Curious, she opened it to find an invitation to a party at George Gerou's house this Friday to promote Beachside at Seaside. She got invites like this occasionally, though the fact Gerou had gotten on board with the project seemed odd. The last time they spoke, he'd expressed concerns about how the development would affect his property.

She and Marcus were supposed to attend the theater on Friday night. Marcus's mom had practically shoved the tickets at them. But this was work, and since she didn't believe Violet and Freddy had an actual conflict, she'd be happy to give the tickets back. Not to mention, it would be one of their last nights before Marcus needed to return to Philadelphia. She didn't want to spend it sitting next to him in a dark theater.

"You can go up now," Barney said.

Ava thanked him and made her way to the second floor. Amanda was waiting when she got off the elevator. "Are you here about Henrick? I just can't believe it."

"I can't either." Ava thought it best to keep her involvement to herself. She couldn't imagine Amanda had anything to do with whatever was going on at the museum, but she had no clue who she could trust.

When they were inside her office, Amanda shut the door and plopped onto the leather couch. She shook her head in disbelief.

"I just can't imagine. Thrown off a balcony? How does that happen?"

Stick your nose where it doesn't belong. Piss off the wrong people. All the outcomes Marcus warned her about.

There was a time Ava would have reacted just like Amanda, but she knew better now. People were mostly good. She had to believe that. But as she was coming to realize, people could also do the most unthinkable things.

Ava sank onto the couch beside her friend and laid a hand on Amanda's leg. "I think the person who killed Patrick also killed Henrick."

Amanda drew back in surprise. "Did they even know one another?"

"I think Henrick was Patrick's source. The one he was meeting the night he was killed."

"That doesn't make sense."

Rather than try to convince Amanda, Ava steered her questions in another direction. "Do you know anyone here at the museum who was close to Henrick? Anyone he had issues with?"

Amanda chewed on her lip. "I didn't interact with him much. He spent most of his time in the studio and rarely came up here."

Ava teased a memory from her subconscious. "I came to see you after Patrick died. I saw Henrick here then."

"He sometimes came to see Mr. Gerou, to show him his work."

"Original work?"

Amanda shook her head. "His restorations."

Restorations. The day after Patrick's death. Henrick was up here. Were they truly restorations, or were they copies? "How often did he come to see Mr. Gerou?"

Amanda shrugged. "Only occasionally."

"Does he do a lot of restorations?"

"He works pretty regularly, if that's what you're asking. Sometimes he'd move straight from one assignment to another. Other times he'd go weeks or months without a project."

Amanda stood. "I'm sorry to cut this short, but I'm due in a meeting with Mr. Gerou and Martin Singh in half an hour."

"Commissioner Singh?"

"Yes, we're meeting to talk about a satellite location at the development they're hoping to build."

Ava paused. "Beachside?"

"That's the one."

"I thought Mr. Gerou was against the development."

Amanda frowned while ushering Ava out of her office and toward the elevator. "They've been batting around the idea of a museum-related gallery for a while now, but I don't have the inside scoop."

Ava gave her friend a quick hug. "Thank you for seeing me and answering my questions."

Ava rode the elevator to the ground floor, said goodbye to Barney and stepped onto the sidewalk. She needed to go somewhere quiet where she could concentrate and write down notes and impressions from her conversations. The colorful tiles on the side of the library building caught her eye. Perfect. She crossed the street.

A notification for an email popped up on her screen. She clicked on it and then froze. Another message from Patrick.

Marcus wiped his face with the bottom of his shirt. Damn, it was hot. Installing the doorbell camera he'd bought for his mom hadn't been difficult, and it hadn't taken very long. Still, thanks to the Florida humidity, sweat seeped through the front, back, and neckline of his shirt.

He twisted the wires around the terminals on the back of the doorbell. He'd adjust the angle after he turned the power back on and got a look at the camera.

The front door popped open. "Here, sweetie. I brought you some iced tea."

Marcus wiped his hands on his pant legs, accepted the glass and drank it down in one gulp. "Let me make sure it's working. Then I'll show you how to use it."

He followed his mom into the house, then stepped into the garage to flip the circuit breaker. His phone buzzed. It was Ava.

The tension he'd been carrying in his shoulders and neck since watching her get into her car this morning released. He didn't like the idea of her being out there on her own, especially after what happened the previous evening. "How'd it go? Learn anything new?"

"A few things." Her voice sounded shaky, strange.

His alert system kicked into overdrive. "What's wrong?"

"I got another message from Patrick."

Now the tremor in her voice made sense. "What did it say?"

"It's an email with an attachment, but I think it's corrupted or something. When I opened it, all I got were a bunch of numbers and letters and symbols. None of it makes any sense."

"Sounds like an encryption." Whatever Patrick had been working on, he'd known it was dangerous.

"So how do we get it decrypted? Can the FBI do that?"

"They can…" He drew the words out. "But it's time consuming. If we had the password, this would be a lot easier."

"It could be anything."

He hated the uncertainty in her voice. "Patrick knew what he was doing. I'm sure he left a clue. Forward me the file and I'll see what I can do."

Setting up the camera had been as much about distracting himself as it had been about Mom's security. "When I finish up here, I can meet you back at your place."

"I'm at the library. About to head upstairs and go over my notes. I'll let you know when I'm done."

They disconnected, and Marcus stepped back inside the house, where he found his mom putting out lunch. "Do you still like roast beef?"

"Sure do." He took a seat on one of the stools lined up in front of the kitchen island. An email notification pinged on his phone. He glanced at it. Patrick's encrypted file.

His muscles tensed with the need to investigate, to drive to his hotel room, get his computer, and try every password he could think of. He turned his phone face down. Right now, was for spending time with Mom.

He took a plate and two slices of bread. His mom pushed the horseradish sauce, Swiss cheese, onions, and tomatoes in his direction. It was so like her to have all his favorites. He waited for her to make a sandwich for herself, then watched her come around the counter and sit beside him.

"Can I see your phone?"

She retrieved it from the side pocket of her purse and handed it to him. "Why?"

"I want to download the app for the doorbell camera and show you how it works." For peace of mind, he'd installed it on his own phone as well.

After downloading the app and finishing lunch, he logged in and began explaining. He led her to the front door and handed back her phone. "There is a motion detector in the doorbell that will trigger the camera. Anytime someone steps onto your porch, you'll get an alert."

"Every time?" She had the look of someone realizing she was getting something she didn't really want.

"Yes. Now stay here. I'm going to go through the garage and come up onto the porch."

She stared at the phone in her hand as though waiting for something spectacular to happen.

"I'll be right back."

Still fixed on the screen, she gave a distracted nod. Good enough. He went through the garage, stepped onto the porch and opened the front door. His mom stood in the same place, still looking at her phone.

"Well?"

"It dinged at me."

"That's the notification. See this icon that looks like a house? That means the camera detected movement." He swiped the bar at the top of the screen, then clicked on the notification. The app opened, and a video played.

"That was taken by the doorbell?"

"Yes. Now, anytime someone is at your door, you'll know it."

She stretched up and kissed him on the cheek. "Thank you, darling."

"It's as much for me as it is for you." And that was the truth. Even though she lived in a gated community, he liked knowing she wouldn't have to open the door every time someone rang the bell.

He shifted from one foot to the other, not wanting to run out on her, but getting antsy to get a look at the file Patrick sent.

"Do you need to go? Are you meeting Ava?"

A wave of guilt crested over him. Mom had picked up on his agitation. The last thing he wanted was for her to get the idea he had better things to do than spend time with her. He shook his head. "She's working."

"That's too bad."

"It is?"

"I don't want to kick you out, but Freddy is taking me to Jai Alai this afternoon." She smiled. "Last time I won forty dollars."

If things were different, Marcus might have invited himself along. He'd never actually seen the game played, and under normal circumstances, would have welcomed the opportunity to learn about a new sport.

"I won't keep you then." He leaned over, gave his mom a kiss on the cheek and headed to the hotel room he hadn't slept in for days.

By the time Marcus thrust open the door to his room, he was practically vibrating with excitement. He'd spent the drive between his mom's house and the hotel thinking of everything he knew about Patrick, about Ava, and about their relationship. He'd come up with a dozen possible passwords and variations of each.

Grabbing his laptop off the desk in the corner, he opened it and sat on the bed. Not trusting the hotel Wi-Fi, he set up a hotspot on his phone and connected.

He logged into his email and clicked on the forwarded message. He'd expected to find a clue to the password hidden in the message, but the body of the email was empty. Nothing but the attached file.

Damn. Not ideal, but he'd sit here all night if that's what it took. They needed to get into this file.

He started off with the obvious. *Password.* Thank God. Marcus would've been very disappointed if Patrick had gone with something so obvious. He tried a couple of variations. After that, he moved onto easy number and letter combinations. He shot off a quick text to Eric to ask if he could get Patrick's birthdate for him.

While he waited for the other agent, Marcus moved on to some of the other ideas he'd had. According to Ava, Patrick obsessed over his dog. He typed *BeagleBailey.* Nope. That didn't do it. For the next ninety minutes, he tried anything and everything. The make and model of Patrick's SUV, the name of his condo complex, the newspaper, the names of famous paintings and painters, Walter Cronkite, the brand of Bailey's dog food. Nothing worked.

His phone pinged with a message containing Patrick's birth date. Holding his breath, he typed it in... Same response as every other variation he'd tried. He fell backwards onto the pillow. If only Patrick had included a clue in his email, this would have been so much easier. Of course, that made no sense. No one who used encryption was going to send information about the password at the same time. They'd send it separately—

He stopped. Patrick's text message. The one about taking care of the dog. He racked his brain trying to remember the exact wording.

And suddenly, Marcus knew exactly where to find the password.

Chapter 27

Satisfied with her notes about Henrick, Ava made her way down the stairs, from the top floor of the library to ground level. She didn't know that she'd gotten anything of significant value, but couldn't wait to go over it with Marcus.

The automatic doors opened, and she stepped into the scorching South Florida heat. She walked toward her car, which was parked about half a block away. A tall, handsome figure on the opposite side of the street caught her attention.

Ian Vanderbrook.

The artist bounded down the steps of the museum, but his feet slowed when he caught sight of her. He waved, and then stepped off the sidewalk and crossed the street.

"Ava! It's so good to see you."

"And you, Mr. Vanderbrook."

"Don't think it escaped my attention that you never called to set up an interview." He pursed his lips. "And please, call me Ian."

Did he not know Patrick was dead? Ava shifted her weight, unsure how to say it. "I'm sorry..."

"Ian." His smile was genuine. She saw it in the way the corners of his eyes crinkled.

"Right." She fiddled with her hair and started again. "Do you remember Patrick?"

"Oh, gosh." His eyes went wide and his posture rigid. "Of course, how thoughtless of me."

"Things have been a little hectic since then." Ava momentarily averted her gaze. "We found him at my house."

This time, his handsome face twisted with shock. "How awful. I had no idea."

"It wasn't your fault." But as she said the words, doubt crept in. Could this man—this famous artist—have been involved? Or was she letting her imagination get the better of her? She cleared her throat. "So that's why I haven't been in touch."

"I understand." He rolled back onto his heels. "You know, I won't be in town much longer. We could grab lunch at the café, chat about my work, and anything else you have questions about."

She worried her bottom lip. She wanted to get back to Marcus, to find out if he'd made any progress with the file Patrick had sent. But Patrick wouldn't have wanted her to pass up an opportunity to interview Ian Vanderbrook. The least she could do was spare an hour.

"Sure. That sounds nice."

Ian held out his hand in an after-you gesture, and Ava stepped into the street. When they got to Basket of Bread, Ian held open the door and waited for Ava to enter. Though she'd never dined at the restaurant, she knew all about it and its art-themed décor.

"Have you eaten here before?" she asked when they were seated.

"Once. Had a caprese sandwich."

The walls of the small dining room were crammed with the work of local artists for sale on consignment. Did any of the pieces belong to Henrick?

Ava's phone buzzed. It was rude, but she couldn't stop herself from looking. "Excuse me." She pulled her phone out of her bag and saw a text from Marcus.

—*Heading to your place. Think I know where the password is.*—

An excited tingle shot through her, and she fought the urge to jump to her feet and run to her car. As much as she wanted to be there when Marcus got into the file, this lunch or interview or whatever it was needed to happen. For Patrick, but also for the sake of professionalism.

She sent Marcus a quick thumbs up, then silenced her phone. Every ping of a text would be a distraction. Better to eliminate the temptation.

She stuffed her phone back into her bag, picked up her menu, and smiled at her companion. "The caprese sandwich sounds good. I'll try that."

"I'm thinking it'll be portobello ravioli for me today." He set his menu on the side of the table, and their server approached to take their orders, including two small Caesar salads.

She looked around the restaurant. Other than the couple sitting near the window, she and Ian were the only customers.

With a piercing stare, he steepled his fingers and rested them beneath his chin. "So, what questions do you have for me?"

Might as well go for it. "I understand you and George Gerou have a history."

His warm expression frosted over before her eyes. "I met George at a youth art exhibit when I was twelve years old. He approached my parents, said I had talent, but was unrefined. He offered me a spot in one of the art classes he ran through the museum."

"That must've seemed like quite an opportunity."

"Oh, it did. My parents were young, and money was tight. They wanted to put me in classes, but didn't have anything to spare. Then along comes this man who not only wanted to nurture my abilities, but was willing to finance my development." His gaze fixed on something over Ava's shoulder, though she suspected he wasn't looking at anything specific. "One class turned into several, and before we knew it, he offered to sponsor my enrollment at a fine arts school."

Something about the story raised the hair on the back of Ava's neck. "How did your parents feel about that?"

"They were delighted. He was giving me something they didn't have the resources to provide. We were all grateful for his generosity but felt completely indebted to him."

The salads arrived. They ate for a few moments in silence. Ava practiced some of the memory tips Marcus had shared. In her mind, she created a series of vignettes. A young boy in front of a painting shaking hands with a man in a suit. The same boy working at an easel in a classroom. And finally, a teenage version going up the steps of a fancy-looking school.

"I have questions about the *African Sun* series, but first I'm curious about the other two paintings you donated to the auction. I understand you were young when you painted them. Were they hard to part with?"

"Honestly, no." He looked her directly in the eyes, and she wondered if he wasn't trying to convey some other meaning. "Those paintings remind me of a time in my life I'd rather forget. They'd been in storage for nearly thirty years. It was good to do something useful with them."

"Because they reminded you of George Gerou?"

He nodded. "While there are many things I love about Florida, the memories from when I was a teen and then into my early twenties are not happy. I was young. I made some bad decisions, some of which I still regret."

Ava wanted to ask for specifics, but this had always been one of her shortcomings as a reporter. "What can you tell me about the *African Sun* paintings?"

"What do you want to know?" Ian smiled, and just like that, the heaviness of the moment evaporated.

"Where did you get your inspiration?"

"Have you ever been to Africa?"

She shook her head.

"If you get a chance, you should go. I spent more than a year there, touring as many countries as I could. It's an incredible place. Both the people and the landscape."

"What was your favorite part of the trip?"

They paused their conversation while the server cleared away the empty salad bowls.

"That's an almost impossible question to answer. The Serengeti, Victoria Falls, the Nile. It's all magnificent. I started painting again while I was there and wanted everything I used to come from Africa—the canvas, the stretchers, the brushes, the paint, everything."

"That's fantastic."

He offered a conspiratorial smile. "Not only did I want to use materials from Africa, I wanted my work to *be* Africa. I found a mine in Namibia that excavates a glittery type of mica. I purchased some, had it ground up at a local processing plant, and mixed it into the paint."

An idea formed. "That's why the paintings shimmered."

"You're the only person who knows."

She imagined the subtle sparkle of the painting hanging in William Klein's living room. "I suppose this mineral could be used to determine authenticity?"

"Absolutely." He tilted his head as though considering the implications of her words, but didn't say anything more.

Should she confess her suspicions? At this point, it was only a hunch. Probably better to keep it to herself for the time being. "May I print the information about the paint?"

"I'd be disappointed if you didn't."

Ava's cheeks warmed. Getting a scoop like this was a big deal. Both for her career and possibly the case.

But then...why wait until now to divulge the information?

Straight to voicemail. Again.

With a disgruntled growl, Marcus checked the location sharing app. Thank God he'd thought to have her turn it on. Judging by her icon on the map, she appeared to be at a cafe behind the museum. But who was she with? And why hadn't she texted to let him know? When he told her he knew where to find the password, she'd responded with a thumbs up. As though this one bit of information didn't have the potential to change their entire investigation.

He scratched the dog behind the ears and around the neck where its collar used to be.

Marcus stared at the password printed in black marker on the inside of the band, now flattened on the coffee table.

Pnx!54y%uGC3

His gaze drifted to the open laptop. He rubbed an agitated hand along his jaw. He'd tried to wait until Ava got home to look at the file, but he'd wanted to make sure the password worked, and once he got a glimpse of what was in there, he'd not been able to stop.

As soon as he gained access and saw who Patrick had planned to meet the night of the gala, he called Ava. She didn't answer.

He fell back against the couch. Patrick had meticulously detailed his investigation. One of the first things Marcus noticed was a timeline of the museum going back to the 1980s cross-referenced with featured exhibits and artwork, including *Mon Enfant*. It seemed Patrick came to the same conclusion about the museum and a possible forgery scheme as he and Ava.

Flipping through the documents in the file again, Marcus landed on a scanned picture of a tough-looking man with dark, curly hair. Beneath it, Patrick had written: *Jared Meeks* → *Alario Crime Family (?)*

He opened a subfolder featuring dozens of images. Picture after picture of paintings and sculptures, presumably forged copies, flashed across his screen as he clicked the button on his laptop. He didn't know the artists or the significance of the pieces. And then...a beige canvas with evenly spaced dots.

The same painting he saw at Mickey the Fish's place. That couldn't be a coincidence.

He reached for his phone and dialed Eric's number.

His friend picked up on the first ring. "Hey, what's up?"

"Do you know of anyone associated with the Alario crime family who goes by the name Jared Meeks?"

"No, but some of these guys have dozens of aliases. Why?"

"Remember the reporter I told you about?"

"The one you thought you were going to sleep with but found a dead body instead?"

Marcus ground his teeth. "The one I'm helping with her investigation."

"What about her?"

"We got ahold of her friend's notes, and he'd made a connection between this guy Meeks and the Alarios."

"Got a picture?"

"Yeah. Let me send it to you." Marcus opened his email and attached the image of Meeks, as well as the picture of the colorful dots painting. "I sent it and another one."

"What am I looking at?" Eric asked.

"Her friend's research included the second picture. I'm pretty sure I saw that exact painting at the Mickey the Fish crime scene."

"I told you all the artwork was real, right? Did I mention that none of it was reported missing? The owners all had their art—or so they thought."

Marcus rolled this around in his mind. "So, there's something bigger going on here than someone stealing a few pieces of art."

"Could be some sort of forgery racket, could be random pieces Mickey picked up as payment over the years. Hard to tell, but if there's a mob connection..." Eric whistled.

"Do you have a list of the work in Mickey's apartment?"

"Sure."

"Can you share it? We need to check it against works that were loaned to Fort Lauderdale."

"No problem." Curiosity threaded the other agent's voice. "What are you thinking?"

"That maybe this is all connected. We think someone at the museum is making copies of loaned art, keeping the originals, and returning fakes." The synapses were starting to fire. "Mickey the Fish had connections to the Alarios, and if this Meeks guy does too, plus he's connected to the museum..." He let the thought trail off.

Eric was quiet for a moment. "It's definitely worth looking into. I'll see if I can find a name for your gangster, and I'll get you the list of the artwork seized from Mickey's place."

They disconnected at the same moment a car pulled into Ava's driveway. Marcus was on his feet and had the front door open before she'd even gotten out of the car.

He was about to tell her how worried he was when she caught his gaze. God, that smile. The anger, the worry, all of it melted away. He rushed from the porch and met her on the path with a kiss.

"I'm happy to see you too." She patted him on the chest. "And boy, do I have a lot to tell you."

He took her hand and walked with her into the house. "I called you. Was your phone off?"

"Silenced. So I could concentrate. I was having lunch with Ian Vanderbrook."

"What?" His body went cold, and his voice was hard. He didn't believe in coincidences where criminal investigations were concerned.

"I ran into him outside the museum—" Her brows drew together. "Why? What's wrong?"

"Ian Vanderbrook was Patrick's source."

Chapter 28

"What? No." Ava scoffed. It made no sense. Ian Vanderbrook couldn't have been Patrick's source. "If that's true, why would Patrick have been pushing me to talk to him?"

Marcus stepped forward and grasped her by her shoulders. "I didn't know Patrick well, but based on everything I've learned, I can't believe he would have knowingly put you in danger."

She turned the idea over in her head. Patrick had insisted on going to the gala. And what better place to connect with his source? But Ian couldn't be the killer. For one thing, she'd spent time with the man and knew him to be both considerate and kind. For another, there wasn't time. "Patrick never returned to the museum that night. He was at my house when he was shot. There's no way Ian could have done it."

"I agree."

She blinked up at him. "You do?"

"Maybe he met with Vanderbrook as planned, but Vanderbrook said something that Patrick wanted to investigate." He tugged on her hand.

Half dazed, she let him drag her toward the couch. When she sat, he lifted his laptop from the table, clicked on a link and revealed an old profile piece from a South Florida art magazine. She skimmed the article, which profiled George Gerou as an up-and-coming playboy and entrepreneur. "So?"

Marcus poked his finger at the picture on the computer screen. "Look at this."

Ava lifted the computer and held it closer to her face to study the grainy image. In the background was a grouchy-looking teenager who, despite the glasses and messy mop of hair, was obviously a young Ian Vanderbrook. What was Marcus getting at? This proved nothing. "Ian told me George Gerou had been his benefactor when he was younger."

"Look at the painting he's working on."

Though the canvas was tilted so you couldn't see the full painting, Ian appeared to be working on some sort of Renaissance-style portrait. "Yeah?"

He snatched the laptop from her and opened another article. "Now, look at this."

The story was similar to the one about *Mon Enfant*. A gallerist purchased a painting at a private auction, and hoping to resell it, took it to an appraiser, only to discover it was a fake. Apprehension churned in her stomach like a gathering storm. She clicked back to the picture with Ian in the background. It looked the same.

"You think Ian did forgeries? For George Gerou?"

"It's a theory, but a plausible one."

More than plausible, if Ava was being honest. She liked Ian and didn't want to think he was involved in something like this. But it was hard to ignore the evidence.

A thought—a horrible, unexpected thought—occurred to her. She turned to face Marcus. "Do you think Patrick came here to warn me not to go through with the interview?"

He hesitated, but she could see the answer on his face. "He added both stories to his file on the day of his death." Marcus pointed to the details of the two articles. "He may have felt guilty for getting you involved."

She took a deep breath. "And he knew I didn't want to do it."

"It's not your fault." Marcus drew her in and gave her a soft kiss.

"I'm not sure it tracks. If Ian was Patrick's source, it must've been because he hoped to expose someone. There's no reason to think Ian would have been a danger to me."

"Maybe Patrick knew he was in danger and worried that a connection to Vanderbrook would endanger you too?"

"So, if we're assuming that Ian worked as a forger for George Gerou, would he really want to involve himself in Patrick's investigation? Wouldn't he want distance from it?"

"Maybe he was hoping to nudge Patrick along without directly implicating himself. A lot of informants prefer to give clues to law enforcement rather than incriminate someone outright. It makes them feel as though they are helping, but they can still tell themselves they aren't betraying anyone." Marcus motioned at the computer where the George Gerou profile and the article about the painting were displayed side-by-side. "Maybe he just pointed Patrick toward these articles."

An idea clicked. "At lunch, Ian said he mixed a glittery type of mica into the paint he used for the *African Sun* paintings. What if he did that on purpose, in case Gerou counterfeited one of the paintings? What if he told Patrick about the mineral?" Adrenaline made her twitchy. They were on to something. Now she understood the rush Patrick got when an investigative piece came together.

"Only he would know of the mixture. It's the perfect way to verify authenticity." Marcus's face grew animated. "It's brilliant."

Ava fell back against the couch. This was it. They'd figured it out. They didn't know who killed Patrick, but they had nearly all the pieces of the art scheme.

"So, why would Henrick contact me?"

"You heard him that night at the museum. Gerou made promises he didn't keep, and Henrick thought he had leverage."

The idea that a man died because he'd decided to tell her his story made Ava incredibly sad.

Marcus's phone rang. "It's the agent I told you about. I sent him a picture of Jared Meeks."

Ava's mind reeled. Patrick's file was turning out to be the falling domino. For the first time since all of this started, she believed they might actually solve it.

Marcus finished the call and turned to Ava. "Meeks's real name is Tony Mandera, and he's an associate with the Alario crime family. He must be Gerou's connection to the black market."

Meeks was the developer on the Beachside project. Was that part of this too?

Marcus clicked on an attachment. "Eric sent a list of all the paintings found at Mickey the Fish's place."

"Who?"

"Mickey D'Amico. A moving man for the mob. Someone murdered him the day before I left for vacation. He had an extensive art collection in his house." Marcus gestured toward the list. "This is an inventory of his collection. I'm thinking we compare this list to Patrick's list of works loaned to the museum."

Ava had already asked for a lot of favors, but she guessed she could ask for one more. "I'll contact Amanda in the morning and see if that is something they have."

"No need." He looked triumphant as he clicked on another document in Patrick's electronic file folder. "We already have it."

Hope blossomed inside her chest. None of this would bring Patrick back, but maybe she could provide closure for his investigation and his death. She grasped Marcus's hand and intertwined her fingers. "Thank you."

He pressed his lips to her forehead. "Now we just need to figure out how to get close to George Gerou."

This time, it was her turn to smile. "I think I might have that covered."

Chapter 29

L istening to another sales pitch, even if it was at a swanky Las Olas address, was the last thing Ava wanted to do today. She pulled her hair over her shoulder and turned her back to Marcus. "Zip me up?"

She'd purposely stepped away from her dresser mirror, not wanting him to see the sadness in her eyes. In the few days since they'd discovered Patrick's research, they'd fallen into an easy domestic routine. God, how she was going to miss it. Because regardless of what she wanted to happen, Marcus had a job—a rather important one—that he couldn't just leave. Of course, now wasn't the time for those thoughts. Not when they were on their way to George Gerou's mansion and his Beachside get-together.

Prickles ran up her spine as Marcus lifted the zipper pull and guided it to her neckline. His knuckles brushed her skin as he hooked the tiny clasp, and she fought the urge to shiver. These simple touches shouldn't be quite this provocative. Nor should the way he looked in dress pants and a blue button-down.

He straightened his collar in the mirror. "You sure I'm okay without a tie?"

The top-two buttons of his shirt were undone, revealing the collar of a white undershirt. "Yep," she said, barely able to speak for fear her desire to secure a permanent commitment would be all too clear in the crack of her voice. They still hadn't had the what's next conversation, but she'd decided the safest thing for her heart was to assume they'd be saying goodbye.

"And Gerou is okay with me tagging along? You're not attending this thing as a guest." While Ava conducted her interview, Marcus planned to snoop around Gerou's house, looking for paintings that matched the ones in Patrick's file.

"I spoke to his secretary earlier. She said it was fine."

Ava's stomach did a somersault. "Is this a good idea? Going to the home of a criminal?" She didn't enjoy feeling like a coward, but she also didn't want to put either of them in unnecessary danger.

"He's also a well-known businessman who wants to protect his reputation. Surely you go to parties and events all the time to get information?"

She gave a weak nod.

"Pretend this isn't any different." He stepped forward, put his hands on her shoulders, and kissed her on the forehead. "Besides, I'll be with you the whole time."

True, Marcus was a trained FBI agent, and he had a gun in a holster strapped to his ankle, but those things only heightened her awareness of the possible danger. Not to mention the nagging sense of foreboding she just couldn't seem to shake.

"I was happy to give the theater tickets back to your mom and Freddy. You know they didn't have a conflicting event?"

"She's relentless." His eyes twinkled, and Ava could see the affection he had for his mom. "She thought we needed a date."

Ava snaked her arms around Marcus's neck, went up on her toes, and pressed a kiss to his mouth. "She was right that there's no one else I want to spend time with."

"Same." He caught her lips, nudged her mouth open and drew her into a deep kiss. "More of that, and I won't want to leave."

"Hmmm." Reluctant to let go, she stepped away. "As wonderful as that sounds, we have art thieves to catch and murderers to reveal."

He took her hand and tugged. "Ready?"

She nodded and let him guide her out the door to his truck. She pulled up Gerou's address on her phone. They were heading east toward the Intracoastal Waterway. There was no direct route from Ava's house, so Marcus drove toward the beach, then turned south onto A1A. A pang of sentimentality struck as they passed the turn to Patrick's condo. Her eyes got tight. Nope. She wouldn't cry. Not after she'd spent twenty minutes doing her make-up.

She stared out the window. "I find this very odd."

"What's that?"

"This sudden change of heart on the development. The last time I spoke to Mr. Gerou, he was undecided, but had concerns. Now he's hosting a party to garner support? Don't you think that's strange?"

"A little, but it's within your rights to ask him about it."

She chewed on her bottom lip. "True, but will I get an honest answer?"

"Even if you don't, maybe you'll pick up on something else. Suspects often speak in partial truths."

Despite all the strides she'd made in recent days regarding her professional confidence, it was hard to shake those old insecurities. At least she wasn't alone. With Marcus at her side, she felt like she could do anything.

They turned onto Las Olas, went over a bridge, and then made a right turn into Gerou's neighborhood. After a couple of blocks, they arrived at a palm-tree-lined driveway. Anxious anticipation stirred in her belly as the house came into view. It was enormous.

Several cars were already parked along the circular drive. An attendant directed them to a spot in front of a black luxury sedan. Marcus came around to Ava's side of the truck and helped her down. "You'll be great."

She blew out a gust of air. "I hope so."

He squeezed her hand, and they made their way to the front entrance.

A man in a gray suit and tie answered the door and welcomed them inside. They stepped into a grand entryway that opened into a large common room. Tall ceilings made the room feel huge, and Ava gasped at the opulence. She'd been in the homes of wealthy people plenty of times. Heck, she'd grown up among the one percent. And yet, she'd never seen anything quite this extravagant. The place felt more like a museum than a home. She'd take Nana's tiny two-bedroom over this any day.

Though it begged the question, what was this guy doing stealing art?

Almost as if summoned by her thoughts, George Gerou appeared, his arms wide and walking toward them. "Miss Montoya, I'm so happy you could join us."

She squeezed Marcus's hand but didn't let go. "Thank you for inviting me. You have a lovely home."

"My pleasure, though I'd be lying if I didn't say I had an ulterior motive."

"Oh?" She used the solid warmth of Marcus's hand to ground her.

Gerou chuckled. "You don't invite the press to a promotional party without hoping for some good publicity."

"Right." Ava's cheeks warmed. Could she actually do this? The fact that she'd so thoroughly forgotten herself because of one innocuous comment was concerning.

Marcus released her hand and offered his to the museum executive. "Thank you for including me on the invitation."

"Of course, and welcome." Gerou regarded Marcus for a moment. "You attended the gala? I believe Freddy introduced us?"

"That's correct. You have an excellent memory."

"Freddy and I go way back. He's a good man."

Ava glanced at Marcus, wondering how this criminal's assessment of his mom's paramour would land.

"I'm glad to hear it. I'd worried Mom was going to be lonely down here, but she seems to have found her footing quite easily."

"Lovely woman..." Gerou's words trailed off as he surveyed the gathering. Ava also glanced around the room and spotted twenty or so other guests. Gerou's gaze bounced back to her. "Perhaps later we can find a quiet place to talk."

A chill ran up Ava's spine. There was something almost predatory in the way Gerou stared. "Whatever works best for you."

He offered an aristocratic bow and a tip of his chin. "Now, if you'll excuse me, it's almost time."

Gerou turned down a hallway, returning a few minutes later with Jared Meeks and Martin Singh. She felt Marcus stiffen beside her when the gangster strode into the room.

A spoon clinked against a glass. The quiet murmur that had filled the space since they arrived died down, and the entire room turned to look at their host. "Please refresh your drinks, grab some hors d'oeuvres, and make yourself comfortable. We'll begin in about five minutes."

Marcus turned to Ava. "Want anything from the bar?"

"Maybe a soda."

She watched as he got in line at the rollaway counter in the back corner of the room. He was so handsome. Nearly everyone he passed stopped to stare, probably wondering who he was and who he was with. An irrational sense of pride filled her insides and threatened to spill over. She shook her head. He wasn't hers, not really, and she needed to pull the plug and drain away every stupid fantasy about having a future with this man. Because, assuming he stuck to his schedule, in two days, he'd be gone.

By the time Marcus returned with two colas, the seats had all been taken. Just as well. She wasn't here as someone who needed convincing. She was here to learn about the project and gather quotes.

Gerou stepped to the front of the room, flanked by Jared Meeks and Martin Singh. "Thank you all for coming today. I know most of you came for the booze, but I hope you'll leave with a new appreciation for the proposed development known as Beachside at Seaside."

He rotated as though taking in every face in the room. "I'm sure some of you are wondering why I changed my tune on this project, when just a week ago, I was more opponent than proponent, and I think once these gentlemen make their case, you'll understand why." He motioned to the two men. "Please allow me to introduce Jared Meeks and Seaside city commissioner Martin Singh."

After allowing for a moment of polite applause, Martin Singh stepped forward, and Ava wondered if this presentation would be any different from the one she saw at the Seaside Rec Center two weeks ago. They'd not persuaded anyone that night, and she couldn't imagine a man like George Gerou finding their arguments all that compelling.

"I was born in Seaside," the commissioner began. "And there are so many things I love about it. But, as much as I love the city I call home, I see missed opportunities..."

Marcus's phone buzzed. Looking at the screen, his brows squished together. "It's my mom. I'm going to take this."

She watched as he stepped through the open sliding glass door and onto the patio.

Marcus glanced at his watch. His mom and Freddy should be at the show. It was too early for intermission. "Mom? Is everything okay?"

Someone cleared their throat, and a male voice echoed through the phone. "Hello. I'm trying to contact someone connected to the owner of this phone."

Marcus's heart thudded in a hard, slow rhythm. "I'm her son."

"I don't know how to say this, but your mom was in an accident."

He forced the words past his suddenly tight windpipe. "What kind of accident?"

"I'm not sure, but it looked serious. I picked up her phone and have been trying numbers until I reached someone."

Marcus reeled. "Where is she now?"

"She was taken to the hospital."

"Which one?"

"I don't know, but Community East is nearby."

"Okay. Thank you."

The voice on the phone was halting. "What should I do with the phone?"

Shit. Marcus pinched the bridge of his nose and inhaled. "Do you mind holding onto it for the time being? Until I can find out what's going on?"

"You want to call when you're ready to make arrangements to get it back?"

"That would be great..." Marcus didn't know the good Samaritan's name.

The guy picked up on the question in his unfinished sentence. "Joe."

"Thanks. I'll be in touch."

Marcus turned toward the house and saw Ava through the sliding glass door. Rather than listening to the presentation, she was watching him, concern etched into her face. He wanted to tell her what was going on, but he needed a moment first. If anything happened to his mom—

He couldn't finish the thought, couldn't let himself go there.

Why had he been such an asshole about her relationship with Freddy? Come to think of it, why didn't Freddy call to tell him what had happened? Was he hurt too?

Question after question tumbled through his brain. Finally, he took a deep breath, slid open the door, and motioned for Ava to join him on the patio.

Without hesitation, she stepped outside, sliding the door shut behind her. "What happened? Is your mom okay?"

He shook his head, not knowing where to start. "That was someone who found Mom's phone. He said there was some kind of accident—"

She gasped and gripped his wrist. "Is she hurt?"

"The guy didn't say, but she's been taken to the hospital." He paced away from Ava, one hand on his hip, the other buried in his hair. "I need to go."

"I'll come with you."

He clenched his jaw. Though he wanted her with him, if she could find something tonight that tied George Gerou to the forgeries, they could put all of this behind them and focus on the future. "I think you should stay. You need to interview Gerou."

Her lips parted just enough to register her confusion. "I want to be with you."

Gratitude filled him at her words. He'd never had a person to lean on—not in his personal life, anyway—and hadn't known what he was missing. "I can't tell you how much that means."

Torn between his mom and the search for Patrick's killer, he glanced through the glass door at the crowded room. There were a lot of people here. He didn't know what to expect when he got to the hospital or how long he'd have to be there. "We don't know when you'll get another shot with Gerou."

She nodded, and he could see it was with reluctance.

"You'll let me know when you get there and you know something?"

"Of course." He dragged her against him, not wanting to let go.

Stretching onto her toes, she gave him a kiss. "Go find out what is going on with your mom. I'll take a rideshare if you can't get back here before it ends."

He took out his phone and mapped a route to the hospital. Looked like it would take about twenty minutes.

Taking her hand, he led her back inside the house, where the presentation was still going. "I'll call as soon as I can."

Ava kissed him again. As he walked across the back of the room, a rush of agitation left him feeling exposed. He glanced over his shoulder. Every head in the room angled toward the men giving the presentation.

But if that was the case, why did he get the sense he was being watched?

Chapter 30

Worried about Marcus's mom, Ava couldn't concentrate on the rest of the pitch. Not that it mattered. This was almost identical to the other two presentations she'd attended.

She twisted her fingers together. Why hadn't she insisted on going with him? Her throat constricted as she thought of Marcus, alone and unsure if his mom was okay.

Surely Freddy would have checked in by now. He had to know Marcus would be worried. Maybe she should step outside and see if he'd gotten any updates.

Light clapping drew her attention back to the main event. People were getting up and moving toward the plastic model. Ava watched for a moment, realizing these didn't look like the typical concerned residents. They were all well-dressed and young, at least compared to the residents who'd turned up to the presentation at the rec center. Of course, she couldn't imagine there was any way George Gerou would want any of those angry people in his home.

She checked her watch. Twenty minutes since Marcus left. He should be getting close to the hospital. Hopefully, he'd call as soon as he had news.

She milled about the room, stopping when she came upon Martin Singh. The commissioner seemed an unlikely partner for a thug like Jared Meeks and the posh museum chairman, but they'd probably wanted someone on the city council in their corner. Still, she had to wonder what was in it for him.

"Well, what did you think?" A bead of sweat trickled down the side of his face. "Quite the vision, eh?"

Ava shrugged. He was clearly hoping that a party at a swanky address would be enough to earn them some good press. "To be completely honest, I'm surprised Mr. Gerou came on board."

Singh gave a nervous laugh. "We've made him a partner in the venture. Also, Jared promised he could open a gallery on the premise."

"I heard something about a satellite location. It'll be a gallery? Like another museum?"

"Oh no, this one will be for selling art, not just displaying it." He glanced over his shoulder, probably looking for Gerou. "It'll be very high end."

"Of course," she mumbled while trying to work out what the scheme might be. Would this be another way for him to acquire artwork to sell on the black market? Perhaps he was looking for lesser-known artists whose work he might hold on to until it grew in value. "And the partnership? Is he providing capital?"

Another nervous laugh. "Not initially, no. The hope is that later, when we show a profit, he'll be encouraged to invest in additional projects and improvements."

A rather unconventional arrangement, by the sounds of it. Ava could only assume this agreement came about in exchange for his endorsement. Singh shifted on his feet.

"You didn't answer my question the other day about your change of heart. I'm trying to understand why you would support something that goes against everything you've claimed to believe. I'm sure your constituents want to understand it too."

The commissioner pressed his lips into a line and crossed his arms. "I believe everything I said during the campaign, but sometimes development is necessary."

Ava remembered what Marcus had said about criminals speaking in partial truths. "Assuming the project goes forward, are you worried about unhappy residents? I believe you have two years left in your term?"

"I was elected to make Seaside a better place to live, and I believe the Beachside development is part of that."

A practiced answer if she ever heard one. She still didn't know how he got involved. "Why—"

George Gerou appeared and laid a hand on the commissioner's shoulder. "Martin, thank you for keeping our guest entertained."

"Of course. My pleasure." Singh tipped his head to Ava. "A delight, as always, Ms. Montoya."

She smiled and watched him scurry across the room to speak with Jared Meeks.

Gerou glanced around. "Did your companion leave?"

"Family emergency." She said, surprised he would notice.

"I'm sorry to hear that." He motioned for her to walk with him. "I was thinking we might have a real sit-down interview. Does that work for you?"

That was far more than she expected. "Yes, fantastic."

They wandered across the room, and for the first time, she realized most of the guests had vanished. A room full of people, gone.

He took her down a hallway and led her into a parlor with a single piece of furniture—a divan in the center of the room. Art hung on the walls, a statue stood in the corner, and sculptures in recessed shelves built into the paneling. Strategically placed lights illuminated the artwork and made the place feel like a gallery.

"I need to say goodbye to the stragglers, but I'll be back in a few minutes and we'll move to my study. In the meantime, please enjoy yourself. Have a look around. This is one of my favorite rooms in the house."

Ava nodded dumbly, her senses on overload as she took in the artwork.

Gerou chuckled. "I know it's overwhelming. Go one piece at a time."

"Thank you, I will." She turned to find him staring, the look on his face somewhere between annoyance and amusement. "Thank you for sharing this with me."

His responding smile looked genuine. "Believe me, it gratifies me more than you know."

Something about the comment sent a shiver up her spine. Ava watched him leave, then turned back to the artwork. She started with the first piece on the south wall. A mix of blues, grays and white, the painting simultaneously appeared to be a cloud and a wave. She studied it for a moment and considered what Ian Vanderbrook had told her at the gallery—pretend you can take one painting home. She studied the turbulent image.

There was something angry and aggressive about it, and while she appreciated what the artist had accomplished by giving a static image momentum, it was unsettling. She wouldn't want to look at that piece every day.

She moved on to the next. An abstract with scary faces. She tilted her head. There was something sinister about this painting. It conjured feelings of foreboding.

Again, she slid to the next framed piece of art. This one depicted a man and a woman in a forest painted in varying shades of blue. Though faint, the woman had what might have been wings, and the man looked haggard and weak. An angel of mercy? Or the Grim Reaper?

She shivered. So far, she didn't like any of these pieces. What did the themes say about the man whose house she was in? Unfortunately, she didn't want to analyze it. Not right now.

The next piece was a creepily realistic three-dimensional face. A woman with long curly brown hair.

"Interesting, isn't it?"

Ava jumped at the voice, deep and assertive. She pressed a hand to her chest and turned.

Jared Meeks stood a few feet away, a somewhat hostile smile on his face. He held up his hand. "Sorry, I didn't mean to startle you."

Though in truth, he didn't look sorry at all.

***

Marcus paced away from the emergency room desk, hand gripping a fistful of hair. He turned back to the polite and patient woman who'd just told him his mother hadn't been admitted to their hospital. "Are you sure? Can you look again?"

"I've checked and double checked, but I'll do it one more time." She offered a smile he supposed was meant to be reassuring and started clicking her keyboard.

He stared at her sunflower-printed scrubs, willing her to come up with a different answer this time around.

She shook her head. "There's no Violet Anderson in our patient directory."

"Any Jane Does?"

"I'm sorry, no."

"Is there another hospital she might have been taken to?"

"You could try South Florida General. It's about fifteen minutes from here."

An anxious knot formed in his stomach. Where was she? And was she okay?

He thanked the woman at reception and raced from the hospital, mapping the route on the way to his truck. It was a Friday night, and traffic was heavy.

Marcus made a right-hand turn off of Broward Boulevard and into the hospital parking lot. He drove slowly, searching for the main entrance, and parked as soon as he saw it.

His phone chirped. He took his hand off the door lever to look at the notification.

The doorbell camera at Mom's house.

He clicked on the alert and saw a recording of his mom and Freddy on her front porch.

Tension oozed from his muscles. He put a hand over his mouth and rubbed it down his chin.

Oh, thank God. Mom was okay.

And then an icy dread assaulted him, suffocating him with his own stupidity. His chest felt heavy. He couldn't draw a deep breath.

The call had been a ploy to get Ava alone. And he'd fallen for it.

Throwing his truck in reverse, he tore out of the parking spot. Adrenaline crackled through his system, heightening his senses and increasing his situational awareness. He shot onto the main road and mashed his foot into the accelerator, driving fast but alert.

"Call Ava." The hands-free system initiated the call. It rang once. Twice. Three times.

"You have reached Ava Montoya—"

Fuck! He disconnected. Where was she? She wouldn't have silenced her phone. Not when she was waiting to hear from him.

Next, he tried his mom's house number. She answered on the first ring.

He blurted his question before she said hello. "Are you okay?"

"Yes...why?"

He felt an irrational surge of annoyance. She had no reason to know the hell he'd gone through. "I thought you'd been hurt."

"Hurt? No. Why would you think that?"

"A man called from your phone and told me you'd been in an accident. I've been driving all over trying to find you."

"I lost my phone somewhere at the theater, but otherwise I'm fine. Could it have been a prank?"

Not a prank, a diversion. "I've got to go. I'm glad you're okay."

His mom's voice wavered. She'd picked up on the fact that something was wrong. "You sound upset. Is everything alright?"

"I don't know. I need to find Ava."

Chapter 31

Ava stepped to the side while eyeing the door. Unfortunately, Jared Meeks, who seemed bigger and wider now that they were standing face to face, blocked the way. When he stepped forward, she fought to control a flinch. Then he shifted past her toward the artwork.

"I never appreciated art before."

"Before what?" Her voice was tentative.

"Before I met George. He opened my eyes to its value." He flashed a devious smile. "Intrinsic value, that is."

"Of course," she murmured. She needed to get out of here.

"I quite like the art he keeps in this room. Really speaks to me."

She bet it did. Every single one of these pieces gave her the creeps. Just like the man standing beside her.

"You know, if you like these—" He leaned over as though sharing top secret information. "You should see the rest of the collection."

Her hands trembled. She clasped her fingers behind her back. "Really? There's more than this? Another fancy room?"

"Fancier, but that room isn't for visitors. Only a few select friends and acquaintances even know of its existence." He stalked toward her. With each of his steps, she took a step backward.

A hard, dry lump rose in her throat, and she forced it back down with a swallow loud enough to be heard in Key West. Meeks walked around her, reached behind a sculpture in one of the recessed shelves, and flicked a switch.

A mechanical grind sounded from inside the wall, followed by a whirr, and then a wall panel moved. She gasped and stepped back, fascinated to see an opening materialize.

There was a gleam in Meeks's eyes as the door revealed another room.

"Go ahead, take a look." He urged her forward.

She took a hesitant step, not wanting to get too close.

"Go on."

Another step. No way was she setting foot inside there. About six feet spread between Ava and the door, but she was close enough to see another room, larger than the one she was in, with free-standing walls, each featuring pieces of art.

"Come on, what are you waiting for? It's a once in a lifetime experience."

End of a lifetime was more like it. What were the chances if she went into that room she'd come out alive? "I can see from here. Amazing. A real-life mini museum."

"Kind of like Scooby Doo, don't you think?"

"Really, Jared? Scooby Doo?" Gerou's voice came from behind her. "It's clearly an homage to Sherlock Holmes."

Ava hadn't realized the museum chairman was back. She spun to find him pointing a firearm. She tried to inch away from the two men.

"You don't think you're leaving, do you?" Gerou looked amused.

"W-w-why are you doing this?" She stammered, holding up her hands.

"Because, my dear. You know too much." He motioned with the gun. "Inside."

Ava stilled. "Please, I don't know anything."

"You're not a very good liar, and if your reporter friend could figure it out, why would you be any different?"

Some sick part of her thrilled at the notion that this man—this madman—assumed she was as good a reporter as Patrick. She almost laughed. Was she so desperate for validation?

"Get. Inside." Gerou punctuated each word with the thrust of his gun. While he'd stopped short of admitting he killed Patrick, going inside that room seemed like a bad, bad idea.

"Now." He surged forward, quick and angry.

Not seeing another option, Ava did as she was told, stepping onto the polished concrete floor and into Gerou's home muse-um. Gerou followed her inside. He didn't shut the door, likely assuming the weapon would keep her put. He was right.

"Give Jared your phone," Gerou demanded.

Her lifeline. She almost cried as she pulled the phone from her bag. With great reluctance, but knowing she had no other choice, she laid her phone in Meeks's palm, then almost wept as the man switched it off and stuffed it in his pocket.

Gerou gestured with the gun. "Now the bag."

Meeks took the satchel and pulled out her tablet. He handed the device to Gerou.

"Take it in." Gerou spread his arms wide—gun in one hand, her tablet in the other—and turned in a slow circle. "Magnificent, isn't it? All pieces I've collected over the years."

Stolen was more accurate, but Ava didn't respond. There'd be no point. Whatever Gerou planned to do to her, she didn't think there was anything she could say that would change that. He was obviously determined to protect his empire of ill-gotten art.

"What's the matter? No more questions? Not planning an exposé like your friend?"

"I never wanted to get involved." She motioned to the nearest display. "I just wanted to know why Patrick was killed."

"He died because he was sticking his nose where it didn't belong. I couldn't take the chance he'd reveal my secrets." Gerou shook his head as though killing Patrick had been nothing more than an unpleasant necessity. "Just like I can't take the chance you'll pick up where he left off."

"I won't. I swear."

"You say that now, but you're a journalist, and journalists can't be trusted." His voice was calm, matter-of-fact.

"What if I write some positive pieces about Beachside at Seaside? Drum up some enthusiasm?" Even to her own ears, the suggestion sounded lame.

Gerou laughed. "I don't give a damn about Jared's development. That was just a cover to get you here. Do you think I'd invest in something so atrocious?"

A low rumble—part growl, part groan—came from the corner of the room where Meeks stood leering at Gerou.

Ava filed away the look of dislike on Meeks's face as he stared the other man down, then turned her attention back to the man with the gun. If only she could get a message to Marcus. Maybe she could buy some time if she could keep Gerou talking. "How does Martin Singh fit into all of this?"

"With the art? He doesn't. Jared's been blackmailing him for his support of the project. Turns out Marty's been having an affair with his secretary. Not only that, he gave her a bunch of gift cards that were originally donated for charity." Gerou laughed. "Weak people doing stupid things are the easiest to manipulate."

Well, that explained the commissioner's new pro-development stance.

"What about the beach residents who were here today?"

"Actors." Gerou waved his hand. "Jared, get the duct tape."

Meeks strode to a table in the corner. "Shouldn't we just kill her?"

Ava froze like an animal about to be flattened by a minivan. This was it. They were going to murder her. Like they murdered Patrick. She'd known it the moment Gerou forced her into this room, but to hear it discussed so casually?

"In good time, Jared. But not here. Too messy." Gerou scrunched up his face as though he couldn't imagine anything more distasteful. "We'll be taking our reporter friend for a ride on my boat."

Meeks ripped a two-foot-long silver strip from the roll in response.

Ava's heart pounded like a machine gun, loud and fast and recoiling against the wall of her chest. "Please, no." Her breaths came quick and shallow. She backed away from the big man stalking toward her. "Don't do this."

Meeks kept coming. Her skin heated to what had to be an unnatural temperature. Her vision darkened. She gasped for air.

"Oh, come now. This is no time for hysterics. Cooperate and this will be over before you know it." Gerou marched closer, still pointing the gun. "If anyone should be upset, it's me. Because of you, I had to deal with Henrick, and now I have to find another forger. Not an easy task. Identifying the right person with the right skills takes time."

A heavy weight pressed into Ava's chest. She couldn't breathe, and her body shook. Her eyes darted across the room. She had to find a way out.

Tears pricked her eyes. The only obvious exit was the door she'd entered through, and there were two men—one huge and scary, the other deranged and holding a firearm—blocking her way. All at once, the fight drained out of her, and all that was left was exhaustion and fear and the unpleasant realization that her life was about to end.

Meeks dragged a chair to where she stood and forced her to sit. Yanking her arms behind the chair back, he took the strip of duct tape and bound her hands together, then ripped another strip with his teeth. She kicked as he held her leg in place and taped her bare ankle to the chair, then repeated the process with her other ankle. Ava struggled, but didn't have the strength or the leverage to put up an actual fight. Lastly, he unspooled the tape and wound it around her shoulders and the back of the chair. This was it. She was one hundred percent fucked.

And Marcus was out there somewhere, worried about his mom and unaware of the trouble she'd gotten herself into. Wasn't this what he'd feared when she first started investigating? Well, maybe not *this*. Who would have guessed she'd end up tied to a chair in a hidden room filled with stolen art?

"What about Marcus?"

Gerou waved the gun dismissively. "Obviously, I don't relish the idea of killing a federal agent—"

Relief filled Ava with gratitude. At least Marcus would be safe.

"But we do what we have to do." He motioned toward Meeks, now leaning against a wall and regarding Gerou like he was a gnat about to be squashed.

She studied him for a moment. An ally, perhaps? Did he hate Gerou enough to double-cross him?

"Jared will take care of it. Like he took care of your friend. And Henrick. And next he'll take care of you."

Ava's body turned to lead. The guy she'd been thinking might be an ally had killed Patrick. And Henrick. Something heavy squeezed at her chest, and it wasn't the tape holding her to the chair.

"But why?" She rasped the words. "Why'd you have to kill them?"

"You know who is to blame for all of this? That ungrateful prick, Ian Vanderbrook." Gerou paced in front of Ava's chair, his gun hand now hanging at his side. "Not even twenty-years-old and he was the darling of the art world. And do you know why?" His stare pierced her like a knife to the gut.

She shook her head.

"Because of me." He poked his finger into his chest. "I made him who he is. So he had to commit a few crimes, forge a few paintings. So what? You'd think I'd asked him to assassinate the president. All he had to do was paint ten pieces for me and, in return, I gave him piles of cash." Gerou snorted and shook his head. "He wanted out of the deal almost as soon as he started."

"You don't need to tell me this." Again, Ava was close to tears. The less she knew, the better. Though at this point did it matter?

"No bother. They say it's good to get it out." A serene and satisfied look settled on Gerou's face. "I didn't see or talk to Vanderbrook for years. It wasn't until I heard about his magnificent new series of paintings that I got in touch."

"So that's how you got him to exhibit at the museum?"

"Once I reminded him of his past and the things I knew about him, he was more than happy to agree."

Ava doubted that. "You blackmailed him."

"A crass description." He paced the room like an actor on the stage, except rather than an adoring audience, this performance was for Ava.

"Everything was progressing perfectly, and then he contacted that reporter friend of yours." Gerou shook his head with obvious disgust. "And you know what Ian did?"

He stared at Ava. She wanted to draw back, to get far away from Gerou and his angry glare, but it was impossible given her current predicament. Unable to get words past her constricted windpipe, she shook her head.

"He told him everything. Everything!" Spit built at the corners of Gerou's mouth, making him look like a rabid dog. "The night of the gala, I had Henrick follow Ian. They met behind the museum, and Henrick saw Ian hand your friend a memory stick and tell him everything he needed was on it."

Ava closed her eyes and inhaled. Poor Patrick. Had he looked at the memory stick and realized the danger he was in?

"Naturally, I had Jared take care of things." He motioned to the other man, still glaring at Gerou. "Then *you* started poking around."

"I only wanted to know what happened. Patrick was waiting for me when he died. I had to know if I could have stopped it."

"If you'd been there, you'd be dead now too."

Little comfort, considering the current predicament. Marcus was right. She should have left it alone.

Gerou continued, lost in his storytelling. "When Henrick reported back to me about what he'd seen, I knew I had to do something, so I sent Jared after your friend. He followed him to your house and found him sitting in his car with his laptop, looking at the info Ian had given him."

Some of this made sense, but not everything. "The police said the shooter was in the car with him."

"Jared may look like the Kraken, but he knows how to get people to do what he wants."

Ava's gaze slid to Meeks. His eyes were narrowed and fixed on Gerou with a laser focus that suggested he wasn't enjoying the retelling as much as the museum executive.

"Told him he could corroborate Ian's story. And your friend—who wasn't as smart as everyone thought—let him in." Shaking his head in disbelief, the museum executive laughed. "Jared got Ian's jump drive, shot your friend, and grabbed his phone and laptop."

"What about the drugs?"

"That was Jared. He's been doing this for a while—for people far worse than me."

Somehow, she doubted that.

"There was no reason to think the police would suspect us, but it doesn't hurt to be safe. Turns out, give investigators something to focus on, they'll chase their tail to make it fit." Gerou stretched his neck to one side, then the other. He rolled his shoulders as though needing to loosen tight muscles. "Anyhoo...then you got involved, stopping by the museum, asking questions. I realized you might also be a problem, and I needed to know what—if anything—your reporter friend had shared with you."

God, Patrick had been smart to encrypt the files and send them to her. Maybe she could use it as a bargaining chip, convince Gerou to let her go. Maybe she could stall long enough for Marcus to find her.

"Then I heard you saying you wanted to talk to Henrick. He'd already become a problem, so obviously, he had to go too." Gerou tipped his chin at Meeks. "I think that's enough chit-chat for the time being."

Meeks ripped a piece of tape that was a few inches long off the roll. Ava twisted and bucked against her restraints. But it was no use. She was completely immobilized.

"No, don't. Please. I promise—"

The sticky tape was pressed against her face. She stared in disbelief. This couldn't be happening.

Gerou stalked forward and spun her chair one-hundred-eighty degrees. "We'll be back. In the meantime, enjoy the view."

The door whirred shut. Ava looked up to see *Masai Mara Reserve in the Morning* glittering like a newly polished diamond.

Chapter 32

Gerou had set him up, taken Ava, and he was going to pay.

Marcus slammed his foot on the gas to get through a yellow—okay, red—light, then turned left into Gerou's neighborhood. Turning onto the palm-tree-lined drive, he drove faster than appropriate, but he couldn't find it in him to care.

Practically driving onto the porch, he killed the engine and dashed up the steps to the front door. Locked. He pressed his finger on the doorbell and held it there.

When no one came, he banged the side of his fist. Finally, movement on the other side. The door flung open to reveal an irritated-looking museum executive. Marcus didn't bother with pleasantries. He shoved his way inside. "Where is she?"

"What are you talking about?" Gerou's voice had a clipped, aristocratic air to it. "And how dare you barge in here."

"I want to see Ava. Now."

"I don't know what you're talking about." Condescension oozed from Gerou's words, and his calm delivery felt like a slap to the face.

"Cut the crap. I know she's here, and I know you tricked me into leaving her alone."

The other man laughed. "You have quite the imagination."

"Where is she?"

"Well, I assure you, she's not here. Got a ride about forty-five minutes ago. There's no one here but me." He motioned with his arm. "See for yourself."

"I will." Marcus marched into the sitting room, where the presentation had taken place earlier. Everything had been cleaned up and put away. Next, he slid open the door to the patio and stomped outside. No Ava. Not even a shed or anywhere he might have stashed her.

Gerou followed him outside, hands shoved into his chinos. "I told you she wasn't here."

Marcus again pushed past the man and stomped back into the house. Ava was here. He could sense it. He turned down the hallway, checking closets, bedrooms, bathrooms. Then, he came upon a gallery room. He stepped inside. Leave it to a pompous asshole like Gerou to set up a museum in his own house. Marcus bristled. Something about this room gave him a bad feeling. He gave the artwork a cursory glance. None of them looked familiar. Of course, Gerou wasn't likely to keep the stolen stuff where anyone would see it.

He gritted his teeth. Nowhere to hide her here.

When he turned, he found Gerou leaning against the door frame. Marcus stalked toward him. "I know you have her, and I'm going to find her."

The other man chuckled. "If you say so." He straightened. "Now, allow me to show you to the door. Or do I need to call the police?"

Though tempted to tell him to go ahead, the truth was Marcus was trespassing. Involving the police would only waste time and distract him from finding Ava.

"This isn't over, Gerou." He poked his finger at the other man and stalked out of the house. Back in his truck but still in Gerou's driveway, he pulled out his phone, wanting to see if Ava had made it home. He dialed her number. Nothing. Then he called his mom.

"Did you find her?"

"Not yet. Will you drive over to Ava's house to see if she's there?" Marcus stared at Gerou's front door, willing Ava to appear.

"Sure thing, honey. I'll leave right now."

"Take Freddy with you." He didn't want his mom out there on her own. The last thing he needed was to put someone else he cared about in danger.

Sending Mom to Ava's house gave Marcus the sense he was doing something, but deep down, he knew she wouldn't find her. Because Ava was here. In Gerou's house. Almost certainly his prisoner. Marcus turned on his engine and cranked the air conditioning. He may not have seen her inside the house, but he'd felt her presence, and he wasn't going anywhere until he got her back.

Jared Meeks pulled up a chair and sat so close his knees almost touched hers. He stretched a hand forward. Ava wiggled and protested from beneath her muzzle. What the hell was he doing?

His fingers brushed her cheek. Her nostrils flared as she exhaled desperation and fear. Gently, he worked the corner of the tape that covered her mouth and peeled it away.

"I don't know why he thought he needed to do that. No one could hear you anyway. This room is soundproofed."

Ava could only stare at the murdering gangster sitting across from her.

"Truth be told, I think he enjoys being sadistic. At any rate, it didn't need to be done."

"What's going to happen to me?" She spoke so quietly she could barely hear herself.

"Your boyfriend was just here, so that means we're going to move soon."

Marcus, here? Her heart lurched. Was he okay? "Did he leave?"

"I'm not sure. I came back so he wouldn't see me. George was going to get rid of him."

She nearly choked on a sob. Meeks laid a gentle hand on her knee. "Not like that."

Again, she held back tears. Marcus had been here, and now he was gone. "What will happen to him?"

"Right now, nothing. Later?" He sighed with a resigned shake of the head. "It won't be good."

Tears were now streaming down her face. She tasted the salt on her lips.

"I guess he's planning to take me out into the ocean to shoot me? Dump my body overboard?" Would Marcus ever know what happened? Would her family?

He gave her a sad smile. "I committed my first crime when I was nine, stole my first car at twelve, and killed a rival gang member at sixteen."

What was she, some sort of reluctant therapist for these men?

"I joined the Alario crime family when I was nineteen. Since then, I've worked with and for some of the worst people you can imagine. I've killed and tortured for them, and none of them have been as inhumane as that man out there." The gangster pointed at the secret door. "He has no conscience, no mercy, no remorse." His gaze held steady. "He's a monster."

Ava shivered. If Gerou troubled Jared Meeks, he must truly be despicable. "If that's the case, why are you working with him?"

"Officially, the boss sent me to stake a claim in George's art scam, to make it clear that he and Mr. Alario were partners. Leaning on a museum exec sounded like an easy gig. 'It'll be beaches and bikinis,' Mr. Alario said." Meeks let out a humorless laugh. "The truth was, George ripped off the wrong guy. One of the boss's ancestors was a famous Italian artist, and Mr. Alario owns one of the few remaining paintings. George desperately wanted to include it in a Mediterranean exhibit and courted Mr. Alario for over a year."

Goosebumps trickled up Ava's arms. She suspected where this was going, but could scarcely believe it.

"Finally, Mr. Alario loaned his painting for a six-month period. When he got it back, because of its value and because he's naturally distrustful, he had it analyzed."

To give a mob boss a fake painting required audacity. "Did he know who Mr. Alario was?"

"He did. That's the thing about George. When he wants something, he goes after it until he gets it. I was sent down here to recover Mr. Alario's painting. When I got home and reported what I found, Mr. Alario sent me back down here to inform George that he now worked for the family."

"How does Mr. Alario make any money? Or does he get originals for his own collection?"

"The copy-and-replace scheme is entirely George. What we're doing is using his forger to create new paintings in the style of deceased artists. Then we fake the provenance and put the pieces up for sale."

"If that's the case, killing Henrick seems like a bad idea."

"It wasn't just George that Henrick planned to sell out. He also wanted to blow the whistle on the Alario connection. George may think I was acting on his order, but Mr. Alario had already told me to take care of it."

Ava's jaw slackened as she tried to make sense of the new information. A bewildered sense of awe settled on her. Had Patrick realized what he'd uncovered?

"If you work for Mr. Alario, why did you kill Patrick?"

"Mostly the same reason. Anything Patrick discovered that implicated Mr. Alario was going to be a problem. But also, the fence and I left a couple of the paintings we sold off the ledger. George found out and threatened to tell the boss I was stealing from him. That would've gotten me killed."

"What about Beachside at Seaside? How does that fit into any of this?"

Meeks shrugged. "I heard about the development and re-alized there was money to be made. Taxpayer-funded projects can be very lucrative." Meeks let loose a heavy sigh. "If you're wondering, it's also why your friend was waiting for you the night he was killed. Somehow, he found out who I was and wanted to warn you away from me."

Ava's stomach twisted into a spool of regret. Patrick never would have been there if she hadn't told him about the Beachside at Seaside story. And if he hadn't been there, maybe he would've had time to come up with a plan to protect himself.

Whirrrrrr. The door rotated open, and Gerou appeared. "Chop, chop, Jared. It's go-time."

Chapter 33

"This is how this is going to work." George Gerou shoved the duct tape into a bag. "We're going to take you outside, and we are all going to climb onto my yacht, and you're going to do exactly as I say."

She watched him pack the bag. An idea formed.

Unless they planned to carry her out strapped to the chair—and she seriously doubted it—they'd have to cut the restraints. Gerou didn't close the door when he came in. That might be her chance to get away. Granted, it had been a while, but she'd played soccer growing up. She could move quickly, and if she timed it right, maybe she could dart around him, get to the front door and make it to Las Olas. From there, she'd flag down a car.

Or maybe Marcus was outside waiting for her.

Gerou had a gun, but she would have the element of surprise on her side.

"Get her up." Gerou barked orders like he wasn't talking to a man who could snap him in two and probably had a gun of his own.

Meeks was a criminal and a killer. He'd never denied it. But they had a common enemy. There was no guarantee, but how likely was it that he'd try to restrain her if she ran? Of course, letting her go would be foolhardy, considering what she knew. She slumped as much as the tape around her shoulders allowed. She was kidding herself if she thought she could get away. Neither of these men could afford to let her go. Still, she had to try.

She steeled herself, tensed her muscles, and prepared to spring.

Meeks cut the tape at her ankles. The shoulder restraints were next. She waited for him to release the strip cinching her wrists behind her back. He didn't.

What were the chances she could get the door open with her hands tied like this?

Looked like she'd have to make do. She wiggled her arms, testing how difficult it would be to clear the back of the chair.

Now!

She lunged forward. The chair crashed onto the concrete floor. Running as fast as her legs would carry her, she went through the door to the hidden gallery, then the mini museum and the hallway.

Keep going.

Adrenaline propelled her forward. "Help! Marcus! I'm here!"

"Get her!" Gerou shouted.

The front door came into view. *Almost there.* She was going to make it. Oh, thank God, she was going to make it. "Marcus—"

Something knocked into her and slammed her into the wall, forcing the air from her lungs. Jared Meeks compressed her body with his own, and for a moment she couldn't breathe.

"Not smart," he rasped, then yanked her backwards by her bound wrists.

Her feet slid against the slick tile floor as he dragged her back to the secret room where Gerou waited.

"You stupid little bitch." He tugged her from Meeks's grasp, grabbed her by the hair and jerked her head back. A knife—probably the one Meeks used to release her restraints—appeared in her peripheral vision.

Gerou pressed the sharp tip of the blade against her cheek. "You need to decide whether you want a quick death or a long, painful one. Do you understand?"

What she understood was that the outcome for her was going to be the same regardless of how she behaved.

He pressed the knife further into the fleshy skin on her face. She felt a prick, followed by a thick drop of blood. "Now, tell me you understand."

"I'll cooperate, I promise." Until she saw another opportunity to get away. She'd rather die trying to escape than give up and let them kill her.

"Good, because I have nosy neighbors who spend all day going up and down the channel. I don't need them involving themselves in my business." He spun her around and sliced through the tape at her wrists. "When we get outside, you are going to act as though you can't wait to get on that boat, and if we see anyone, you're my niece visiting from Greece." He held up the knife again. "And you will keep your mouth shut because if you involve anyone else, you will be responsible for their deaths too."

Ava swallowed and let his words seep in. If he thought she was willingly going to get on his yacht, he had another think coming. With her hands free, she had more options. She just needed to pick the right moment.

Gerou threw the bag at Meeks's feet. "Get her ready—we need her restrained, but not looking like a hostage."

Meeks dug through the bag and pulled out the duct tape. She recoiled, but with him standing between her and the door, she had zero options. He tore off a strip and yanked her toward him. Then, holding both her wrists in one of his big meaty paws, he bound her hands, this time in the front.

"Don't try anything cute." He yanked a towel from the bag and draped it over her bindings. Grabbing her by the arm, just above the elbow, he dragged her toward the open door.

Gerou was already on the boat when they got outside. Ava scanned her surroundings and saw no one. Meeks tugged her toward the stern of the boat and hustled her onto the flat platform.

"Lock her in the cabin," Gerou ordered.

Ava was wrangled down a set of stairs and thrust into a room. She fell to the floor. The door slammed shut, and she heard a lock engage before she even knew what had happened.

Chapter 34

S till parked in the driveway, Marcus clenched and un-clenched his fists while staring at Gerou's front door. The first thing he did after asking his mom to check Ava's house was walk the perimeter of Gerou's mansion, sneaking around, checking windows and doors, looking and praying for a way inside. Nothing. Not even a glimpse, thanks to the curtains shielding the mansion's windows.

So here he sat.

Keeping an eye on the house, Marcus pulled up the dossier on Tony Mandera aka Jared Meeks, the guy who might be hurting the woman he loved. Meeks had worked as a bagman for the Alario crime family, a bodyguard for Vincenzo Alario, and was moving up the ranks to captain. Extortion, corruption of public officials, assault, murder, gambling. The list went on and on.

And to think this man had Ava.

His phone buzzed. It was Eric. "What do you know?"

"Two of the paintings we found at The Fish's place match paintings on the list you gave me, so whatever it is you've stum-bled into down there, there seems to be a connection."

Marcus had already suspected a link based on the painting he recognized, but this confirmed it. "What's your theory? Obviously, Mickey was moving the art, but what's it doing in his house?"

"I don't know. Storage maybe?"

Hidden in plain sight. "Or maybe it was a showroom? Somewhere to bring prospective buyers."

"Doubt we'll ever know for sure. How are things on your end?"

"Not good." Marcus filled Eric in on Ava's abduction, including his catastrophic mistake of falling for Gerou's ruse.

"Man, I'm sorry."

The other agent's sympathetic tone had Marcus admitting something he'd not wanted to say aloud. "I've never been this scared." And that was saying a lot.

"Another reason you won't catch me falling in love with someone connected to a case."

"Not helpful."

Eric cleared his throat. "The Miami field office is aware of the forgery scam, as well as a possible connection to Alario."

"Can you make sure they know about Ava?"

"Yeah, no problem."

Marcus disconnected and went back to glowering at the house. He sat like that for what felt like hours, but the clock on his dash showed only a few minutes had passed.

His phone rang again. He answered immediately, recognizing regret in his mom's voice. "She wasn't there. I'm sorry. I can't believe they would use me against you."

"It's not your fault. I was the idiot who fell for it."

A gruff baritone barked across the speaker. "What's the plan, son?"

Blinking away his fury, Marcus focused on Freddy. Mom said he had connections? Could he help with this?

Cold determination threaded through Freddy's voice. "Very few people know this, but several years ago, I did a stint as an FBI asset..."

The words drifted onto Marcus like snowflakes. "Mom mentioned you knew criminals, but didn't say you were an informant." And here he'd sized the guy up as a total putz.

"It seems like a lifetime ago now, but yes."

Marcus sat back in his chair. "What are you proposing?"

"Most of my contacts are retired, but I'll call around and see if I can't find out if there's any intel on Meeks or George Gerou."

"I've already got information on Meeks. His real name is Tony Mandera. He works for Vincenzo Alario."

Freddy whistled. "Alario? He's the worst of the worst."

He wasn't wrong, but it wasn't what Marcus needed to hear. "If you want to make some calls, I'll take all the help I can—"

Movement. Past the house. On the water.

Marcus's heart dropped into his stomach. "Gerou's on the move. In a boat."

He got out of his truck and ran past the house to the backyard. Drawing up short at the water's edge, he saw a forty-foot yacht gliding down the canal. *Fuck!*

The reality of it slammed into him like a nine-millimeter slug to Kevlar. He had no boat and no idea where Gerou might go. A deep, hollow ache took root in Marcus's chest. Gerou was getting away. And he was taking Ava with him.

"Which direction is he going?" Freddy asked.

Marcus clenched his fist. "South."

"Head to the 17th Street Marina. Maybe we can follow him."

—————

The boat continued its never-ending rocking. The smell of fuel filled Ava's nostrils and made her head throb. She curled into a fetal position on the edge of the bed and moaned. Pressing the back of one of her still-bound hands against her forehead, she inhaled, hoping to quell the nausea rising into her throat. Though, come to think of it, it would serve Gerou right if she vomited on his silky, soft comforter. She choked out a laugh, imagining his million-thread-count linens covered in barf. At least she'd be leaving behind forensic evidence.

A sobering thought.

Her first action after being thrust into the cabin was to conduct a thorough search of the small, plush room, with its rich wood paneling that concealed drawers and cabinets. Desperately, she'd searched for anything she could use as a weapon or a means of escape. Instead, she found nothing but empty storage spaces. Not so much as a dust ball.

Narrow windows on both sides of the cabin offered little in the way of information, given the inky blackness of the ocean at night. She guessed they were heading south, but that was all she managed to ascertain before seasickness set in.

Get it together, Montoya.

She stood and staggered to the small bathroom to wet a towel. Pressing the cool cloth against her cheeks and then her forehead, she forced herself to consider her options. There weren't many.

Maybe she could bargain with Gerou. Marcus had already forwarded Patrick's file to the FBI, but Gerou didn't know that. Would he trade her life for the information Patrick collected?

Her mind raced through a series of possibilities. Convince Gerou that Patrick's dossier would be sent to every major newspaper in the country if anything happened to her. Tell him the FBI already knew everything and that he was going down either way. Argue that another murder conviction would only add time to his sentence.

She slumped against the cabin wall. Who was she kidding? She was going to die. Whether Gerou killed her now or later, her life was over.

Knowing death was near didn't scare her as much as she thought it might. At the moment, resignation was the overwhelming sentiment, but there was a healthy dose of regret in there as well. Regret that she'd never told Marcus her feelings. Regret for the rift that had developed with her family. But also, regret that the world might never know what happened to Patrick.

But Marcus knew. He'd make sure the truth got out.

A tear slipped down her cheek. *I tried, Patrick. I really tried.* She gulped down the cry inching up her throat and blinked away tears.

Footsteps reverberated from above. Someone was moving across the deck. A chain clattered. Was that the anchor? Ava tilted her head to listen. *Clank, clank, clank. Thud.*

She trudged as fast as her nauseous body would allow to the window. Though still mostly dark, a soft pink glow was cracking above the horizon. In the distance, she saw what looked to be a house in the middle of the ocean. She blinked. Was she hallucinating?

Voices carried from beyond the cabin door. Ava crept closer, straining to hear.

"You need to find another forger. You're still in debt to Mr. Alario." Meeks's voice conveyed anger and impatience. "This is your mess, and you need to clean it up. If you hadn't brought Vanderbrook back, none of this would have happened. I don't know what I was thinking going along on this quest of stupidity."

"You went along because you're a greedy sonofabitch who wants to get paid."

"Given what I know now, no amount of money is worth this volume of fuckery. Especially now there's a Fed involved."

"Get her in the dinghy and transfer her to the house." Animosity and condescension swirled in Gerou's words.

"You must not have heard me. You need to handle this. I'll come along to make sure you don't screw it up any more than you already have, but this is your problem."

Footsteps stomped away. A few seconds later, the clank of the lock on the outside of the door jolted her into action. Pressing her back against the wall, she held her breath and waited. The door flew open, and Gerou stepped inside. She leaped behind him to dash up the steps.

"Not so fast."

A hand wrapped around her ankle and yanked. Ava tipped forward. She shoved her tethered hands out to stop her fall, but her right knee banged against the edge of a stair. The sharp sting emanated from the soft, fleshy bit just below her kneecap. Tingles of pain radiated down her leg.

Gerou let go of her ankle and laughed. "Where do you even think you're going to go?"

She marveled at the man's transformation from respectable businessman to ruthless criminal. "Why are you doing this?"

"Oh, I don't know. One less person to testify?" He tugged her elbow roughly. "Get up."

Ava didn't resist. What would be the point? She needed to get off the boat. Then she'd reassess her options.

"I have the notes from Patrick's investigation. I'll give you everything, but I have to get it."

"Nice try." Gerou let out a humorless laugh and pulled a gun from behind his back.

They arrived at the back of the boat, and with the gun in his hand, Gerou nudged her into a small inflatable vessel.

She squared her shoulders. "It's true. I just got access, and I haven't verified everything yet, but there's proof of your scam, how you bring paintings into the museum, create a copy and return the fake."

His expression registered surprise, then rage. A dark purple flush crawled up his neck and face. "Move!"

Ava stepped into a hard-bottomed raft. Meeks sat at the stern, hand on the motor. Gerou landed in the boat with a thump and motioned for her to sit on the single bench seat. He sat on the side.

"We've got a problem." Gerou said to the gangster. "This little bitch has that reporter's notes. Says she's got proof."

"As I've explained, *we* no longer have an official association, so you'll have to solve this on your own." Meeks's voice and demeanor remained calm. He twisted the throttle, and the boat took off.

Gerou, on the other hand, was turning into a root vegetable. He clenched his hands into fists and shouted over the motor, "You're part of this too! You and your money-grubbing boss!"

Ava looked over the side. The water was shallow. Maybe only a few feet. What were the chances she could get away and swim?

Meeks slowed the raft and angled toward the dock of a tiny house on stilts. "You're one to talk. My God. I've never met anyone with your particular mix of avarice and stupidity. You're like King Midas, except everything you touch turns to shit."

Ava's gaze bounced from one man to the other. Where Meeks appeared poised and in control, Gerou looked like a volcano about to blow.

They bumped against the wooden platform. Meeks picked up a coil of rope and wrapped it around the cleat.

"Go." Gerou poked her with the gun.

Ava stepped onto the dock and looked around. The platform was about fifteen yards long. The raft flanked one side. The other was the underside of the house. Stairs led to a wraparound porch.

Should she go into the water or take her chances upstairs?

Too late. Gerou hopped onto the dock and pointed the gun in her face. "Looks like you may have bought yourself some time. You're going to get me that file. Now climb."

Ava ascended the stairs with Gerou close behind. He forced her along the balcony toward a door on the side of the house, then shoved her inside a sparse but comfortable-looking living room.

He gripped her biceps and yanked her across the room, pushing her onto the couch. "Where's the information?"

"It's in an email."

Meeks entered the room.

"Jared, do you still have her phone?"

The big man nodded.

"Give it to her."

Meeks pulled her cellphone out of his bag and handed it over.

"Can you untie my hands? Please?"

Before Gerou could object, Meeks stepped forward and sliced through her bindings.

Oh, sweet relief. She took a moment to rub her sore wrists, then held down the power button. The phone came to life, and after a moment, a series of notifications popped up. Calls and texts from Marcus. Dozens of them.

A sharp pain stabbed her in the chest.

With the phone now on, he could use location sharing to find her. She breathed a sigh of relief. There was still hope.

"I want to see it, and then you're going to destroy the file and the email it came in."

She navigated to her email, then clicked on the attachment and handed the phone back to Gerou. He stared at it, nostrils flaring. "It's encrypted."

Ava pushed down her fear. This was her chance to bargain.

"What's the password?"

"I don't know. Marcus has it."

Chapter 35

They flew across the water at full throttle. Freddy piloted the speedboat, while Marcus braced both hands against the top edge of the windscreen. Not only did Freddy keep a boat at a small private marina along the Intracoastal Waterway, but he'd been right about tailing Gerou's boat. They'd spotted the lights of the small yacht not long after they got into the Atlantic. After following for several miles, Freddy had a strong suspicion of where they might be taking Ava. Marcus called the Coast Guard with the approximate coordinates and a description of Gerou's yacht.

Freddy took one hand off the wheel and clapped Marcus on the shoulder. "We're almost there."

There was a wood-frame house located off the southern tip of Florida. Stiltsville, as Marcus had learned, was a collection of stilted homes located within the boundaries of Biscayne National Park. While the homes were generally off-limits to the public, Gerou sometimes rented one and enjoyed bringing collectors out for the novelty of the experience. Apparently, this was part of how he finagled artwork out of unsuspecting aficionados.

Right now, Marcus's entire focus was on Ava's safety and getting her back. But later, when things calmed down, he would do some soul searching about his initial reaction to Freddy. He also planned to make sure that the man knew how much he valued his help.

Marcus's phone pinged. He checked his notifications. Ava's location sharing had just reactivated. Finally, some good luck. This would help pinpoint her location. "Bear west," he told Freddy.

They passed the yacht anchored about a half mile from the house where Ava was being held. Freddy slowed. Marcus's heart kicked into overdrive. Didn't look like anyone was on board.

"That's George's boat," Freddy said. "Don't see a tender. Must've headed for the house."

A buzz shot through Marcus's veins. They were here. This would be over soon.

Still, he worried that whatever Gerou had planned, he'd want to do it before the sun came up and the tourists came out. The pink glow on the horizon concerned him. He tapped his hand against the fiberglass hull.

"The water is shallow here," Freddy said as he eased up on the throttle and a powder-blue house with a wraparound deck came into view.

The raft tied to the dock indicated they were in the right place. Prickles of restless energy danced up and down Marcus's skin. He tightened his grip on the metal trim framing the windscreen. His breath quickened. He needed to see her, to know she was okay.

Freddy switched on the trolling motor, and their boat began an easy bob.

The slower speed only ratcheted up Marcus's skyrocketing anxiety, and it took all of his willpower not to fling himself into the water and swim. "Can't you go faster?"

Freddy clasped a hand on Marcus's shoulder, and somehow it calmed the storm gathering inside him. "This is quieter. He won't hear us coming."

The reassurance did little to calm his apprehension, but Marcus nodded. Alerting Gerou of their approach would absolutely be the wrong thing to do.

Gerou's face went crimson. "The damned FBI agent has the password?"

"If he doesn't hear from me soon, he'll send the file to the Feds." Ava tried to sound calm, confident. Meanwhile, a Cat 5 hurricane roiled her insides.

"I want that password."

Ava prayed the gamble would work. "Let me go. Patrick hid the password. I know where it is. I'll get it and destroy it. Then the file will be unreadable."

"No." Gerou stepped forward, grabbed a wad of her hair and held the gun against her cheek. "Tell me where it is. I'll go get it. If it's where you say it is when I get back, I'll make your death as quick as possible."

"If you kill me, you'll never get the password."

Gerou released her hair and mimicked a look of pensiveness with his index finger pressed against his chin. "Then I guess I'll have to find your boyfriend and force him to watch while I torture you. That ought to get it out of him."

Ava's heart took off like a heavy metal drum solo, beating fast and loud, thundering in her ears. What was she going to do? She looked at Meeks and silently pleaded for him to intervene.

He gave Gerou a fed-up look. "George, stop."

"Excuse me?" Gerou turned to look at the other man. The gun slid from Ava's cheek.

"The information in the file? Ian Vanderbrook has a copy. Are you going to kill him too? What about the next guy he gives it to? And the one after that?" Meeks stood, drew a gun from his belt and pointed it at the floor. "It's over."

"Not for you to decide." Gerou aimed his weapon at Meeks, who took a step closer.

"You might as well just give yourself over to the police. You'd be better off in prison."

Ava eyed the door. Could this be her chance? Steal the raft? Get away?

"How do you figure?" The gun in Gerou's hand shook.

"You ripped off Vincenzo Alario. There will be consequences."

Ava stood and side-stepped softly behind the museum executive.

"I don't think so." There was a smile in Gerou's voice. He spun, capturing her wrist, pulling her in front of him, and bracing his forearm across her chest. "Because I have a hostage."

As useless as a fish caught in a net, Ava thrashed against him, wriggling and kicking, desperate to get away. It was no use. He held her in place, his arm pressing against her chest like a vise.

"The FBI agent will trade the password for her. Then, when I get it, I'll kill them both."

Gerou pulled Ava out of the house and across the deck toward the stairs.

Beeeeeeeeeep.

Gerou turned his attention to the water. A small vessel approached.

She could hardly believe her eyes. *Marcus!* A rush of relief shot through her, and in an instant, the love and affection she felt multiplied, expanding her chest and filling her up.

"That fucking FBI agent." Gerou's face twisted into even more of a sneer. He released her and pivoted to point the gun at the boat.

Her entire world slowed as she followed the angle of Gerou's arm, now extended over the banister, the barrel of the gun pointed at Marcus. Her breath caught. She couldn't breathe. And then something inside her exploded like a clap of thunder.

Anger pulsed in Ava's veins. Something about this asshole threatening Marcus gave her courage she didn't know she had. She rushed forward, slamming into the man and knocking him off balance.

"Ava!" Marcus yelled from below. The boat took off around the side of the house.

"You little bitch!"

She sprang, pushing off her toes and sprinting away from Gerou. The porch followed the perimeter of the house. If she kept going, she'd end up at the stairs.

Footsteps on the steps shook the deck. It had to be Marcus. She didn't stop to look.

"Drop the weapon," Marcus shouted.

Her vision narrowed on the corner of the house.

Almost there. Get to the corner.

Pumping her arms, she moved like she'd never moved before.

Her breaths were quick.

Her heart rate quicker.

Two more steps.

She was going to make it.

The crack of gunfire sounded at the exact moment something stung her in the shoulder.

Chapter 36

T his wasn't real. It couldn't be real.

A muffled roar filled Marcus's ears and his sight grew hazy. Ava falling forward filled his vision and, in that moment, nothing else existed.

And then his training kicked in. He lifted his gun and pointed it at Gerou. "Drop your weapon! Turn around! Now!"

Gerou turned but didn't drop the gun. At least it was no longer pointed at Ava.

Marcus's gaze skirted past Gerou to Ava, who had somehow gotten herself into a sitting position. She was pale and sweaty and slumped against the house, a streak of blood smearing her shirt. She pressed a bloody hand to her shoulder. He needed her to move, to get out of the way.

He motioned with his head, but she didn't acknowledge the gesture. Her eyes fluttered shut.

"Stay with me. We're going to get you help."

"Cold..." Her words were a mumble, but those caramel-colored eyes were open.

"Focus on me. Stay awake."

She responded with a weak nod.

Marcus's vision grew blurry. Was he crying? Surely not. He'd seen people shot before.

But not Ava. Ava was different.

The truth of it slammed him in the gut, nearly knocking the wind out of him. He loved her. So much. If anything happened to her—

"This is all so very touching. Truly, a feel-good movie in the making." Gerou realigned his aim at Marcus, squinting one eye and lining up a shot. "Roll credits. This story is over."

Marcus tightened his support hand, realigned his thumbs and adjusted his aim. "You think so?"

A motor roared to life.

"It's Meeks! He's getting away!" Freddy's footsteps shook the wooden deck as he ran toward the stairs at the other side of the porch.

Sure enough, the inflatable dinghy had pushed away from the dock and was heading south.

"That goddamn motherfucker," Gerou shouted.

Dammit. Where was the FBI? He'd called Eric before they set out for Stiltsville with the coordinates for where they thought Gerou was going. So why wasn't anyone here?

Ava moaned. Her eyes fluttered closed again.

"Over here, sweetheart. Eyes on me." He needed her conscious to assess her condition, though there wasn't much he could do about it at the moment.

Her head lolled to the side. Time to end this. He took two steps forward and reset his stance. Gerou let his gun drop, but Marcus wasn't about to be fooled into thinking this maniac was giving himself up.

The man spun, once again pointing the firearm at Ava. He twisted to look at Marcus. "Give me the boat, and I won't kill her."

"Not happening. Drop your gun, or you die."

"Nice try. If there's one thing I know, it's the intrinsic value of an asset." Gerou laughed. "It's clear to me you value her life more than anything, probably more than your own. Unfortunately, the market value of her life is that boat." He leveled a condescending stare at Marcus. "Key. Now."

"Sorry, no."

"Freddy!" Gerou shouted. "I need that damned key."

Freddy didn't respond, but Marcus saw his head peek around the corner of the house behind Gerou's back. He was only a few feet from Ava. Maybe if Marcus could get Gerou to direct the gun at him, Freddy could drag Ava around the corner, and Marcus could get a shot off without worrying he might hurt her.

"We know everything. We know about the stolen art, the deal with a mobster. All of it. You're done. You're going to jail for the rest of your life."

Gerou turned back to him. "I don't think so because you're going to tell me where I can find the password, and once that's destroyed, there won't be any evidence. I'll go back to being a humble museum executive fulfilling my life's mission of sharing art with the public."

Now it was Marcus's turn to laugh. "That's the best part. Even without Patrick's information, you're through. The Vanderbrook painting? The original had a rare type of mica mixed into the paint. What are the chances your forger knew to get the exact mineral found only in Africa?"

For the first time since this began, uncertainty flashed across Gerou's face. He swiveled to point the gun at Marcus—just as Marcus wanted.

"You're lying."

"Am I?" Marcus took another step closer, careful not to let his gaze wander to Ava. In his periphery, he saw Freddy emerge from behind the corner, but he couldn't let himself watch, couldn't give away what was happening.

Freddy grasped Ava around the waist and lifted her to her feet. She hissed in pain. *Don't look.* He didn't acknowledge the sound, and Gerou didn't seem to hear it. Finally, she was out of sight. Marcus didn't speak for a long moment, wanting to give Freddy the chance to get her to the boat.

"Looks like it's just you and me."

Gerou's gaze darted to the spot where Ava had been sitting and bit out a curse. He turned back to Marcus. "I'm going to kill you—"

A bright white searchlight illuminated the side of the house. "This is the Coast Guard," came a voice over the loudspeaker. "We have secured the area. You are surrounded. Please release your weapon and surrender peacefully."

Marcus bent to put his gun on the wooden deck, then stood, hands in the air.

Gerou's wide-eyed gaze darted from side to side. Then, his lips curled into a snarl, and Marcus knew this guy would rather die than go into custody.

"Don't be stupid, Gerou."

The man grunted in response, lifted his arm and aimed his weapon at Marcus.

A single *phfttt* from a sniper rifle sounded from the Coast Guard vessel. Gerou crumpled onto the wooden planks of the porch.

Marcus didn't stop to check for vitals. The man was dead.

He raced around the house and practically fell down the stairs. Somehow, Freddy had gotten Ava to the dock. She was lying on her back, still holding her shoulder. He fell to his knees and gathered her into his arms. "It's okay. You're going to be okay."

Please, God, let that be the truth.

Coast Guardsmen thundered onto the dock and bounded up the stairs. Noise and commotion filled the air.

"We need a medic," Marcus shouted to no one in particular.

The faint *thump-thump-thump* of a chopper carried over the chaos.

Marcus's body slumped in relief. He heaved Ava against him, burying his face in her neck. "I love you. I love you so much."

"Love...you...too." Her voice was weak, but she was alive. And to think he'd almost lost her.

A man and a woman with a backboard had somehow materialized. "Air support is on its way," the woman said. "We need to stabilize her and get her ready for transfer."

Blinking back tears, Marcus nodded. "I'll see you soon. And every day from now on."

He kissed her, then moved aside to let the rescue team work. He watched as they secured her to the board.

The helicopter hovered. After an agonizing few minutes, the team on the dock gave the signal. The operator dropped the hoist, and the ground crew fastened the straps to the rescue board. Before Ava was lifted to the helicopter, Marcus stepped forward and squeezed her hand.

"I told you it would work out." His voice broke.

Ava squeezed back.

"Sir, I need you to move aside." The female medical officer motioned for Marcus to move away.

He took a step back to stand beside Freddy. This man who had been with him from the beginning tonight. The man he'd not trusted with his mom and hadn't wanted to like. He owed him an apology. Freddy was the reason they'd found Ava. Freddy was the reason she was still alive. Marcus cleared his throat.

"You don't have to say it," Freddy said.

"Say what?" Marcus watched a medic pull Ava's board into the helicopter.

"What you're working up to saying. Don't worry about it. We're good."

A lump stuck in Marcus's throat. He nodded as the helicopter faded into the distance.

Chapter 37

Ava sat on the edge of the hospital bed and glanced around the room. There'd been a constant rotation of visitors for the last few days. But now, everyone was gone. Her parents had said goodbye just a little while ago, leaving with Marcus, who'd offered a ride to the airport.

Once she was stable and out of surgery, he'd called them to explain the situation. Their arrival had been a welcome surprise. A tear sprang to Ava's eye as she recalled the stress on her mother's face, her furrowed brow, and the quiver in her chin when she stepped into the room. Her father revealed his worry in a different way, demanding her doctors justify their recommended treatments. Oncology was his specialty, and he knew little about traumatic injuries, but everyone appeared to recognize it for the coping mechanism that it was.

Now, for the first time in days, she wore regular clothes. She stood and slid her feet into the shoes Marcus had fetched for her, a pair of slip-on sneakers. He was always doing things like that, taking care of her in little, thoughtful ways, like realizing she couldn't tie her shoes with her arm in a sling.

There was a light rap on the door. She glanced up to find an anxious-looking Ian Vanderbrook hovering at the entrance.

They'd spoken once since she'd been in the hospital, but she hadn't expected to see him again. "I didn't know you were in town. What are you doing here?"

A sheepish look crossed his face as he stuck his hands into the front pockets of his jeans. "Amanda asked if I'd shoot a TV promo for the exhibit, and I didn't want to miss a chance to see you while I'm here."

Since Gerou's arrest, Amanda had taken charge of running the museum. The board was voting on an interim director later this week, and she seemed a shoo-in. "That's great."

"It's been sold out every day since your article was published."

"I'm so happy to hear that."

Despite being hospitalized, Ava had wanted to be the first to publish the story. Because of her injury, she'd had to dictate the article—a new and challenging experience. But it was worth it. The story was picked up by the wire and published in newspapers all over the country. It had even made the TV news. She'd insisted on giving Patrick a posthumous byline, and there was something bittersweet about seeing his name beside hers.

"I noticed you didn't mention my connection to Gerou or the forgeries."

She'd written that Ian's painting was one of the pieces recovered from Gerou's secret collection, but she'd not said anything about his prior involvement. "I didn't think I needed to dredge up the past. It was a long time ago, and you were a kid, hardly in a position to tell him no."

"I appreciate the sentiment." He rubbed a hand against the back of his neck. "But I've decided I want to come clean. Keeping this secret is too much of a burden. I want to tell my story regardless of the consequences, and I want you to write it."

Her mouth dropped open. "Are you sure?"

"Absolutely. It's my fault you're here and Patrick is—" His voice cracked. He cleared his throat. "Gone."

Ava could see the anguish in the hard lines of Ian's face. "You didn't know..." She didn't finish her thought. It didn't need to be said. "How long are you in town?"

"Just a few days."

"How long will you be wearing that thing?" He motioned to the sling, then dragged over a chair.

"Probably another couple of weeks. I was lucky the bullet didn't hit the bone, but there was some muscle and tendon damage. For now, I have to keep it immobilized to help it heal." She didn't mention the nerve damage or the fact that she was having trouble using her hand. He didn't need another thing to feel bad about.

"And Marcus? What's going on there?"

Things with Marcus were fantastic. Just thinking about him had her grinning like a fool. "He'll most likely have to return to Philly, at least for a bit, but he's put in for a transfer to Miami."

"That's fantastic."

They chatted for a few more minutes before Ian stood, returning the chair to its spot against the wall. "I'm glad I got to see you. I wish you a speedy recovery."

Ava hesitated. There was one more thing she wanted to know. "Can I ask you something?"

"Shoot."

"That picture of George Gerou with you in the background working on a forgery? How did that end up in the newspaper?"

"It was a picture my mother took. She gave it to the reporter, not realizing the implications." He shook his head at the long-ago memory. "George was furious."

"I bet."

"That's another reason to tell the truth. Now that everyone knows about the forgeries, there's a chance that picture will resurface. Might as well get out in front of it."

Ava nodded. Crime aficionados were already delving into the case. "We should try to do our interview sooner rather than later, then."

"Agreed. I'll check my schedule and let you know." He came forward and drew her into a gentle hug. She wrapped her free arm around his shoulder. "Take care of yourself."

"You too." And then he was gone.

A few minutes later, Marcus entered her room. He pointed over his shoulder with his thumb. "I just ran into Vanderbrook at the elevator."

"He came to see how I'm doing."

"Pretty sure he left a trail of swooning nurses."

She laughed. "He is handsome."

"Hmm." Marcus narrowed his eyes.

"Not as handsome as you, of course."

"Good save." He drew her in for a long, sweet kiss. "Ready to leave?"

"Let's go home."

Epilogue

Three Months Later

Ding-dong.

Marcus looked from Ava to the door and then back again. "Are you ready for this?"

"No, but it's too late now." She looked beautiful in a short green polka-dot dress with ruffled sleeves that covered the scar on her shoulder. "Let them in."

The doorbell rang again, somehow louder and longer this time, almost as though channeling the impatience of the person on the other side. Mr. Belvedere took that as his cue and bolted from the room. The cat had the right idea. "We can still slip out the back."

"Just do it." She shooed him toward the door. How did she make annoyance look so cute?

Jokes aside, he was looking forward to hosting their first dinner party. He grabbed the doorknob, and before he knew it, his mother shoved her way into the room.

"Took you long enough." Mom pulled his face down for a kiss. "But I get it. Young love. You can't keep your hands off one another." She gave them both an exaggerated wink.

"Seriously?" For once, there was no bite to his words. This was just Mom being Mom.

"Darling!" His mom hurtled toward Ava with arms wide to draw her in for a hug. "This dress is adorable. When are we going shopping?"

Ava laughed. "Whenever you want."

"We brought wine." His mom gestured to Freddy, still standing just inside the entrance holding two bottles of red and a bottle of Champagne.

"Let me help you with that." Marcus grabbed two of the bottles and carried them to the kitchen. Freddy followed with the Champagne, trying not to trip over an excited Beagle Bailey.

Marcus turned back to his mother. "You didn't need to do that."

She gave him the oh-please wave. "We have much to celebrate. Your move to South Florida. Ava's recovery. The two of you living together."

He threw his arm around Ava's shoulder and hugged her to his side. His mom wasn't wrong. The last few weeks had been a whirlwind. Though he liked his job in Philly and enjoyed working with the team there, ultimately, the decision was easy. Being near Mom was a bonus.

"The food is done, so if you're ready to eat, we can move into the dining room." Ava motioned to their new table, the first piece of furniture they picked out as a couple.

In the weeks leading up to his move, Ava decided it was time to put her own stamp on the house. Though she would always miss her nana, she set about sorting her grandmother's belongings, deciding what to keep, what to discard and what to donate. Marcus offered to help, but understood when Ava said it was something she needed to do by herself. The process was emotional, especially considering she'd just organized a memorial to spread Patrick's ashes at the beach. Marcus did what he could to be there when she got overwhelmed by memories, and when the task was done, he set up a home office in the second bedroom for her, freeing up the dining room for its intended use.

"Don't forget the wine," his mother called as she took a spot at the table.

Marcus carried stemware and the bottle of Malbec to the table, then returned to the kitchen to help Ava with the food—meatloaf, potatoes, and roasted Brussel sprouts.

"This is delicious," Freddy said between bites.

Marcus squeezed Ava's hand under the table. She chose this menu, knowing it would be easy to eat with a fork. She'd been diligent with her physical therapy and had made huge improvements, but using a knife was still difficult, and she hadn't wanted to feel self-conscious.

"I read your article about that commissioner fellow." Marcus's mom refilled her glass and took another sip of wine. "So, he stole gift cards donated for a children's charity and gave them to his lover? Is that right?"

For someone who'd been so insecure about her abilities, it turned out Ava loved to talk about her work. "Thousands of dollars' worth."

"And that gangster fellow was blackmailing him for his support on that Beachside project?"

"Correct. The gangster is still at large, but Martin Singh resigned from his job as a city commissioner."

"He ought to be ashamed of himself, stealing from needy children."

"I think he probably is. He pleaded guilty to third-degree felony theft."

"Good." Marcus's mom popped a Brussels sprout into her mouth. "Now, what about you two? What are your plans?"

"I'm starting my new position on Monday," Marcus offered.

"That's wonderful, sweetheart, but not what I meant." His mom gave him another conspiratorial wink. "What I want to know is when I can plan an engagement party."

Marcus should have expected she'd start a conversation about this. Little did she know, he already had a ring.

"Vi, dear." Freddy offered a gentle admonishment, and Marcus appreciated him for it. They'd made huge strides in their relationship since Ava's kidnapping. "Why don't you leave the kids alone?"

She glared at him. "We both know it's what they want."

"And it's none of our business."

"I consider my son's happiness very much my business." Her voice was terse and tense.

Ava stood, breaking the tension. "How does everyone feel about German chocolate pie?"

She made a beeline for the kitchen. Marcus cleared the dishes, glancing at Ava from time to time, trying to figure out whether the topic had caused discomfort.

His mom put her hand against his forearm. "I'm sorry, honey. I guess I shouldn't have said anything."

He glanced at Ava, stacking plates and getting silverware. She knew what his mom was like. He couldn't imagine the topic would upset her. "We'll talk about it when we're ready." Probably as soon as his mom and Freddy left.

Because while he hated to admit it, his mom had given him the opening he'd been waiting for. Suddenly, he couldn't wait for them to leave. He carried the dishes and empty wine bottle to the kitchen, putting the bottle in recycling, setting the plates in the sink, and leaning over to kiss Ava on the cheek. "Dinner was great."

"I'm glad." She handed him the dessert plates and forks. "This was fun."

"Sure, but I'm ready to have you to myself." He looked over his shoulder to find his mom staring at them.

Ava picked up the pie and carried it to the dining room. She dished, and Marcus distributed the slices. As soon as they were done eating, he snatched up the plates and put them in the dishwasher. "Well, it's been fun. Thanks for coming."

"What about the Champagne?" Mom stood and walked toward the kitchen. "I wanted to make a toast."

"Can we do it another time? It's been a long day." He shot Freddy a get-her-out-of-here look.

Thankfully, Freddy caught Marcus's meaning. "If you don't mind, Vi, I think I'm ready to go."

Mom turned a concerned eye to her companion. "Is something wrong?"

"Just tired."

Her eyes darted from Marcus and Ava to Freddy. "There will be more invitations, I assume?"

Ava rushed forward to hug her. "Of course, you're welcome anytime."

"But call first," Marcus said. The last thing he needed was Mom showing up unannounced.

She tugged him into a hug and whispered in his ear. "She's going to say yes. Call me tomorrow and tell me all about it."

His mouth gaped. She couldn't possibly know. He gave a noncommittal response. "Drive safe." He urged them out the door.

Ava strode to the kitchen to finish cleaning up after dinner. "You were in a hurry to get rid of them."

He leaned against the counter, trying to look nonchalant. "Want help?"

She shook her head. "It'll just take a couple of minutes."

With Ava distracted, he made his way to the bedroom, unlocked the security box in his nightstand where he kept his firearm, and removed the velvet box. Glancing over his shoulder to make sure Ava wasn't coming into the room, he opened the lid and a little light came on, illuminating the oval diamond and making it sparkle.

He snapped the box shut, shoved it into his pocket and stalked back to the living room. The idea had been to plan a grand gesture, but he realized a big, elaborate moment wasn't necessary. All he needed was Ava, and he couldn't think of a more perfect place to ask her to marry him than the house where they were starting their future together.

She was drying off her hands when he got back to the kitchen. "How'd you feel about a glass of Champagne?"

She gave him a suspicious look. "You just told your mom you didn't want any."

"I didn't want any with her..."

He moved around her to pull two flutes from the cabinet, then tore the foil off the top of the bottle and untwisted the metal fastener. Covering the top with a towel, he twisted the cork until it popped.

"Why are you acting so strange?" Ava took a glass.

He didn't respond but guided her to the couch. When they were sitting, he took her glass and set it on the coffee table next to his own before taking her hands. He took a deep breath and began.

"When I first came to Florida, it was because I thought my mom was incomplete without my dad. Instead, I found you, and I realized I was the one who was missing my other half. I love you so much—" His voice broke. "More than anything, I want to spend the rest of my life with you."

Tears shimmered in Ava's eyes. He let go of her hand and reached into his pocket. She gasped when he pulled out the little box and revealed the solitaire.

"Marry me?"

She wiped her eyes. "Yes, of course."

He took her hand and slid the diamond onto her ring finger. The moment he saw the ring, he'd thought it was pretty, but seeing Ava wearing it filled him with a new sense of wholeness. A symbol of their future, from this day forward, forever intertwined.

It was perfect. Just like Ava.

About the Author

Evie Jacobs is an award-winning author of romantic suspense who loves grumpy heroes, forced proximity, and a good sex scene. She lives in Colorado with her husband, two cats, and seven bicycles.

Visit Evie online at:
eviejacobsauthor.com
@eviejacobsauthor on Instagram and Facebook